FINDING
Brooklyn

FINDING *Brooklyn*

M.J. RICHARDS

Sage Circle

PUBLISHING

For my mom, my first reader—
until we meet again.

CHAPTER 1

didn't dare move. I knew once I did, she would be gone forever. Thunderclouds rolled overhead, and the skies released another round of unrelenting rain. I stared into the sea of black attire. An older woman dabbed at her nose with a wrinkled tissue. Our eyes met, and she looked away. Everyone seemed to look away, their faces pitying me.

I clenched my teeth. My jaw ached against the unending vice, but I couldn't release it. I couldn't give in. I feared if I did, it would start again. The tightening in my chest rushed to my head and released in a heartbroken whimper. I was afraid if I dared to move, the sadness would consume me.

Infinite drops fell in all directions from heavy clouds pushing themselves toward the eastern horizon.

I held a pink umbrella over my head, opposing the low, gray sky. Beads of water cascaded off its plastic spokes, threatening the curls I had worked so hard to put in. I pressed my fingers against the cold, rose-colored steel in front of me. I let my fingertips trace along the rolling design of the beveled edges. I wanted to see her one more time, but I knew I couldn't.

I looked over at two men who waited in the distance. They stared back, but if they were losing patience, they didn't show it.

They simply sat there, legs dangling over an open tailgate, the service truck sheltered under the awning of a maintenance shed. They had likely watched this scene play out many times before, but I doubt they found many nine-year-olds playing the role I was. At least I hoped they hadn't.

"Brooklyn?" My father's voice shook me from my thoughts.

He marched toward me. His suit, wrinkled and worn, clung to his frail body, weighed down by the rain.

"We have to go."

He turned toward the men and raised an apologetic hand.

I tilted the umbrella up slightly and stared at his face. My heart pleaded with me to hurt for him, but my mind controlled the anger which shot from the narrow slits of my eyes.

"No."

"Now."

"No."

He took a step toward me but glanced at the two men, then hesitated. He rubbed a hand over his forehead and through his hair. A cascade of water sprayed onto his shoulders.

"I've given you enough time, so stop it. She's gone, and she's not coming back. Stop crying and get in the car."

He reached for my arm but caught the sleeve of my dress. He pulled hard. I heard the tear of fabric, the sound echoing straight to my heart. We looked at each other in disbelief.

"You ruined my dress."

"Brooklyn…"

"Why would you do that?"

"Brooklyn, it was an accident."

"This is my dress. The dress Mom gave me. The last thing she ever gave me, and you ruined it."

This time when he reached, he caught my arm. He pulled me close and stood over me.

"The last thing?" He stole another look toward the two men. I felt the warmth of his breath before it cooled in the fall air. "The last thing? Look at you. Your blonde hair. Your blue eyes. Brooklyn, you're a spitting image of her. So don't tell me you have nothing left of hers. You're a walking reminder that she's not here."

The truth hung heavy between us. I clenched my teeth again and looked up at him. "I hate you." I regretted the words as soon as they left my mouth.

He nodded slightly and turned to walk away. "Hurry up and finish your goodbyes. It's time to go."

I stood alone. The only sound was the hollow chorus of raindrops as they clapped against my mother's casket. I knew my life would never be the same. Everything I had known and everyone I loved—was gone.

CHAPTER 2

The drone of a car engine hummed through the morning air. The rhythmic pop of its muffler grew louder for a moment, then faded into the distance.

I drew in a deep breath and blinked away the heaviness of sleep. A streak of light slipped through a gap in my bedroom curtains, catching a steady stream of dust dancing through the air. I rubbed my face and stared at the ceiling, letting my eyes trace the pattern of its popcorn texture.

The house was quiet. Nearly silent. I could hear the beat of my heart echoing gently in my ears. I didn't have any siblings, so most of the noise in our home came from me anyway, but I missed the mornings of hearing my mom making breakfast in the kitchen, bacon popping in a frying pan, and my dad singing whatever tune had gotten stuck in his head as he got ready for work; his voice always slightly off-key.

I yawned, got out of bed, and tiptoed onto the matted runner that stretched across the creaky wood floor. It connected my bedroom to the bathroom, and then to my parents' bedroom.

From that distance I stared into the darkness of their room, the long shadows matching the sadness of the space. The last time I saw my mom before she took her life, I was peeking my head into their room to say goodbye before I left for school.

"Goodbye, baby girl, I love you," she had said, then seemed to quickly fall back to sleep.

I love you.

I held these words, her last words, close to my heart. They helped calm the storm of doubts and fears that circled endlessly around my mind in the nearly six months since she had died.

I turned from the bedroom and walked into the kitchen. The smell of burnt toast lingered in the air, and a ring of spilled coffee on the counter revealed my father had been there.

"Dad?"

I leaned through the narrow opening that led into our family room. A pillow slumped at one end of the sofa, a crumpled blanket on the other. He had been doing this a lot lately, sleeping on the couch.

"Dad?"

I stepped around the countertop and the low, overhanging cabinets in the kitchen, into the small space occupied by our table. The spot had become a catchall for discarded mail, fast food wrappers, and anything else my father didn't care to throw away. I lifted the edge of one envelope. The words *Past Due* were stamped across the front in bold, red letters.

What does "past due" mean?

A familiar uneasiness tightened in my stomach. I placed the envelope where I thought he would see it.

I maneuvered through the mess and lifted the corner of the curtains, exposing the arch window concealed behind them. I leaned close and peeked through the haze of the worn panes, my eyes followed our driveway toward the carport. His car was gone.

More than once, I had asked him to wake me before he left. I told him I didn't want to be late for school, but really, I just wanted to see him. I wanted to know I wasn't alone.

He wasn't the same anymore, not like he used to be. Something in him had changed. He was angry a lot now. Not always at me, but at everything. At the mail. At the dishes. At the way the bathroom light flickered when it shouldn't.

I used to get so excited when he came home from work. It was "our time," as he called it. We'd eat popcorn on the couch and watch movies, or he'd make up stories with wild voices that made me laugh so hard, my sides hurt.

Those nights felt far away now. I waited for him to come home only because I hated being alone in the dark. The house got too quiet, and I noticed shadows in the hallway I hadn't seen before.

I sighed and released the curtain, watching it drift back into place. As I walked past the table, my elbow caught one of the cluttered piles, and a stack of envelopes slid off the edge and tumbled to the floor. I reached to gather them and knocked my knee hard against a chair. The sharp jolt made me wince.

I gave the table an angry shove knocking over a long-forgotten plastic cup filled with soda. Its lid broke on impact, and I watched as the sticky contents dripped to the floor.

I moved to catch it but stopped. I wanted him to find it, to see the mess I had made. Maybe then he would notice me.

I heard the effortless tick of the kitchen clock. I had slept later than I'd thought, so I quickly walked to my bedroom.

Clothes covered nearly every inch of the floor. Most of them had been worn two or three times since they were last washed. I thought it would be helpful if I taught myself how to do laundry, but my father didn't like it.

"Why do you need clean clothes every day?" he had asked. "You're just a kid. Stop wasting water and electricity, you're not the one paying the bills. Wear 'em a few times then wash them."

I found some jeans and a top I had worn earlier in the week. They smelled like grass stains and the musty dampness that seemed to live in the corners of our house. I rubbed a smear of dry peanut butter off the shirt hoping the stain wouldn't be too noticeable. It would have to do.

I rushed into the bathroom and flipped the switch. In the dim glow I caught sight of my tangled hair. My dingy clothes struggled to keep pace with my recent growth spurt, and I tugged at the bottom of my shirt. I feared if I bent or moved in the wrong way, something would tear. I stared at the girl in the mirror and quickly turned away.

I ran back into the kitchen, pulled my lunchbox from my backpack, and swung open the pantry door. The shelves were nearly bare. My father had promised he'd start going to the store more often, but even when he did, he only came back with a few meager essentials.

I lifted an empty bread bag from one of the shelves and crumpled it in anger. Without a sandwich, I was going to starve all day. I grabbed a napkin from the counter, used but clean enough, and folded a handful of cold cereal into it. The crumbs from the bottom of the bag clung to the shelf in a dusty rainbow. I swiped my finger through the colors and licked it, the sugar sweet on my tongue.

I opened my lunchbox to find a peanut butter sandwich sealed in a plastic bag. I stared at it for a second, then smiled. He had given me the last of the bread, and for a second, I felt a twinge of guilt.

I zipped my backpack and slung it over my shoulder. I stood by the picture window in our front room and looked down the road toward the Timmons' house.

Chatwin, Colorado, was a small town, but I still didn't like walking to school alone. If I timed it right, I could follow Sophie Timmons and her two brothers from a distance. That way, I wouldn't have to be by myself when I passed the Johnson's house, who's ugly, mean, pit bull was never on a leash. I hoped I wasn't too late.

Jacob Timmons bounded out the door first, with Ryan not far behind, catapulting himself over the guardrail as he ran out. Sophie followed at a quieter pace, her graceful style a far cry from the tomboy who used to walk back and forth with me along the narrow, broken asphalt between our homes. She stepped down their tiered walkway and looked toward our house. I instinctively dropped below the window.

Had she seen me?

I peeked my head just above the sill. I watched as she reached the end of their walkway, then turned to follow her brothers toward the main road.

I moved to our front porch, the screen door slamming behind me, and waited until she neared the end of the street. Once she was a safe distance ahead, I began the long walk toward Chatwin Elementary.

CHAPTER 3

The school lunchroom was old and dimly lit, tucked away beneath the gym like a forgotten utility room. Fluorescent tube lights flickered in and out, humming weakly in time with the stomping footsteps from the basketball court above.

I held my lunchbox close to me and walked in, the scent of reheated chicken nuggets, sour milk, and stale gravy thick in the air. Voices echoed off the cinder block walls as more students poured in, their laughter and greetings rising in a wave of noise.

I scanned the tables, watching as the other students found their friends. Their smiles came effortlessly, their conversations clicking into place like pieces of a puzzle I no longer belonged to. I had never been popular, but I used to fit in. After my mom's death, I was treated like I had a disease, as if the sins of my family might be contagious. The girls were worse than the boys; their comments seemed to be aimed at my greatest insecurities.

I smoothed my shirt and ran my hand through my hair. I turned away and took my usual spot at the far end of one of the tables.

Sophie called from the other end of the table, "Hey, Brooklyn, why don't you sit by us?"

For a moment my heart lifted at her kind invitation, but the smile on her face and the poorly concealed laughter of the girls around her gave away her intentions.

"Why?"

"Why?" She looked around in mock confusion. "Duh, 'cause we want to sit by you. We miss you."

The laughter grew louder, and Sophie slid down her side of the table toward me. "Come on, we can trade lunches."

She craned her neck to look over my meager meal. "Except… you don't have anything I want. Yuck, what is this? Did you take this out of a garbage can? Is that mold on your sandwich?"

She stuck out her tongue and turned to the other girls. She looked back at me, smiled, lifted her nose, and pretended to smell me. "And what's that smell? Is that you?"

I slammed my lunchbox closed and quickly stood. The girls laughed harder, and I stared at Sophie, hoping my eyes would convey the hurt she was causing me.

She didn't even flinch. "Do us a favor and take a bath once in a while."

I glared at her. "Shut up, Sophie."

She snickered and looked back at the other girls. "What? I'm just trying to help you out."

I tossed my lunchbox into our class bin and made a beeline to the doors at the back of the room. The heavy steel resisted for a moment, then opened. I was greeted by the peaceful quiet of the outside world. I squinted toward the sun, letting its warmth press against my face.

In the small playground next to the school, a pair of swings swayed lazily in the afternoon breeze. Beyond that was a large open field for games of kickball and football. Worn baseball diamonds blended with patches of dirt, where the sprinklers couldn't reach, so the grass was never green.

I walked toward the outer edge of the fields and ran my fingers along the chain-link fence that bordered the school property. Twisted vines grew along the diamond pattern. If I walked far enough, I could disappear for the lunch period, away from the others and their burning words.

I heard a laugh in the distance and saw Doyle Penrod and Josh Hatfield approaching me. Doyle was the biggest kid in school, due in part because he was spending an extra year in the sixth grade. He had a scar that ran from the bottom of his nose to the right side of his upper lip. He claimed he got it trying to escape a mountain lion, but we all knew his father beat him.

He walked around like he was the king of the school. One day I walked past the open door of his classroom, and he was just sitting there, staring. His teacher was rambling on about nouns and pronouns, and he didn't seem to be getting any of it. His eyes were glazed over. He probably spent most of his days counting down the minutes until the next recess, if he even *could* count. Part of me wondered if his anger came from the realization that with a family like his, he was destined to spend the rest of his life working as a farmhand in Chatwin.

As he and Josh neared, I considered making a run for it, but I was too far from the entrance of the school. They would catch me within a few strides and punish me for my escape attempt. A tightness gripped my throat, and I kept my gaze low to the ground.

"Hey, Brooklyn, how's your mom doing?" Doyle smirked.

"Go away, Doyle."

"Oh, wait, that's right, she went crazy and killed herself."

He laughed and nudged Josh, who gave a half smile. I stared at him, and my lips tightened. Anger burned in my chest.

"Just tell me, how'd she do it?" Doyle asked. "Did she hang herself or did she use a gun?"

My fingers curled, and I dug my nails into my palms.

He looked down at my hands and smiled.

"My dad said you was the one who found her. Said that'll stick with you for the rest of your life. What's it like to see a dead body?"

I took a step toward him and stared into his hollow eyes. He moved toward me and towered over my small frame. His eyes flashed with excitement, and his breath stank behind his yellow teeth. He looked like he wanted to hurt me.

Josh started to walk away. "Come on, Doyle, let's go."

I turned away from his piercing gaze and walked past him. My hands shook, and the burning receded to my stomach. I grabbed the fence, took a deep breath, and teetered on the brink of vomiting.

I heard rustling behind me and looked back. Doyle was pulling on a long stick tangled within the links of the fence.

I turned and ran toward the school.

For a moment I thought I was going to make it, then I heard the stick cutting through the air. The side of my back exploded in pain, dropping me to my knees. I screamed toward the playground, but I was too far away. My fingers grasped the dead grass as I tried to pull myself up. I looked at Doyle in disbelief.

Josh's eyes were wide, and his mouth hung open. He slowly backed away and nervously looked toward the school. He seemed to be calculating whether to run. "Doyle?"

Doyle stood over me. His dumb smile was gone, replaced by his quivering lips. "Don't you ever walk away from me."

He raised the stick, and I tried to scramble away, but before I could, I heard the air separate again, and my right thigh crumbled beneath me in a spray of pain. I screamed out and collapsed to the ground again.

"Doyle!" I heard Josh plead again.

I knew I was going to die. Doyle was going to kill me right here, in plain sight. Through clouded eyes I stared in the direction of the school hoping that someone—anyone—would come to my rescue.

"You used to think you were so special, Brooklyn," he said. "Like you was better than everyone."

He bent down close to me.

"I guess your mom couldn't handle being with a loser like your dad and a kid like you."

He stood and started to laugh. He looked over at Josh and slapped him on the back.

Josh started to laugh too but kept his gaze over his shoulder toward the school.

A sharp pain stabbed at my side. I searched for the source, and my hand rested on a rock protruding from the ground. My fingers slowly gripped it, but I continued to stare at the boys. In one quick motion, I yanked the rock free from the ground, spun my body to face Doyle, and side-armed the stone toward him.

Everything seemed to slow down for a moment. I saw his eyes widen then he shifted the weight of his body and cowered in fear. The rock barely missed the brim of his nose and continued its flight path.

Like a line drive in a baseball game, Josh never saw it coming. The rock collided with his face, just below his eye. I heard him scream, and then he was down, rolling around on the ground.

As quickly as my rage had arrived, it was gone, and I sat there in stunned silence.

Doyle looked at Josh and then turned to me. The smile returned to his face.

I ignored him and jumped to my feet. I ran to Josh and crouched down next to him. "I'm sorry, Josh. I didn't mean to…"

His screams turned into a loud moan, more dramatic than the small welt developing under his eye deserved.

"Shhh, you're fine." I surveyed the playground. I hoped no one had noticed, but a small crowd of students were walking our way. "Please, Josh. Please stop, you're gonna get me in trouble."

It was too late; our audience had arrived. They pushed and positioned themselves in a circle around me, Josh, and Doyle.

Their eyes were wide, but an odd sense of excitement seemed to fill their faces.

"What happened?" Sophie asked.

Of course, she would be here.

Doyle scoffed. "Brooklyn threw a rock at Josh's face."

I looked at him in disbelief, then looked up at the crowd. Every eye was focused on me. I scrambled for words. I wanted to tell them about Doyle and what he had done and how I never meant to hurt Josh, but I saw the looks in their eyes; to them, I was already guilty. If only they could see the welts forming on my back or notice the stick that Doyle had quietly dropped beside him, but they just stared in anger.

Brynn Adams looked puzzled. "What's wrong with you, Brooklyn?"

"I can't believe you would do that," said Sophie.

What was happening? Doyle Penrod had made life miserable for every one of them, but now they rallied around him and scorned me.

Sophie continued, "What would your mom think if she saw you acting this way? Actually, what would she think if she saw you at all? You look homeless with your raggedy hair and dirty clothes."

"It's called soap, why don't you buy a bar." Brynn sneered.

With that, the silence from the crowd turned into laughs. I bit my lower lip hard. I wasn't going to give them the satisfaction of crying.

"Bet your mom never thought her only child would turn out like you," said Sophie, and the laughs grew louder.

I turned away from them and took a final look at Josh, whose moans had turned to sniffles. I gave him a compassionate look.

"I'm sorry, Josh."

I got up and began running toward the school. The jeers from the crowd faded behind me.

Sophie yelled, "Runaway little orphan girl, nobody wants you now."

I had nowhere to go. If I ran home, the school would call my dad at work. That would make him mad because he told me his boss didn't allow personal calls. There was nowhere to hide on the playground, and students weren't allowed in the school during lunch, except to use the bathroom. I could hide in one of the stalls, but I feared that would be the first place Sophie and the other girls would look. I ran toward the school anyway.

I went in one of the back doors and stood at the end of a long hallway. Classrooms ran endlessly along both sides. We weren't allowed to run in the school, so I walked as quickly as I could, my heels never touching the ground. The dim fluorescent lights cast shadows on the tired linoleum as I passed the locked doors of the classrooms. A few were open, and teachers stared at me curiously.

I finally reached my classroom and paused outside the door. A plaque glued to the wall read, "Room 112—Mrs. Harper." The name didn't seem to fit, as all of Mrs. Harper's students called her Miss Amy. She had insisted on this from the first day of school, saying with a smile that Mrs. Harper was her mother-in-law's name.

I stared at the closed door and said a silent prayer. I slowly turned the handle, expecting to feel the resistance of the lock, but the door sprang open. I hesitated for a moment, then slid through the narrow opening.

Miss Amy was at her desk, reading a book and holding the corner of a sandwich in her hand. Her eyes met mine, and I debated sneaking back out, but it was too late. We stared at each other in silence for what seemed like an eternity. Finally, I closed the door behind me and quickly sat at my desk.

I knew she wasn't going to let me stay. The only thing I could think to do was keep my back turned to her and hope she would ignore me.

"Brooklyn, are you all right?" she asked.

I couldn't reply. My emotions were raw, and the sincerity of her simple question, the gentleness of her tone, overwhelmed me. A lump painfully pushed its way up my throat. I closed my eyes.

One, two, three, four, five. Breathe.

I was losing the battle. My chest felt tight, my thoughts scrambled and loud. No, I was not all right. Everyone I had known and everything I had come to expect in the first nine years of my life were gone. My mom was gone, my father may as well be, and the people who were supposed to care spent more time reveling in the mistakes of my parents than being there for me.

I felt Miss Amy's hand on my shoulder. "Brooklyn, talk to me. What's wrong?"

I turned and looked up at her. Her expression softened, the pain in my eyes reflected in her own. I wrapped my arms around her waist and buried my face against her.

My mind told me to stop, to breathe, to remember where I was, but I couldn't control it. Sobs shook through my body.

"It's okay, sweetie. It's okay."

I held onto her for a long time, then finally released my grip and wiped my eyes. She stroked the top of my head, then walked away. I knew I was in trouble. I was sure she was going to call my father or go get the principal, and everyone would make a big deal about it. Then my classmates would begin to trickle in from lunch and see what was going on and all hell would break loose. For a moment I thought about running away, but I would be lucky to walk let alone run as the muscles in my abdomen held a tight grip on me.

From the corner of my eye, I saw her walking toward me again. She pulled a chair from the desk next to mine and sat down close to me. I could feel her warmth. She smelled like fruit and flowers and everything that was good. She leaned forward and held out a box of tissues. My bleary eyes looked up at her, and she smiled at me.

"Brooklyn, what's going on? Did someone hurt you or say something to you?"

I thought about Doyle and whether I should tell her. Yet, if he got in trouble, I would be his number one target. Maybe not at school, but for sure on the walk home.

I shook my head. "Nothing that I haven't heard before."

"Are you sure? Because if someone's hurting or teasing you, please come and tell me. I can take care of it without any of your classmates ever knowing you told me."

"It's okay. I'm okay."

"Then what is it?"

"I don't want to be alone anymore." The words escaped before I could stop them.

She frowned and nodded her head in agreement.

"Oh, sweetie, I can't imagine how hard it must be to lose your mom, but I promise you, you're not alone. You have your dad and…"

"My dad isn't home."

"Of course. I'm sure he works a lot, doesn't he? It's not really fair when you need him, especially now."

I debated how much to share. Should I tell her that on most nights my father didn't come home until the early hours of the morning. That he would stay out late with his "drinking buddies," as my mom used to call them. He had started doing this before she died, and it had only gotten worse since then. Should I tell her that I have to plead with him to come home? That I'm scared and I need him, but that the pull of the bottle is stronger than my tears? That I've learned to fall asleep with every light on and sixty watts shining in my face? I wanted to say all of this and more, but I couldn't.

I simply said, "Yeah, it's hard when he's gone."

She nodded her head again. "I don't like being alone either, but you know what?"

"What?"

"I'm always here for you. Even when we're not at school."

One, two, three, four, five. Breathe.

I picked at my fingernails and stared at the floor, my tears drying. When I looked up, Miss Amy was watching me, her brows pinched, and lips parted like she'd been holding her breath. The moment our eyes met, she blinked quickly and offered a soft smile.

"I'm so happy that you came in here today," she said. "You must have known I needed help on our class project."

"You do?"

"Have you ever tried to cut out twenty circles with a pair of scissors?"

I shook my head.

"Let me tell you, it's next to impossible, and I could really use your help. Are you good with circles?"

"I'm great with circles."

"How good?"

"Like, really good," I said. "Seriously, circles are my best shape."

"Well, aren't I lucky that you came in here today? Do you want to help me?"

A feeling of relief flooded my body, and I nodded my head with excitement. I was safe with her.

She winked at me. "And, Brooklyn, you can come in and help me anytime you want to."

CHAPTER 4

A splash of sunshine burst through the picture window in our front room, cutting through the shadows. The joy of Saturday morning pulsed through me. The lazy comfort of pajamas and cartoons, and the thrill of knowing I didn't have to go to school. It was the one day a week when things almost felt normal.

I yanked my jacket off the hook near the front door and shoved my arms through the sleeves. The tattered cuffs barely reached my wrists. I tugged the zipper up and pushed the door open.

The warmth of the morning sun surrounded me as I stepped off the front porch. I stopped and smiled. The bright, morning sky was a welcome reprieve from what had felt like an endless winter. I took my jacket off and faced the rising light. I closed my eyes and stretched my arms out as far as they would go. My body basked in the rays of my long-lost friend.

I blinked away the streaks of afterlight racing across my vision. As the dark specks began to fade, I noticed something in the stretch of dirt that bordered our driveway. I stepped closer. Two narrow, green stems pushed just above the surface, their heavy tops reaching toward the sun.

My mom's lilies.

My breath caught at the sudden sign of life and a memory flashed in my mind.

My younger self sat cross-legged on a patch of dark green grass in our front yard. The shade of our locust tree danced around me as I watched my mom kneel by the flowerbed. She worked the ground with her narrow shovel; its wooden handle darkened from years of use.

"This soil's not the best," she had said as she dusted a cloud of dirt from her gloves. "Especially if we want these lilies to bloom next spring. But it'll do. With a little love and care, we can bring life to this space. We can create something beautiful."

She had looked at me and smiled, gently reaching toward a strand of loose hair covering my face. I curled my nose at the sharp, earthy scent of the garden soil on her gloves.

"You can make anything beautiful if you try hard enough." She tucked the golden curl behind my ear.

I could picture the flowers in my mind, their vibrant colors dancing in a gentle breeze. This was the real Angela Blair, warm, bright, and beautiful. She hadn't gone crazy, no matter what her so-called friends whispered at her funeral. I remembered the way their eyes widened when they realized I was standing there.

If only I could curl up next to her again, like I used to on those days when I would come home after school and find her lying in bed. If I could go back, I would wrap my arms around her in the tightest hug and tell her everything was going to be okay. If only I could have made her happy again.

I used to listen to my parents talk at night. Their hushed voices echoing through the house. There were many laughs, which were always loud at first then quickly muffled, my mom probably burying her face in a pillow, trying to hold back her giggles.

There were also conversations I wasn't supposed to hear.

"You're too hard on yourself," my father had said one night.

"I don't know why you think you're a failure."

"Because I am," my mom said.

"But you're not. Look at all the things you have…"

"It's not about that, David. You keep saying that, and it just makes me feel worse. Like I'm not grateful enough."

Her voice was rising, and I tiptoed toward the crack in my door to listen.

"Don't you think I know what I have?" she asked. "That I should love every day? I should, I know that, but do you know how hard it is for me just to get out of bed in the morning?"

"Everyone has bad days," my father said. "There's lots of times I hate going to work."

She let out a heavy sigh. "It's not the same thing. You're not listening to what I'm saying."

"I'm trying to."

"You just don't understand." Her footsteps echoed across the wood floor. The slam of her bedroom door filling the house.

I was mad at her that night. I didn't like her being mean to my father. She was the one who couldn't decide whether to be happy or sad. One look at her face each morning and I knew what kind of day she was having.

Then, all at once, everything seemed better. I came home from school one day and found her standing with her back to the door, talking on the phone. When she turned around, I smiled. Her face was lit with a brightness I had forgotten; a genuine, glowing smile that reached the dimple beneath her cheek.

"Brooklyn just walked in," she said. "I'll call you later."

She bit her lower lip, stepped toward me, and took my face in her hands.

She smiled. "Guess what?"

"What?"

"You know how you've always wanted to be a big sister?"

"Yeah."

She paused, and my mind raced with excitement.

"Wait, really?"

She nodded her head.

"You're going to have a baby?"

"Yep."

I pulled my backpack off and leapt onto the couch. I threw my arms in the air and jumped back and forth between the cushions. My mom laughed and jumped onto the couch with me. She was back.

That happiness didn't last as long as I hoped. I don't know what happened, but something went wrong, and I never got my little brother or sister. One day Mrs. Timmons stopped me on my way home from school and told me I needed to come play at their house for a while.

"Did my mom say that?"

"Yes, sweetie."

"Where is she?"

"She had to go see the doctor with your dad, but don't worry about that. She just wants you to come over to our house for a little while until they get home."

"Is my dad okay?"

"Yes, Brooklyn, everything is fine. Now come on in."

A little while turned into hours. I woke up later that night on the Timmons' couch to the sound of soft voices.

"I'm sorry to hear that, David," Mrs. Timmons was saying.

My father answered, "Thank you. And thanks for watching Brooklyn."

"Anytime."

My father cradled me in his arms, and I hugged his neck. He carried me the short distance to our house and laid me in my bed.

"Hey, Brooklyn, let's let Mom sleep tomorrow morning okay?"

"Okay, Dad."

He started to close my bedroom door.

"Why?" I asked.

"Why what?"

"Why does Mom need to sleep? Is she okay?"

He let out a deep sigh, and in the dim light of the hallway, I saw his steeled expression melt away. He reached for the light switch, paused, and left it off. He walked over and sat at the edge of my bed. He didn't look at me but simply stared into the darkness.

"Brooklyn, the baby didn't make it."

"What do you mean?"

"It died."

"Wait, Mom already had the baby?"

"Not exactly. The baby never came. It died in Mommy's tummy."

I could see the light reflecting off his wet cheeks. I looked at my nightstand where I had propped a small chalkboard against the wall.

"COUNTDOWN TO BABY."

I fought to breathe as tightness gripped my chest, and I leaned my head against my father.

"I'm sorry," he said. "I know how much you wanted to be a big sister."

"Is Mom okay?"

"She will be, she just needs some time."

He was wrong. There were no more good days after that.

A bird swooped overhead and landed on one of the fence posts above the lily stems, bringing me back to the present. I swallowed hard. I missed my mom.

CHAPTER 5

I sat next to Miss Amy, both of us tucked behind her grey linoleum desk, hiding from the world. The room was quiet, except for the rhythmic pop of our hole punchers biting into thick cardstock.

I had started eating lunch with her every day. Once my classmates caught on, they began calling me "teacher's pet," but I didn't care. The things they said to me on the playground would be much worse than a silly nickname. She did make me go outside for the last fifteen minutes of lunchtime to "feel the sun" and "stretch my legs," even though I didn't really want to.

I peeked over a sheet of yellow paper at the remains of Miss Amy's lunch. I had finished my own quickly, much to the disappointment of my unsatisfied stomach.

"Do you want some grapes?" she asked, nudging a plastic bag across the desk. "I can't possibly eat them all."

I grinned. "Sure!"

"And you need to try these new crackers I bought, they're so yummy."

"Thank you."

I set my hole puncher aside and took a handful of grapes. I popped one into my mouth and smiled as the crisp skin gave way to a burst of sweet juice.

"Do you know what I remember most about your mom?"

"My mom?"

"Yeah, I was thinking about her last night."

I looked at her, wondering why she would think about her. What horrible rumor had she heard? I sat up in my chair and stared at my hands.

"You were?"

She smiled. "Did you know, I met her at the school carnival last year? I was trying to run the cotton candy booth, and for the life of me, I couldn't figure it out. The line of students just kept getting longer and longer, and parents were getting frustrated. I had spun sugar in my hair and all over my clothes. Everywhere but where I needed it to go. It was a nightmare."

I laughed.

"And do you know what your mom did?"

"What?"

"She stepped right to the front of the line, and with the kindest smile, she asked if I needed help. I could have cried; I was so relieved. She got in that booth with me and worked her magic."

I smiled, remembering that night and finding my mom covered in her own layer of sugar. My heart filled with pride. I hadn't heard anyone say a nice thing about her since she had died. The memory was a sweet gift for a longing soul.

"She made that night so much fun," Miss Amy said. "I don't think she knew how much her kindness meant. Honestly, I don't think most people realize the impact they have, but everyone plays a role. Every life has a purpose."

She placed her hand on mine.

"Your mom was a kind woman, Brooklyn. She brought a lot of happiness to people. I see that same gift in you."

My eyes widened. "Really?"

"Oh yeah, that great big heart of yours shines bright just like hers did."

"I don't think that's true."

She stopped and set her hole puncher and paper down. Bits of colored cardstock scattered gently across her desk.

"Look at me, Brooklyn."

I lifted my head and stared into her hazel eyes.

"You can't let what anyone does or anyone says to you dim the light that's inside of you. You're going to do great things in your life."

"You're the only one that thinks that."

"Maybe I am and maybe I'm not, but it doesn't change the fact that it's true. You just have to believe it. You have to keep dreaming big."

I furrowed my eyebrows and looked down at the mess of confetti on the desk, then I looked back to her.

"What do you mean? Like when I dream at night?"

She smiled. "Kind of. I mean when you think of what you want to do or what you want to be someday, what do you think about?"

"I don't know, I guess maybe I'll just find some job here in Chatwin like everyone else does."

She shifted in her seat and reached for a purple sheet of paper. She shook her head. "I don't believe you."

"What?"

"Brooklyn Blair, if your dream is truly to stay in little old Chatwin, Colorado, I've got no problem with that. Our dreams are our dreams, and no one has the right to tell us whether they're right or wrong. However, I have a hard time believing that you're just counting down the years until you can go work on old man Mattinson's farm."

I chuckled. I had never thought about what I would do when I grew up. I heard my mom say once that most of the women in town had grown up here and spent their days clinging to a hope that Prince Charming would one day ride through town and take them away to a better life, but these fairy tales never seemed to come true.

"Brooklyn, what do you like? What do you enjoy doing? What's fun or makes you happy?" She paused for a moment and looked up from her hole punching. She placed her hand back on mine. "I'm sorry, that was insensitive of me. I know there's been a lot of sadness in your life lately. I didn't mean to dismiss that."

We looked at each other for a moment, then I quickly looked away. I didn't want her to feel bad.

"What do I really like to do?"

"Yeah."

A memory popped into my mind. I was lying on our family room floor, propped up on my elbows. My mom was standing in our small kitchen making dinner. She was singing, so it must have been before the sad days, and her beautiful voice carried throughout the house. I had pulled a large book of photographs off a shelf, a gift from my grandma. Its worn edges and torn book sleeve were evidence of the many hours I had spent looking through it. It contained pictures from across America. National parks, large cities, popular landmarks, and small towns that looked far more charming than Chatwin.

"I like pictures."

"You do?"

"Yeah, like pictures of mountains and trees and flowers and buildings."

"That's amazing. There's not many kids your age who can recognize the beauty that photographs bring to life. That's a talent."

"It is?"

"Absolutely."

"I didn't know I had any talents."

"What are you talking about, you're exploding with them."

My spirit lifted. It was nice to feel special.

"I have this big book of pictures that my Grandma Belle gave me."

Miss Amy looked at me curiously.

"Have I met your grandma?" she asked.

"I don't think so, she's not from here. Maybe you did, when she was living with us."

"Maybe. She's not living with you anymore?"

"No, she was here when my mom got really sad."

Miss Amy's smile faded slightly, and her eyes softened. "Oh, it must have been nice to have her there, to help your mom."

"Yeah, we had lots of fun."

"It's good to have people in our lives that we can count on."

"Yeah."

I began punching holes again, watching as the circles floated effortlessly onto the desk.

"She always called me Brookie-Cookie because she said I loved cookies when I was little. I still love cookies."

"Who doesn't?" Miss Amy laughed. "Does your grandma live close by? Do you get to see her a lot?"

"No, she's not here anymore."

"She doesn't come to visit?"

"She died last year, just before my mom did."

I turned a sheet of paper in my hands and continued punching, trying to see how close I could get each hole. I began to realize that the room was quiet, the only sound was the faint voices and laughs from the playground. I looked at Miss Amy. She was staring at me, her head tilted and her lips curled into a frown. She shook her head.

"I'm so sorry, Brooklyn, that must have been really sad."

I looked back at the sheet of paper and began punching again. "Yeah, I loved my grandma. She made everything better. I don't know why she died. I heard my dad tell someone it was cancer or something like that. That it spread everywhere in her body."

Miss Amy frowned again. "I hate cancer."

"Me, too, even though I don't know what it is. But anyway, she gave me the big book of pictures I was telling you about."

"Right, sorry, I interrupted your story."

"I'll have to show you this one picture. It's of a big bear. He's standing next to a river, and there's all these giant trees around. It's beautiful. And he's reaching for a fish that's jumping out of the water. It's amazing. Like, I don't know how someone took that picture at just the right time."

"I would love to see it."

"Maybe I can bring the book to school. It's pretty big, but I think I can fit it in my backpack."

"Well, even if you can't, just hearing you describe it brought it to life for me. I can picture it in my head."

I reached back and grabbed a new sheet of paper from behind Miss Amy's desk.

"Brooklyn, I'm lucky because I'm your friend, and I know how smart you are. I know you can do amazing things, if you believe. Don't do things just because everyone else is doing them. Dream big. Use the gifts that God gave you."

It had been a long time since someone had said anything so nice to me. The other kids were wrong; I wasn't the teacher's pet. Miss Amy was my friend. She was my best friend.

"Thank you," I said softly.

"No matter what happens, where you go, or what others say, I want you to remember that you are special."

"Okay."

We didn't say much during the rest of the lunch period. Miss Amy seemed deep in thought, and I was focused on how many confetti punches I could create before the hour was over. Yet, her words kept turning in my head, and I started to think about all the things I could take pictures of. I just needed a camera.

CHAPTER 6

I hesitated outside the closed door, not knowing what memories might be awakened inside. I pressed my thumb against a bubble of peeling paint on the door frame, fighting the urge to run.

I drew in a deep breath and turned the handle, letting the door swing open. The familiar squeak of its hinges echoed through the house. I paused and listened for my father.

He had been coming home early the past week or so. I thought at first maybe he had been fired from his job, but he kept leaving for work every morning. He just wasn't staying out as late anymore.

He didn't say much to me, but I liked having him around. At least I wasn't alone. He'd come home, change his clothes, and head straight for the shed behind our house to work on an old motorcycle he owned in a past life.

A couple of hours later he would come in smelling of exhaust fumes and gasoline. He would search for dinner, offer me a little, and then go to the basement where he would shuffle through old boxes late into the night, long past my bedtime. He seemed to be doing anything to stay busy.

I tiptoed into the bedroom, trying to remember if it was the first or second floorboard that squeaked. I stopped and listened for my father again. I could hear the distant sound of his music coming from the speakers in the shed, his standard selection of classic rock. As if on cue, a guitar began an endless solo, the notes reaching higher and higher.

The air in the bedroom smelled stale, and a fine layer of dust blanketed the furniture. I looked around and braced for a flood of memories but was met instead by its bewildering appearance. It looked completely unchanged, as if expecting my mom to return home at any moment.

A quilt covered the bed, hand stitched by my Grandma Belle. Two skinny nightstands stood on opposite sides of the old queen mattress, each with an accompanying lamp. An alarm clock shined weakly in the darkness.

I turned on the light and stared at the long dresser that ran along the length of one wall. A figurine of a young girl playing with a dog sat in the center of it, next to a marble green jewelry box. I traced my fingers along the glossy details of the porcelain sculpture, remembering how I used to sneak in and stare at it, longing for a puppy of my own.

I slowly opened the jewelry box. There were only a few items inside, including a pair of earrings, two bracelets, and a small hidden compartment containing a necklace. I put the bracelets on my wrist and let them dangle loosely.

I caught my reflection in the large mirror that towered over the dresser. I patted the tangles in my hair and pulled against the worn collar of my dingy shirt. Maybe the kids at school were right, I was trash.

I quickly turned away and began searching through the drawers. It didn't feel right to be going through my mom's things, but I knew she wouldn't mind. She had shared everything with me.

I was searching for a box of memories. A collection of photographs and other items that she had set aside to keep safe. I knew she had kept them in here because she had shown them to me before. Yet, every drawer was the same, with her clothes still neatly folded.

Maybe my father had thrown the box away. It wouldn't surprise me; he never wanted to hear or talk about any memories of her.

I slowly wrapped my fingers around the last drawer pull and made a silent wish. I tugged on it, but the drawer resisted. I pulled harder, and it finally released, sagging under the collection of keepsakes kept in the same box I remembered. My heart flooded with relief.

I bent down and examined the contents. Most of the items would have meant nothing to me if not for the fact that they were hers. Everything took on a special meaning after she died. It was the only connection I had left.

I lifted a folder from the drawer. It was filled with cards and old newspaper clippings. My grandma's obituary sat on top. I stared at her picture, the gray and black image failing to capture the strength of her warm smile.

Behind the obituary, folded neatly into a square was a picture I had drawn for my mom when I was younger. I carefully unfolded it revealing two stick figures holding hands under a rainbow. Scrolled across the top, in my best five-year-old handwriting, I love Mom.

I set the drawing down and saw a newspaper article underneath it. The words curled around a picture of my mom standing next to a boy I didn't recognize. I held it up and stared at this younger version of her. Her face lifted with a light I didn't know she had. The bold font above the article read, *Two Mountain Valley High Seniors Recognized as Sterling Scholars.*

I wasn't sure what the words meant, but with the dress she was wearing and how pretty she looked, it seemed like it must have been a big deal. My heart swelled with pride, and I thought for a moment of marching right over to Sophie's house and shoving the article in her face. I could prove to her that my mom was amazing. Maybe that would finally shut her up, but I knew my mom wouldn't approve of such behavior.

I set the folder down and continued to search the drawer until finally, under a stack of photographs, I saw the glossy edges of my mom's digital camera. It was a gift from my father, and she had cherished it. It was the one thing that I was not allowed to touch or play with.

I looked at the camera, then slowly pulled on its wrist strap, lifting it from underneath the photos. I carefully held it in my hands and examined the series of buttons and dials on top of it. From behind me, I heard a creak in the hallway. I dropped the camera and instinctively jumped to my feet. I looked toward the empty doorway. The house stood silent again.

I turned back to the drawer and grabbed the camera, examining it for damage. I gently pressed the power button, and it began to buzz, coming to life. I held the viewfinder up to my eye and scanned the bedroom.

I stood and quietly walked through the house and out the front door. I held the screen door so it wouldn't slam behind me. I paused at the top step and listened. My father's music continued to play from the shed.

I held the camera firmly in my hands and moved toward the lilies my mom had planted, which were now in full bloom. I lifted it to my eye again, and the flowers came into view. I smiled and pulled it away one more time to make sure my finger was resting on what I hoped was the right button. I lifted it back to my eye, found the lilies, and pushed the button. The camera made a clicking sound. I wasn't sure whether a picture had been taken, so I took another. It clicked again. I stared at the digital screen and could barely make out a grainy, digital image.

It worked.

"Brooklyn?" My father's voice cut through the air. His tone was sharp, instantly pulling me from the camera. I quickly turned it off and ran toward the house.

"Brooklyn!" This time he yelled.

I walked through the kitchen, jumping as my feet hit the hardwood and a stack of dirty dishes shifted in the sink. I heard the soiled water drip and then curl down the drain.

I passed through our narrow laundry room, to the bedrooms on the other side.

"Dad?" I asked.

"Brooklyn, get in here."

He was in the bedroom, standing over the open drawer. My heart sank.

"What were you doing in here? Have you been going through Mom's stuff?"

"No."

"What's in your hand?"

I followed his eyes to the camera and instinctively took a step backward.

"I didn't touch anything else, I promise."

"That's expensive. You know you're not supposed to be playing with it."

"I wasn't playing with it. I was taking pictures. My teacher told me I might be good at it."

I took another step back and prepared for my punishment. He stepped toward me, and I closed my eyes. He pulled the camera from my hands.

"I'm sorry, Dad. Please don't be mad."

He stepped back and sat down on the edge of his bed, staring at the camera.

"Your teacher told you to use this?"

I hesitated, not wanting to get Miss Amy in trouble.

"No, sir. She just said I might be a good photographer someday 'cause I like pictures."

He examined the camera and held the viewfinder up to his eye. He adjusted the lens, something I didn't know it could do.

"That's good of her," he said. "I'm glad they're teaching you the important stuff. Teaching you how to work with your hands and things you can actually use."

His reaction surprised me. I relaxed and stepped into the room.

"Do you remember when we bought this?"

His tone was soft, a gentleness he used to speak with.

"Kind of."

He looked at me. "It was Christmas Eve, three years ago."

"Wasn't it two?"

"No, I remember, because the steel shop had waited 'til the last possible minute to give bonuses that year. I was worried it wasn't coming, but we finally got 'em just before Christmas."

"Didn't we go early in the morning to buy it? I remember it was so cold in your car."

"That's right, I'd forgotten that. You loved the snow and all the decorations on Main Street."

He turned the camera over in his hands and rubbed his thumb against the smooth edges. He looked at me and smiled, one side of his face rising higher than the other.

"I wanted to get your mom a camera 'cause she'd always liked pictures, but I had no idea what to look for. Old Gary there at Dalton Thrift tried to talk me into financing some fancy one that came with three different lenses and a carrying case." He shook his head. "I'll tell you, that man's as slick as they come. I wasn't falling for it. Who needs all that extra stuff? Just more junk to throw away. I just wanted to get your mom something nice, I'd never been able to do that for her and she deserved better."

I watched him, slouched on the bed, lost in his thoughts. He looked tired. I sat down next to him. I used to never leave his side, but I couldn't remember the last time I had been this close to him. I gently leaned against his shoulder.

"I loved the look on her face when she opened this. Wish I coulda seen it more often."

I said, "You know what else I remember?"

"What?"

"I remember we drove to the Mayfield Bakery after the store, and you bought me a donut and chocolate milk. The donut had red and green sprinkles on it, and I called it my Christmas donut."

He nodded. "That was a good day."

"Yeah."

"Not too many good ones since," he said.

"I guess not."

He drew in a deep breath and seemed to release himself from the grip of the memories. He handed the camera to me.

"You can have this."

"Really?"

"Yeah, it's not gonna do any good in the bottom of a drawer. Everyone uses their phones now anyway. You need a new memory card or something though, this one's full."

"I know, I took the last pictures."

"You did?"

"Yeah."

"Of what?"

"Mom's flowers out by the driveway."

"You noticed those too, huh? Good choice."

He stood and stretched his back then made his way to the doorway.

"Dad?"

"Yeah?"

"I don't know what to do with the pictures. Like, how to get them printed. I know Mom usually took them to the pharmacy, but I don't know how to do that. Do you think you could show me sometime?"

He looked away, down the hallway, then back to me. "Um…ya know, Brooklyn, I'm not really good with that kinda stuff. Maybe you could ride your bike down there. I'm sure Melanie will help you."

"Okay."

He looked at me for a moment then left the room. I stayed on the bed and adjusted the lens, just as he had.

"I guess we could figure it out," he said, standing in the doorway again.

He surprised me. "Really?"

"Yeah, let's go."

"Right now?"

"Why not?"

"Okay." I jumped off the bed and brought the camera with me. I grabbed my shoes and put them on as I hurried out the door. I didn't want to give him time to change his mind.

<hr>

You could walk just about anywhere in Chatwin without breaking a sweat. My father said if a person was driving along Highway 160, Main Street would seem to appear out of nowhere. A short, two-lane stretch lined with angled parking and faded brick buildings standing shoulder to shoulder. It served as a connector between Interstate 25 and the coal mining town of Ellis. Each day brought a steady stream of eighteen-wheelers hauling coal back and forth, long into the night. When I lay in bed waiting for sleep to overtake me, I could hear the distant growl of their engine brakes as they rumbled into town.

Despite the short distance, we climbed into my father's car and made the quick drive to the pharmacy. He pulled in along the side of the building, the front tire brushing the curb. I looked up at the faded orange and blue sign, *Chatwin Rexall Pharmacy*. I used to spot it from a block away when my mom and I went on walks. It was one of my favorite places to go with her. As soon as we stepped inside, I'd dart off to the little toy aisle. Without fail, Mrs. Jenson, the kind older lady at the register, would find me and give me a piece of candy.

"Now, don't go telling your friends about this," she would say. "I only give these to you because you're my favorite."

Eventually my mom would find me, and I would show her the candy and beg her for whatever toy I had found. "Maybe next time," she would say, and we would leave together.

I hadn't been inside since she died.

As I pushed open the heavy glass door, I heard the familiar bell ring above it. I could almost picture my mom there with me.

"Well, what a nice surprise," I heard a voice say. I recognized the warmth in the tone immediately.

"Hi, Mrs. Jenson," I said.

"Look at you," she said. "Looking more and more beautiful every day, just like your mother. Is your daddy with you?"

I assumed he was behind me, but when I turned to look, I saw him standing outside the door. He held his hand against the handle, ready to push, but hesitated. We locked eyes, he looked down and came in.

"Hello, David," she said.

"How are you, Melanie?"

"It's so nice to see you. It's been too long."

She pulled him in for a hug, and I noticed his body tense. She squeezed tight, and he gently placed a hand on her shoulder, giving her a couple of unaffectionate pats. She released him, and he took a couple of steps back.

"I've been so worried about you…the both of you. I still can't believe Angela's gone."

We stood in awkward silence.

"You know, my niece lost her husband a couple years back," she said. "So, I understand a bit what you're going through."

My father glanced at me. I could feel his energy wanting to storm from the store. People were always saying stuff like this to us, acting like they knew our pain. I don't think they meant anything by it, I just think they didn't know what else to say.

"Course he was the breadwinner," she continued. "Left my niece with two little girls and no way to care for them. Can you imagine?"

"You know, we're actually just here to get some film developed," my father said.

"Oh yes, of course. You didn't come here to listen to me ramble on."

"Brooklyn's started to take up photography."

My heart soared. Maybe he was trying to make himself look like a better father, but I sensed a hint of pride behind his words.

"You are?" Mrs. Jenson asked.

"Yes, ma'am."

"Good for you. I hope you'll let me see them when they're ready."

"Most of the pictures my mom took, I think. I only took the last ones."

"Really? How fun. Do you know what she took pictures of?"

I hadn't thought about this, but the question was all at once exhilarating. The finality of death is swift and abrupt. This reality cornered me the moment my mom died. Her memories could live on, but that's all they were. Stories of what was and what might have been, but her ending was written. Her epilogue complete. Yet, the pictures were a mystery. Something new and unknown. I was torn between wanting Mrs. Jenson to develop them right then and wanting her to take as long as possible. Draw it out, because once I had them, they would never be new again.

"Do you know what they are?" I asked my father.

"No. Probably just some random things, birthdays and such."

"It'll be a gift from your mom, whatever they are," said Mrs. Jenson. She looked around the store and crouched down to me. With her finger, she waved for me to come close.

"Because these were your mother's and she was one of our favorite customers, we're going to do these for free."

"Really?"

"But don't tell anyone, it'll be our secret."

"Thank you, Melanie," said my father.

"Give us two days and we'll have these ready."

"Thank you."

I jumped into the passenger seat of my father's car and reached to close the heavy door. It required a delicate balancing act of pulling hard enough to close the door without letting it pull me out of the car.

"Do you wanna go eat at The Kween?" my father asked.

The Ice Cream Kween, or The Kween as it was called, was one of only two restaurants in Chatwin. Its sign said it had been serving up the same burgers and fries since 1955, although its faded white exterior hardly resembled its once vibrant past as a drive-in diner. My stomach rumbled at the thought of a real meal.

"Yeah."

I assumed we would go to the drive thru as usual, but he pulled into one of the parking stalls.

"Should we go in?"

"Sure."

The air inside hung with a haze of deep-fried grease. The cracked windows provided little relief. We stared up at a hand-painted sign above the register. The limited offerings were the same as seventy years ago. Hamburger, cheeseburger, add bacon, add onions, corn dog, fries, onion rings, and a variety of shake and malt flavors. A teenage girl stared at us blankly from behind the counter.

"Can we get two hamburgers, an order of fries, and…do you wanna share a shake?" my father asked me.

"Sure."

"Strawberry?"

"Yeah."

"And a large strawberry shake."

"Is that all?" the girl asked.

"Yes."

"That'll be $17.73."

My father paid, and we surveyed the restaurant. There was a young couple sitting at one of the booths, but the rest were empty. He chose one on the opposite side. A large crack in the teal-colored seat exposed the stained foam underneath.

I watched as he stared out the window. He looked anxious. His fingers worked tirelessly against each other, gently pulling the skin around his fingernails. I wondered what he was thinking about. I wondered if he would ever be the same…if *we* would ever be the same.

"Dad, can I tell you something?"

"What's that?"

"You promise not to get mad?"

He turned to me. "Is something wrong?"

"Just promise, please."

"Okay, I promise I won't get mad."

"I don't like being alone."

"What'd you mean?"

"When you don't come home from work until late."

He stared at me, then looked past me. "Well, it's hard, Brooklyn. Sometimes I have to work late. I can't always be around."

"You said you wouldn't get mad."

"I'm not mad."

"You sound like you're getting mad."

"I'm not, I promise. I know it's hard not having your mom here. I miss her, too, but I have to work extra hard to support us."

"But why do you have to go to the bar every night?"

He looked at me again, his eyes seemed to be searching for an answer.

"You're a different person when you drink, do you know that?"

He smiled, letting out a faint chuckle. "You sound like your mom." He looked out the window again, then turned back to me.

"I'm still your father, Brooklyn, that hasn't changed."

"No, the Dad that I know, came home every night."

His gaze lingered on me for a long moment, then he looked away. He grabbed the salt shaker from the edge of the table and turned it in his hands. "I know you're getting older, but you're still a little girl. You don't know as much as you think you do."

The couple stood up from their table, and the man walked their tray over to a trash bin. He emptied it while the woman refilled the drink they were sharing. My father watched them as they left, but I kept my eyes fixed on him.

"I know more than you think," I said.

"What?"

"I know more than you think."

He looked at me and leaned in close, his pupils forged of steel. I refused to turn away. I was not going to back down. "How do you know that isn't the real me?"

"Because it can't be. Because if that's who you are, then I have no one."

His eyes closed, and he held them that way. He cupped my hands in his. I nearly jerked away but relaxed in the warmth of his grasp.

"I will not leave you, Brooklyn. I will always be here for you."

A weight lifted from me, a tightness I hadn't even realized was there. For the first time in months, I could breathe. I lowered my head, resting my forehead against his hands.

My father was back.

CHAPTER 7

I stepped along patches of dense crabgrass, making my way through the forgotten landscape of our backyard. Weeds crept along the dry flowerbeds, consuming the life that had once thrived within them.

I approached our old hammock that hung twisted between two large maple trees. It was stiff with the residue of winter. I patted off a mess of broken leaves and a dusting of fresh pollen from its worn mat and boosted myself in. The ropes groaned as they flexed between the two trees.

I stared into the afternoon sun and swung lazily back and forth. Wisps of white clouds moved aimlessly across the blue sky.

This was our special space, me and my mom's. I could picture myself curling up next to her side, feeling the gentle rise and fall of her breathing, remembering how my head rested against her shoulder as she read stories to me late into the summer evenings.

I settled into the hammock and lifted a tattered book I had brought with me. The spine was cracked, and the edges of the pages curled outward, the wear from years of abuse in and out of the school library. I opened to a dog-eared page and let the words pull me into their fictitious world.

A faint breeze drifted through the yard, rustling through the leaves of the towering trees and rocking the hammock as I read. The rhythm gently tugged at my tired eyes, slowly guiding me into sleep.

Suddenly I stood inside the school doors of Chatwin Elementary. I pressed the palm of my hand against the cold, worn steel and entered the outside world. The low hum of school buses echoed in the air.

A gust of wind blew, and I watched as a cluster of fallen leaves danced around each other in wide circles along the pavement. The cold was biting, made worse by the steady breeze.

A row of cars idled in front of the school, as parents waited to chauffeur their children home. The steam from their exhausts billowed in the air. The line seemed exceptionally long, not unexpected with the cold. I scanned the row, holding my hand out in front of me to shelter my eyes from the wind. I hoped my mom might be there, but I was not surprised that she wasn't. Envy filled my mind as I thought of those already thawing in the comfort of mechanical heat.

I looked to my right, down the wide road leading away from the school, where other hapless souls had already begun to trudge home. I zipped my coat to my neck and took my place in the march.

One by one the group peeled away, running toward their homes off the narrow side streets of Chatwin. My family lived in the north end of town, on Whitmore Street, where the homes gave way to the barren landscape. Most days my mom would meet me somewhere along the journey, and we would walk the final stretch past the Timmons' house to our home. I hurried to find her, but when I was close enough to see the pitch of our roof peeking above the trees, I knew she wasn't coming.

My shoulders slumped, and my pace slowed. I hoped it was the cold that kept her in and not the draw of her bed.

A loaf of fresh-baked bread sat perched on the top step as I approached our front door. I lifted it up and felt the plastic wrap squish against my fingers. A scent of bananas stirred with a hint of cinnamon to awaken my hunger. Attached to the loaf was a handwritten note.

Miss seeing your smiling face at book club!
Thinking of you, love Lindsey & Becca.

"Mom, I'm home," I said as I walked through the door. No answer. The only sound was the hum of our refrigerator.

"Mom?"

I crept toward her bedroom, not wanting to wake her if she was asleep. The light was off, and the curtains were closed, but through the glow of daylight, I could see her head resting on her pillow. I reached to close the door but stopped at the whine of its hinges.

I walked into the kitchen. The cereal bowl I had used for breakfast was still sitting on the countertop, the leftover chocolate puffs fat with milk. I rinsed it out and placed it in the sink next to the coffee mug my father had used that morning.

Peppermint, my bunny, stirred restlessly in his cage next to the kitchen table. He pulled at an empty water feeder.

"Hey, buddy," I said and reached for the cage door. "Did Mom forget to give you water today?"

I pulled the empty water bottle and filled it in the kitchen sink. He hopped toward it as soon as I replaced it. The cage rattled as he took heavy licks from the feeder. I looked toward the bedrooms and listened. I didn't want to wake my mom; she needed to sleep. She was happier after she slept.

"Let's go outside and play," I said. "Then Mom can sleep."

I lifted him from the cage and stepped through the family room toward the sliding door leading to our back patio. I drew in a deep breath and tugged on my coat zipper, readying myself for another round with the cold air.

I walked through the backyard and pulled the rusted pin holding the latch on our gate. I sat Peppermint on the ground and let him hop through the empty fields behind our house. We hid in the tall grass, unseen from the world. Peppermint drank from a shallow stream, then we skipped to an open meadow on the other side. I laid down on the cool grass and watched the trail from an airplane slowly dissipate in the afternoon sky.

I could have stayed there forever, if not for the cold and the fact that Peppermint kept hopping away. I jumped back to my feet and did my best to keep him moving in a straight line.

Eventually we reached an abandoned barbed wire fence, lost in the overgrowth of dead grass. I traced my fingers along the rusted wire, gently pressing a fingertip against one of the barbs. The edges were still sharp.

I looked over my shoulder and saw the sun beginning to drift toward the western horizon. Long shadows stretched across the field. I turned toward our house and started walking home.

As I broke through the tall grass and into the open field, our house came into view. It stood dark. The lights were still off.

Why were they still off?

The fear I'd been trying to suppress since the moment I got home from school, surged in my chest. Something was wrong. I knew it now. My heart pounded in my ears, and I wanted to run, but I couldn't will my legs to move.

"Mom?" I whispered to the emptiness around me.

I scooped Peppermint up and began to make long strides across the field. I mistimed my leap across the stream, landing one shoe in the water. Its cushioned sole squished like a wet sponge with each heavy step.

I fumbled with the latch on the gate, my fingers shaking as I tried to pull the pin. I took a heavy breath to calm myself and finally got it opened.

I ran to the sliding door and stepped into the silence of the house. I dropped Peppermint into his cage and turned to face the dark hallway of the bedrooms. I listened intently, hoping for a sound, praying for any sign of life.

The clock in the kitchen ticked just past five o'clock. It would be an hour before my father got home.

I reached for our phone, which was tucked beneath the kitchen cabinets, rarely used. I picked up the wireless receiver and listened to the steady dial tone. Written on a worn sticky note, in my mother's careful handwriting, was a list of emergency contacts. I ran my fingers along the names until I found David's Work. I dialed the first digits, then hung up.

I couldn't call him. He wouldn't be happy to find her like this. Sleeping so long. Isolating herself from the world. He didn't need to know.

I carried the phone with me and tiptoed toward the bedroom again. I leaned in. Through the fading light I could see her shape on the bed. Lying in the same spot she was earlier.

"Mom?" I asked. She didn't respond.

I stepped away and began turning on all the lights in the house, letting their glow fill the darkness that threatened to consume me. I paced the hallway, panic tightening its grip, suffocating me. I stepped back to the door.

"Mom! Mom, it's time to wake up."

Silence.

I stepped toward her bed. A pill bottle, tipped on its side, lay open on her nightstand. A trail of pills were strewn across its surface. My heart raced.

"Mom? Mom, I really need you to wake up now, okay."

Nothing.

My legs gave out beneath me, and I dropped beside her bed. I pressed a hand to her face and recoiled at the chill of her skin.

"Mom, please. Please wake up. I need you to wake up right now."

My eyes shot open, and I gasped for air. The hammock twisted beneath me, and the book fell from my hands. The warmth of the spring air surrounded me again. I steadied myself. My heart pounded in my chest. I pressed my palms to my forehead, as if I could force the memories out. I couldn't relive them anymore, but like a broken record, they played over and over in my dreams. In my nightmares.

"Mom, why did you leave me?" I whispered to the empty world around me.

CHAPTER 8

I sat at my school desk and peeked over my shoulder at the clock on the back wall. The second hand made its slow, methodical sweep around the face. It seemed to be moving at a snail's pace.

The room buzzed with the usual noise that came with the end of the school day, but I tuned it all out. I slid my notebook into my backpack and shifted to the edge of my seat, ready to bolt the moment the bell rang. Normally, I didn't mind lingering, but today was different. My photos were ready. It said so right on the receipt Mrs. Jenson had given me. The anticipation was all-consuming.

I was so excited, I even swallowed my pride and rode my bike to school, something I hadn't done in a long time. It had been a gift for my sixth birthday, but now it made me feel like a baby. It had princess-pink paint, a wicker basket on the front, and rainbow tassels flaring from the handlebars. My legs were too long, and my knees constantly bumped the frame, and worst of all, it still had training wheels.

Not wanting anyone to see me, I came early, before most kids arrived, and locked the bike at the farthest rack from the entrance. Now all I needed was to be the first one out when the bell rang.

"Everyone listen up, please," Miss Amy said, her words lost in the chorus of conversations and laughter. "Hey," she said louder.

"Before you go, remember that your final book reports are due tomorrow."

Final.

The word pulled me back into my seat. Time was running out, and I knew it. The school year was almost over. This was not a surprise, just an acknowledgement of its reality. A voice lurking in my mind, whispering that things were about to change again.

I'm sure the other kids were counting down the days until summer break, but I wasn't. I wished for time to stop or at least slow down. I looked forward to my lunches with Miss Amy. She was my best friend, and I didn't want to say goodbye. I feared that next year I would be forgotten again.

Sometimes I would lie awake at night and fantasize about her adopting me. I pictured her arriving at my door, holding my hand in hers, and the two of us driving away from Chatwin forever. We would make sure to go by the school on the way out so all my classmates could see us. They would be jealous, because I was escaping, and they were stuck.

I knew this was a fairytale, it wouldn't be so grand, but I had convinced myself that Miss Amy would at least let me come live with her if I needed to. I had it all planned out. I would tell her how little space I needed, that I didn't eat much, and that I could work harder than most teenagers, let alone nine-year-olds.

Yet, I was also starting to think I couldn't leave my father now. I was helping him get better. Things almost felt normal again. As normal as they could be. Besides, even though Miss Amy wouldn't be my teacher anymore, I could still see her. There was no reason we couldn't spend our lunches together next year. Maybe I could even ride my bike, hopefully a new one, to her house during the summer. The more I thought about it, the more I realized we didn't need to say goodbye.

The clock hit three, and the chime of the school bell echoed through the building. I pounced through the door and into the hallway, where a steady stream of students were already gathering. I lifted my backpack high into the air and cut through the crowd, my momentum carrying me toward the double doors. Finally, I was out, into the crisp Colorado sunshine. I hurried to my bike and pedaled away.

The photos were ready, just like Mrs. Jenson said they would be. I wanted to open the packet right there at the pharmacy but decided to wait until I was home where I could be alone. I didn't want anyone to ruin the moment.

I worried they would get bent in my backpack, so I carefully clutched them in one hand and steered my bike with the other. I wobbled along the uneven sidewalks of Main Street, and in little time, I was turning down Whitmore Street toward my house. I sailed past the Timmons, where Sophie and Brynn Roberts glared at me as I rode by.

"Nice bike, teacher's pet," Brynn yelled.

I reached my house and jumped off the bike just before the dirt road met the unkept edge of our grass. The bike sailed forward, continuing its momentum until it slowly drifted to the side, stopping just short of the hedges bordering the front of our house.

I dropped my backpack on the ground and sat down on the steps of the front porch. I caught my breath and looked around for Sophie and Brynn. They couldn't see me.

I lifted the edge of the envelope and carefully peeled back the self-sealing glue, the soft crackle of paper breaking the quiet around me. Inside was a narrow stack of glossy photographs, cool and smooth against my fingertips.

I slid them out and held them like something fragile. A visual timeline spilled into my hands, snapshots of our family over the last two years. My seventh birthday, with frosting on my nose, the Fourth of July, and the Halloween when I insisted on being a mummy, even though my mom begged me to be a princess.

I paused on one from Christmas morning. There we were, me, my mom, and Grandma Belle. I was in new pajamas, grinning wildly, mid-laugh, holding up a big, wrapped box. My mom sat beside me, her smile wide and warm, glowing with life. Just looking at her made my chest ache. What I wouldn't give to step back into that exact moment. To feel her arm around me. To be that happy again.

I continued through the stack and came across photos of my Grandma Belle's funeral. There was one of my mom and her brother TJ, who we hardly ever saw, and another of my mom standing solemnly next to my grandma's casket. Dark sunglasses concealed the pain that clearly shone through her eyes that day.

I reached the end of the stack and found my photos of the lilies. I got part of my thumb in one and more of the fence than I wanted in the other, but they were good for a first try. I couldn't wait to show Miss Amy.

I grabbed my backpack and went inside. The house felt stuffy from the warmth of late spring and smelled of stale coffee. I left the front door open, closing only the screen, and made a quick snack. Then I pulled a sheet of scrap cardstock I had taken from school, wiped off an area of the kitchen table, and pasted a photo of the lilies to it. I cut a clean edge around it, leaving enough room to fill in the border with colorful designs.

I stared again at the photos of my mom. I knew my father would be excited to see them. I wanted to call him to see what time he would be home, but I knew it wasn't up to him.

"Work ends when the boss tells us we're done," he always told me.

I started to worry when the last rays of the sunset gave way to the shadows of night. He hadn't been this late in a while. Finally, I heard a car door close, and then the slam of the screen door. Relief filled my body.

He dropped his lunch cooler on the table where I was sitting. Its edges were scuffed, and it was stained with the dirt and grease from years of use. He sat on the chair opposite me and brought his hands to his chin. He rubbed his calloused palms along his face, pausing over his eyes, and let out a heavy sigh.

"Why'd you use the front door?" I asked.

"What?"

"Why'd you come through the front door?"

"'Cause the stupid car stopped working. Piece of junk radiator went out on it. Of course, 'cause heaven forbid I catch a break."

"I'm sorry."

"I think that dumb, hick Phil did something to it when he helped me with the alternator. It was working fine, and now all of a sudden, I've got this massive repair on my hands."

He looked to the side and stared vacantly into the distance. "Where am I gonna get that kind of cash? I already advanced everything I could to pay for your mother's…"

He stopped and looked at me.

"I'm sorry," he said. "You don't need to worry about stuff like this."

"It's okay."

"How was your day?" he asked.

"Good," I said. "I got the pictures."

"What pictures?"

"The ones we took to the pharmacy."

"You did?"

"You can look at them if you want. This one's my favorite."

I handed him the picture of Mom and Grandma Belle. He glanced at it briefly, then gave it back to me. I looked at it, its edges still warm from where I had been holding it for so long. I thought it would mean more to him. I thought he'd feel something.

I reached for one of the other pictures. "Here's one of the lilies that I told you about."

"That's really good, Brooklyn."

"Thanks."

He was there, but not there. His leg nervously bounced on the ball of his foot, causing the table to rattle. He stared at his hands and pushed his thumb up the palm of the other, toward the end of each fingertip.

"I'm gonna go spend some time in the shed, all right?"

"Okay."

"Then we'll scrounge up some dinner."

I picked up the picture of Mom and Grandma Belle and wiped off a smudge left by my father's hand, a perfect capture of his fingerprint. I walked over to the refrigerator, placed the photo against it, and held it in place with a Chatwin Valley Bank magnet. I wanted their memory to live in our home forever.

CHAPTER 9

The early afternoon sun warmed the broken asphalt of the school playground. I looked to the sky as tiny beads of sweat formed along my forehead. A trail of silky, white clouds attempted to provide relief, but they couldn't compete. It felt more like July than May.

I followed a step behind Miss Amy as we weaved our way through the crowded playground. Students ran in all directions, filled with reckless excitement that only the last day of school could bring.

The tradition at Chatwin Elementary had always been for the students and teachers to gather for field day, the annual end of the school year celebration.

Miss Amy came up with the idea that she and I should have our own party, with one final, special lunch. She had planned a picnic for just the two of us.

I eagerly moved with her as we continued to zigzag through the chaos. She looked back and said something to me, but I couldn't hear it over the laughter and screams around us. The Beach Boys, "Surfin' USA" blared over the PA system. An odd choice, since I didn't know anyone in Chatwin who had ever been surfing or even been to a beach, but it was one of Principal Giles go-to summer songs.

I tried to get closer to Miss Amy. "What?" I asked, but she had already turned back around, and she didn't hear me. She pointed to an area of open grass in the distance. I nodded with understanding and continued to follow. With each step, the peacefulness of the outlying schoolyard began to settle over me.

"This looks like a good spot." She set a small, nylon cooler on the ground and unfurled a thin blanket. She pulled its corners tight on the grass.

"Have a seat."

I sat down on the checkered blanket and tucked my legs underneath me. The grass beneath it was soft and slightly damp.

She handed me a plastic bag with a carefully wrapped sandwich inside. "I hope you like chicken salad."

I raised an eyebrow and tilted my head. "What's chicken salad?"

"It's my grandma's recipe, and you're going to love it. Every time I eat it, I feel like a little girl again, sitting in her kitchen, eating sandwiches on a hot summer day."

I unwrapped the sandwich and stared at its unusual shape. Miss Amy smiled. "Haven't you ever had a croissant before?"

"A what?"

"A croissant. It's good, try it."

I pulled off a small corner and placed it in my mouth. The pastry melted on my tongue. It was flaky, buttery, and soft. "Yum, it's a lot better than bread."

"I'm glad you like it. I also brought some chips and two éclairs…"

I laughed. "What's an éclair?"

She leaned toward me with a crooked smile. "If you think the croissant is good, just wait. An éclair is like heaven. It will blow your mind."

I smiled, and my stomach growled with anticipation. I took a bite of the sandwich. The creamy chicken blended with bits of crunchy celery and something tangy I couldn't quite name. It was delicious.

We sat in silence, enjoying the meal. I felt like royalty, sharing this special moment with my friend. Yet, our impending goodbye loomed in the background.

"Isn't it beautiful?" she interrupted my thoughts.

"What?"

She turned my attention to the schoolyard. "The Maypole. Isn't it beautiful?"

I watched as members of the sixth-grade class weaved long ribbons into a colorful pattern on a large pole. Moving in opposite directions, up and over, in and out.

"Yeah."

She wiped a napkin against the corner of her mouth and looked at me. "Hey, what's up with you today? Is everything okay?"

I'd learned I could be honest with her, but I didn't want to today. I didn't want to ruin our picnic by telling her how much I dreaded the loneliness of summer, or that my dad seemed sad again. He was home every night now, which was good, but he had less and less to say to me. More than anything, I didn't want to say goodbye to Miss Amy.

"I'm good."

She leaned closer and looked into my eyes. "Are you sure?"

"Yes." I nodded and smiled. "Thanks again for lunch."

"Well, thank you for the company."

We sat quietly for a while longer, eating our sandwiches and trying to stay ahead of the heat which was rapidly melting the chocolate frosting off our éclairs.

Miss Amy broke the silence. "Brooklyn, I've got something to tell you."

"Okay."

"I have some bad news."

My head shot up from the chocolate I was inconspicuously trying to wipe off my hand onto the grass. I hated bad news. She had my full attention now.

"I'm leaving Chatwin."

Her words hit like when I was playing kickball and the ball slammed straight into my stomach.

My breath vanished. My world stopped. "What?"

"I have to leave."

"Why?"

"My husband and I moved here so that we could help his grandpa, who's been really sick. We thought we'd be here for a few years, but he's gotten worse, faster than anyone thought. They're going to move him to Mayfield where he can live in a place that's kind of like a hospital. The nurses there can help him better than we can."

I heard her talking, but the words were lost on my shattered heart. I had never thought about why Miss Amy was in Chatwin. I guess I believed she was here just for me.

"You're leaving," I said more than asked.

"I know. It's breaking my heart, too. How in the world am I going to leave my best friend?"

She brought me close with one arm and placed her forehead against mine. I could feel her love radiate through me, soft and warm like sunlight. We stayed like that for a moment, then she slowly pulled away. Thoughts of my mom swirled in my head.

Why does everyone keep leaving me?

"You can't go. I can't lose you, too. I can't. You're all I have left."

One, two, three, four, five. Breathe.

"Please take me with you."

She stared at me in silence. The happy face she had worn to break the news faded, replaced by something I couldn't quite read. Confusion or maybe embarrassment, I wasn't sure. She turned away and looked the other direction.

Was she laughing?

Heat rushed to my cheeks.

What a stupid question to ask. What was I thinking?

She reached for a napkin and turned back to me. Gently, she dabbed beneath her eyes where a single tear had carved a faint trail down her cheek.

"That's probably one of the sweetest things anyone has ever asked me."

My heart grew hopeful.

"I would love to have you come with me, sweetie, but we both know you can't."

I scrambled for my sales pitch, but it was lost, and all I got out was, "I can work really hard."

She held the tissue to her nose and laughed through her tears. "Oh, Brooklyn, you are so unbelievably sweet. I would take you with me in a second if I could and hard work wouldn't be required, but you've got a daddy at home who loves you and would miss you if you were gone."

She was wrong, he wouldn't miss me. I hadn't told her enough. He probably loved me, I think, when he could, but he couldn't raise a daughter. He would be happy to see me go.

My heart was breaking. "But I can't lose you."

"I don't want you to worry. I've talked with the other teachers, and they're going to look out for you. They're going to keep you safe here. And Brooklyn, if things ever get bad here or at home, you go and talk to Mr. Giles. He'll know how to help you."

"But…but you wouldn't even know I'm there. I can be really quiet, and I don't eat much food. Please."

She took hold of my shoulders and pulled me close to her. I hadn't been hugged by anyone since my mom died, and I collapsed into the warmth of her embrace.

"Please don't leave."

She held me close, and I stayed there, clinging to her, letting the tears fall freely. Through my heartbreak, I began to understand, Miss Amy was leaving, and I wasn't going with her.

"It's going to be okay," she whispered, pulling away and smiling at me. "I'm going to give you my phone number, and I'm going to write to you. No matter where I go, I will always be there for you."

She looked at me the way she had so many times before, gentle and kind. Her eyes softened, and she pressed the napkin to them again.

"You're going to do great things in life, Brooklyn Blair, just you wait and see. God's got a plan for you, and it's bigger than this crumby old town. Don't settle, be better than this place."

I nodded, but Chatwin had already sunk its claws into me. I wanted to believe what she was saying, but feelings of doubt and hopelessness seized my mind.

Suddenly the bell rang, and it was time for the entire school to gather for a final farewell from Mr. Giles.

Miss Amy began packing up our lunch. Hesitantly, I pulled a gift from my backpack. I had wrapped it in a brown paper lunch bag and did my best to color it with crayons and markers, but in the end, it was still just a brown bag. I handed it to her anyway.

"Well, what a nice surprise," she said. "And I love the wrapping paper."

She carefully opened the bag and reached inside. She pulled out the picture I had taken of the lilies. I watched closely as she looked at the photo. I wanted to show her that I had taken a picture of something beautiful, just like she said I could.

"Oh, Brooklyn…wow, this is amazing."

I smiled, and my heart burst with joy.

"Did you take this?"

I nodded my head with pride.

"How did you know how to do this?"

"I just took the pictures like my mom always did and then took it to the pharmacy. Mrs. Jenson helped me from there. She even told me exactly what day to pick them up, and I did, all by myself."

"That's very impressive. And you told me about your mom's lilies, but I had no idea how beautiful they really are."

She remembered. I couldn't believe it.

"She would be so proud of you."

I rushed to her and gave one more hug. "I love you," I whispered, then turned and ran away.

In the late afternoon, the low hanging sun filled our backyard. Its blinding rays reflected in a spray of light. I stood on the perch of our sliding glass door holding Peppermint in my arms and squinted into the horizon.

I looked at my bunny. "That's too much sun for me. What about you?"

Peppermint wiggled his nose against the open air.

"Let's have our tea party inside today, and then next week, since I don't have school anymore, we'll have it outside." I stroked the top of his head. "Does that sound okay, buddy?"

My tea set was a gift from my Grandma Belle for my seventh birthday. It came with four cups, four saucers, and a teapot, each with matching, intricate designs. I pretended the set was made of the finest porcelain, even though I had seen the same one at Dalton's Thrift in Mayfield. I guarded it with my life and kept each piece wrapped in the packaging it came in.

I sat Peppermint down and spread a blanket on the kitchen floor. I organized the tea set in perfect order. One cup on each saucer, with the handles pointing to the right, just like my grandma had shown me.

Peppermint wasn't much company at my parties because he was always hopping away, so I also set up my dolls around the blanket. This formed a larger group and kept things more sophisticated and proper.

I sat down and looked at my group of imaginary friends. The other kids from school were probably kicking off their summer with something more exciting, like a water balloon fight or a trip to the Chatwin pool. I envied them, but I didn't have a swimsuit that fit or a friend to do any of these activities with. My mom used to tell me not to dwell on what we didn't have and make the best of what we're given. I was trying.

I pretended to serve croissants and éclairs, just like Miss Amy had. I think it was my best party yet.

As nighttime approached, I carefully put everything away then plopped down in front of the TV. I scrolled through the channels, but all the kid shows were ending, giving way to boring news programs.

I checked the clock, it was six p.m. My father should be home. I hoped that maybe he couldn't find a ride or that he had to work late, but as the deep shadows of night overtook the house, I was running out of reasonable excuses. I gave up by eleven thirty and crawled into bed.

I woke up with an incredible urge to pee, instantly regretting my last cup of juice. I tiptoed out of my bedroom, still half-asleep. The cool linoleum sent a chill through my feet as I stepped into the bathroom. I stumbled in, my eyelids heavy, tugging me back toward bed.

Suddenly I heard a noise from the kitchen. I froze. The drip of the kitchen faucet echoed as each drop plinked against a stack of dirty dishes. I held my breath and walked to the kitchen to turn it off. Then I slowly let my breath escape.

I heard a sniffle. My eyes shot to the entryway leading into the family room. A faint glow spilled from the reading lamp beside the couch, casting a soft light across the room. My father was sitting there in his usual spot, holding the photo I had taped to the fridge. The one of my grandma and Mom. I stood still, watching him.

Was he crying?

I didn't want him to see me, so I began to carefully tiptoe toward the bathroom

I must have missed one of the saucers when I was cleaning up. *How could I be so careless?*

My foot found it in the dark, and I kicked it along the hardwood floor, shattering it against the baseboard. My eyes immediately looked toward the family room, connecting with his. Even in the dark, I could see his rage. He leapt off the couch.

"Brooklyn," he yelled, stumbling toward me.

The sound of my name, sharp and slurred, cracked through the quiet just like the saucer breaking. A chill rushed down my arms, into my feet, and rooted me to the floor.

Something was wrong. He was drunk, I could smell it from across the room, bitter and sour, but it was more than that. There was something in his voice I'd never heard before. Not sadness or confusion. It was uncontrollable anger.

"What' you doing? Spying on me?"

He moved toward me, but his drunken legs gave way, and he veered left, barely catching himself against the wall. It gave me just enough time to make a run for my bedroom.

"Brooklyn," his voice boomed. "Get back here, so I can teach you a lesson. I don't need anyone watching me—you understand? You understand?"

I stood at the opening of my bedroom and surveyed my options. There weren't many. I could hide under my bed, but I feared what was hiding under there.

"Brooklyn."

Time was running out, and the only place I could think to go was the back of my closet. I locked my bedroom door and ran for it, shoving aside clothes and the few toys I owned. I crouched in the corner, tucked my knees to my chest, and squeezed my eyes shut.

I heard a loud crash, and my bedroom door slammed open. The sound of wood splinters scattered across the floor.

"I'm gonna teach you some respect. Teach both of you," he slurred. "Your mom ain't here now, so it's my job. Now come on out!"

I tried to be as small as I could wishing the closet would swallow me whole.

"Both of you, always spying on me. Tellin' me what to do. Well, where's your mom now? Huh? Where is she?"

Before my brain could stop my mouth, the words flew out, "Mom went to Heaven to get away from you!"

I buried my face in my knees; I had just given away my hiding place and thrown more fuel on the fire.

Silence filled the room. I could almost feel the twisted grin that must have crept across his face.

"Heaven?" he said with a bitter chuckle. "Your mom in Heaven? Oh, angel… your mom's not in Heaven. She's in hell. That's where people go when they give up. When they walk away from their husbands and families. From their daughters. Hell's where they go when they kill themselves. You hear me?"

In a flash he jerked open my closet door, and I slowly opened my eyes. For one brief moment, I thought my tears would soften his heart, but I didn't recognize the man I was staring at. My father was gone, replaced by the drunken maniac standing in front of me. In one quick motion, he picked me up by the back of my nightgown and lifted me out of the closet. The collar pulled hard against my neck. It felt like my throat was going to explode. He threw me across the room; I hit hard and crumbled against the wall on the opposite side. My bladder released, soaking my night-gown and pooling underneath me.

Suddenly he was standing above me. He yanked me up by my arm. I screamed in pain as the weight of my body pulled in the opposite direction. He cupped a hand below my chin and held me against the wall. I could smell the rottenness of his breath. I closed my eyes and waited for him to slap me or throw me again, but he didn't move. I peeked through one eye and saw his lower lip quiver and tears formed around his eyes. Slowly, he let go of me, and I fell to the floor.

"Don't you ever spy on me again."

And then he was gone.

CHAPTER 10

Nine Years Later

stared through the glass partition of the housing department at Grand Mesa Community College. A woman sat behind it, her expression fixed in a look of mild annoyance, her hair pulled back into a tight ponytail. She seemed more invested in her computer screen than in me. My eyes drifted over to the corner of her desk where a day-to-day calendar rested. There was a picture of an angry cat with the caption, *Of all my lives, this one is the worst.*

She glanced up at me. "Miss Blair, in order to process your student housing request, we must receive a deposit of seven hundred and fifty dollars."

I drew in a deep breath and let out a quiet sigh. My frustration was growing. I had been standing at this window for fifteen minutes, shouting through the worn speaker that separated us, because the woman kept saying she couldn't hear me. My mind scrambled for the right words, something that would get through to her. No was not an option, but the fears and doubts that stalk all dreams had my confidence in their crosshairs.

"I understand what you're saying," I said. "But my financial aid won't begin until Monday. I'm here now, and I'm telling you I can put four hundred dollars down today and pay the rest in a couple of days, once the aid begins."

"I sorry, Miss Blair, that's not possible. If I let every student come in here and do that, do you know what an accounting night-mare that would create?"

I looked to my left and then to my right and stared down the empty hallways. I had arrived at the school a week early so I could get items like this taken care of. Up to this point I had only seen two other people roaming around the campus.

I sighed. "There's no one here. It's just me, and I'm telling you I will pay you Monday morning. I'll be the first in line."

The woman looked up from her computer, finally acknowledging me. Her eyes glared above the purple rim of her glasses.

"Miss Blair, There. Are. No. Exceptions."

She punctuated each word as if I couldn't understand.

"You shouldn't have arrived before your financial aid started; that's your fault. This is the real world now, sweetie. You're in college. Mommy and Daddy can't come and talk to the principal and fight your battles for you."

My mind was spinning.

What was I doing here? Thinking I could be a college student. This is why people didn't leave Chatwin. Just accept who you are and deal with it. Why did I think I could be one of the lucky ones?

I rubbed my palms on the thighs of my jeans and swallowed the lump crawling up my throat.

"I'm sorry I showed up early. I was just excited to get here."

"What's that?" the woman asked without looking up. "You'll have to speak up."

I shook my head and stepped back. "Nothing."

I had waited nine years, made it all the way here, and somehow I already felt like I didn't belong. So much for conquering the impossible.

<hr>

What Grand Mesa College lacked in size, it made up for in distance. Long hallways led in various directions, each one ending at its own, two-story building. Grey brick walls ran endlessly, broken only by the methodical placement of windows. There were seven buildings that spurred off the larger, circular Douglas Administration and Student Building. One was the library and another one was the PE Building. The remaining five consisted of classrooms. None of the buildings were particularly large, but they were spread out, probably to make the campus look more like a college and less like a high school.

Beyond the *Bicycle Wheel*, as the campus was called, was an older building that the school had converted into student housing. It was a cheap option for those who didn't live in off-campus housing or didn't want to live at home. I quickly signed up for a spot after receiving my acceptance letter. There were four to a room, so I knew it would be tight, but so was my budget.

I stood in the college bookstore looking at a large map of the campus. After my run-in with the housing czar, I figured I could at least admire my future living quarters. I really didn't need a map, it was obvious that one of the seven spokes would eventually lead me where I needed to go, but I wasn't in a hurry. I had nowhere to go. I also had nowhere to sleep, a fact which twisted with anxiety in my stomach.

One of the bookstore employees approached me. "Can I help you with something?" I was caught off guard by his appearance. He looked like a human billboard, promoting the college. He wore a maroon Grand Mesa T-shirt, with a matching flat cap, and visible just above his pocket, I could see the college logo stamped on his phone case.

"I'm just looking for the housing building."

"Oh, that's easy. Pretty much any of the east hallways will lead you there."

I knew it.

"Are you a freshman?"

"Is it that obvious?" I joked.

"No." He looked down and rapidly clicked his pen. "Sorry, it's just, campus is pretty basic, so the only people who ever look at the map are new students."

"It does seem pretty easy."

He looked up and smiled at me.

"Are you a local?"

"Yeah…I mean I'm from Colorado." I purposely avoided the mention of Chatwin.

"Cool, well welcome to GMCC."

"Thanks."

We hesitated for a moment, the conversation wilting. I stared at the map again but watched him from the corner of my eye. He didn't leave.

A girl's voice came from behind me. "I can help you find the Harper Building."

I turned and was greeted by a warm smile. She held her hand out to me. "Hi, I'm Ellie Foster."

"Brooke."

"Brooklyn Blair," she said.

"What? Wait, how did you…"

"Your name tag." She motioned to the lanyard hanging around my neck and lifted it. The school had included it with the welcome packet. They recommended wearing it for the first couple of weeks so people can, "get to know you."

My insistence on following the rules suddenly made me feel dumb.

"Brooklyn Blair from, blank Colorado," she said. "Ooh, a mystery girl."

She smiled and let the lanyard fall back against my shirt. She had an aura about her that seemed to command the lowering of all defenses. I suddenly felt at ease and smiled with relief as the weight of my imposter syndrome melted away.

"I can take you if you want."

"Oh…no, you don't need to do that."

"It's no biggie. Life's all about connecting, Brooklyn, and we're the only students here. So, let's walk and talk."

I pulled the lanyard from around my neck and folded it into my back pocket. I wasn't Brooklyn anymore. I had traded in that name when my childhood was taken from me. If someone called me by my full name, it told me they either knew me when I was young, or they didn't know me at all. I had no use for the former group, but I was willing to give the latter a chance.

"Actually, it's just Brooke."

"Brooke. Got it. I like that."

We turned and began to leave. I followed a half step behind Ellie, letting her lead the way.

"I think you have an admirer," she said.

I turned and looked over my shoulder. The bookstore employee was still staring at me. I gave him a shy wave.

"Thanks again," I said.

"Not a problem. Go GMCC!"

I turned back to Ellie, and we both fought a laugh.

"You're freaking gorgeous by the way. Are you like an influencer or model or something?"

I smoothed my hair and looked down at my boring T-shirt and jeans. I laughed. "I've never been accused of that before but thank you."

"Well, just saying, you could be. I wish I had your height."

I shook my head. She was pretty, with light brown eyes and matching, wavy brown hair. She was also petite, especially next to me. Her head barely reached my shoulders.

"Are you kidding?" I asked. "I would kill to be your size. I feel like a giant. Boys don't like girls who can look them in the eye."

She stopped and turned toward me, looking at me from head to toe. "You're not that tall. What are you, like five-eight?"

"Five-ten."

She dismissed me with a wave. "Like I said, you're gorgeous, but maybe we can do like a *Freaky Friday* thing and change bodies for the day. See how it is."

"I loved that movie."

We continued down one of the empty hallways and veered toward a set of double doors off to the side. We opened them to the warm world outside.

"You know on TV when a character goes off to college and their dorm life looks amazing?" she asked. "Everyone is hanging out and they live in amazing, huge rooms?"

"Yeah," I said.

"That's not Harper Hall. Harper's more like a prison. With long hallways and worn-out floors. And doors, so many doors. Just door after door after door. Each one hiding two sets of bunk beds in a space that can barely fit one."

It was clear by Ellie's appearance that she had money and most likely plenty of it, although, this was a judgment I was trying not to make. Her hair, earrings, and clothes screamed wealth. I felt a hint of disappointment. Was she just another, typical rich kid who couldn't understand why anyone would want to be poor?

Like anybody wants to be poor.

"I've probably seen worse," I said. "And beggars can't be choosers."

I appreciated her help, but I suddenly wished she would leave. If the place was as bad as she said, it would be made worse by her pointing out all its defects.

As we approached the building, I was already disappointed. I had learned a few tricks of photography, but there was no way this could be the same building I saw on the school's website. They made it look so inviting. In reality, it was anything but. It was old, but not in a cool historical way. More like 1960s modern architecture old. The exterior was light blue, and there were white, wavy pillars running from top to bottom between the windows.

Ellie ran up and opened the door for me. With her arm sweeping out as if I were royalty, she led me in.

"Welcome to your new home," she said.

She was making this worse.

I stepped inside. The air hit me first, stale, thick, and unmoving, with a faint trace of mildew clinging to the walls like a memory no one bothered to clean.

Ahead, a narrow staircase rose into the dimness. On either side, a maze of dark brown doors stretched out like something from a bad dream. The gray walls made everything feel smaller, and the poorly lit hallways only deepened the gloom.

We climbed the stairs and found more of the same. Same walls. Same doors. Same feeling that this place hadn't been meant to feel like home.

"It's literally a prison," I said. "A very old prison."

"Right?" she asked and then began laughing.

I turned toward her, wanting to be angry at her enjoyment of this, but her laugh was somehow contagious. I frowned but then started laughing, too. Hard, can't catch your breath type of laughing. Something I hadn't experienced in a long time.

We stepped back outside, and I sat down on steps leading to the front door. As quickly as the laughter had come on, the reality of my next year began to set it. I buried my head into my knees.

"Go GMCC, rah, rah, rah," Ellie mockingly cheered and sat down next to me.

"So, here's what I think, Brooke," she said. "I don't know where you're from, and I don't know your parents, but I know they didn't send you to college, even a community college, to live like this. They love you too much to do that to you."

Little did she know.

"This was meant to be."

"What?" I asked. "That I'm finally living my dream of going to college, and it starts out like this?"

"No. It was meant to be that I came to campus today looking to post a listing for an opening we have at my townhouse. When I saw you standing there, I said to myself, 'Ellie, that's the one.' And when I heard you say Harper Hall, I knew you were the one."

I looked up and stared at her, trying to determine whether she was serious or not.

"You have to come live with me, Brooke. I can't leave you here. There's no other way. I live with four other girls in a townhouse my parents own. They bought it when my older brother was pretending to be a college student. He finally decided to graduate after six years, so now the house is mine. We'll not mine. I mean, it's my parents', but you get the point."

She was talking so fast, I couldn't process what she was saying.

"What'd you think?"

"You don't even know me."

"Call it a good first impression. I guess I'm not threatened by tall, pretty blondes with blue eyes that hang out at a small community college in nowhere Colorado. Maybe a bit jealous, but you don't seem like the scary type."

"Wait, are you being serious?"

"Absolutely."

"I don't know, Ellie…"

"No! Brooke, don't do that. Don't think of why you can't do this. Think of why you have to do this."

Who was this girl?

"No, I mean it sounds great. Seriously, like, I can't even believe it. It's just…"

"It's just what?" Ellie asked.

My past beckoned my return to reality. My house, my appearance, the hunger I learned to tolerate. I was an imposter here. I could dig through the clearance racks at Walmart and Target and make myself presentable, but I was still Brooklyn Blair, a white trash girl from a small town.

"I can't afford it," I said.

We sat in silence for a moment. Ellie began to nod her head.

"Totally. Like, I totally get it. But if you don't mind me asking, what can you afford?"

"Harper Hall, unfortunately."

"Which is?"

"Which is?" I questioned. "You mean like cost?"

"Yeah."

"Three fifty a month."

Ellie's body shifted, and she stared directly at me.

"Shut up. They charge you *three hundred and fifty dollars* per month for a bed in this dump?"

I shrugged. "It's a bed."

"Can you swing four twenty-five? That's what my parents charge, and it's so much better than this, Brooke. You'd share a room with me, and we'd have our own bathroom."

I looked over my shoulder at the tired building, then looked back at Ellie.

"Are you sure?"

"Totally."

I laughed. "Okay…I'm in."

"Seriously?"

"Yes!"

She stood and reached out her hand to me. "Then let's get you out of here before this place sucks the soul right out of you."

I grabbed her hand, and she boosted me to my feet. Maybe I could do this after all.

CHAPTER 11

We sat in silence. The only sounds were the soft hum of the air conditioner and the faint buzz of the fluorescent lights overhead. I shifted in my seat and glanced to my left, then right. Three tiers of chairs curved around the lecture hall, every one of them filled.

Our professor paced at the front. "Come on, guys. This one's basic."

I knew the answer, maybe, but no one else raised a hand. I must be wrong.

"Let me repeat the question," he said. "All living things require an input of…what to survive?"

"Energy," I whispered.

I raised my hand, halfway. Dropped it. Then raised it again.

"Yes?"

"Energy?"

He raised an eyebrow. "Are you asking me or telling me?"

I sat up straighter. "Telling you, sir."

"Good. But no need to call me sir."

I flushed. "Sorry."

He gave a small wave. "No apology needed. Thanks for being brave enough to answer."

My heart beat fast. One month into college, and here I was, speaking up like I belonged.

A hand touched my shoulder. "Nice job, Brooke," Ellie whispered from behind.

I was still smiling as class dismissed, and Ellie and I made our way to the student center. The common area was filled with the usual lunch rush. There was a surprising number of students, given the limited food options. Ellie and I managed to find an open table, and I wiped away the crumbs and a smear of ketchup left over from the previous tenants.

"Gross," Ellie said. "You'd think people could clean up their mess."

I tossed the soiled napkin in the trash and sat down. From my backpack, I unwrapped a pre-sliced bagel and spread a small packet of cream cheese onto it. The stale edges crumbled under the weight of the plastic knife. I took a dry, disappointing bite and watched as students filed by. I was surprised by how many knew each other. This was obvious from the first day of the semester, as every classroom felt like a high school reunion. It was as if the students were simply returning from summer break, ready to face another school year.

"I feel like everyone knows each other here."

"That's because we do," Ellie said. "For most, this is basically a glorified high school."

"What do you mean?"

"Well, you've got CSU to the north and CU to the south. Grand Mesa lives in the shadow of both. It's kind of where all us drifters from Carlson go when we don't know what to do next in life."

"I don't think the professors got the memo. I got a 68 percent on my first English paper, and that's my best subject. I'm drowning here."

She leaned forward and smiled, wiping crumbs off her hands from a breadstick that accompanied a sad looking salad she had purchased.

"Yeah, the professors totally have an inferiority complex," she said. "It's like they need to prove they're as good as the universities. If I sit down on the first day of class and they say this will be the hardest course you'll ever take, I'm out, because they're not lying."

We watched people for a while longer as I choked down the rest of my bagel. Slowly the crowds began to thin.

"So, are you coming to the bonfire tonight?"

I knew this question was coming. She had been hinting about it all week. I loved my new roommates, but from day one, every night seemed to be an adventure. Clubs, parties, dinners. It didn't take me long to realize they came from a different world than I did. They spent more money in one shopping trip than I did in six months. Keeping up with their spending habits was proving to be the ultimate test of my frugal abilities.

I also couldn't afford another bad grade. My confidence was already teetering. Inside my mind, a battle raged. One part of me, the part that wanted to protect me from pain, clung to the failure and whispered that I should leave school before it broke me. Yet, deeper still, something burned. A hunger that refused to quit. A voice that seethed at the thought of giving up. I just needed to dig deeper and keep going.

I shook my head. "I don't think I can."

"Come on, Brooke, I feel like I never see you. You're either in class, at work, or at the library."

"That's not true. I hang out at the house—sometimes."

"Yeah, after everyone's gone to bed. We need to see your cute face more often."

I watched as a group of girls walked by laughing at something on their phones. I looked at Ellie, who was staring at me, and looked away again.

"What are you studying anyway?"

"Biology."

"Ugh, I'm with you there. I'm totally stressing Monday's test."

I perked up knowing I wasn't the only one struggling.

"I know, right? It's impossible to know all of this."

"You'll do great," she said.

"Do you want to study with me?"

"I would, but I have a strict no studying policy on Friday nights."

"I wish I could do that."

"Why can't you?" Ellie asked.

"I have to get a good grade."

"Are you worried your parents will get mad?"

I looked away and laughed. "No, my dad doesn't care and my mom's…"

I stopped myself and looked sideways at Ellie. In the month I had known her, I had said almost nothing about my family.

"Your mom's what?"

"She's gone."

"What do you mean she's gone?"

"She died when I was young."

I studied her face to see how she reacted to this revelation. I had come to hate being pitied, which is why I rarely told people. She cocked her head and leaned closer.

"Wait, what? Your mom's dead? Geez, Brooke, how did I not know that?"

"It was a long time ago."

"I'm sorry, that must really suck."

I smiled. "Yeah, kinda, but I don't think about it much anymore."

"How old were you?"

"Nine."

"Woah, you were just a little girl."

"Yeah, it seems like a lifetime ago."

We sat in silence for a minute. I pressed the crumbs from my bagel between my index finger and the top of the table. I instantly wished I hadn't told her. I felt like it changed something between us, but not in the way I had hoped.

"It's crazy that you could go through that and not let it define you," she said.

I looked up from the crumbs. Her eyes were focused on me.

"What do you mean?"

"You're like this amazing person. I mean, I've known you for what, like just a few weeks, and you've never mentioned that you lost your mom. Most people lead with that. It becomes their identity. They just kinda get stuck in their trauma, you know?"

This girl who played the life of the party, always having fun and seeming to never take anything serious, had just shared with me the most profound summation of who I hoped I was.

"Wow, your philosophy class is really paying off," I joked.

"I know, right? I'm full of deep thoughts. But no, what I'm saying is that you're just like this totally centered person. You give off this great aura of calm and peace."

"I hide it well. There's a lot of demons running around this head of mine."

"We all have our demons. But I can't imagine how hard you've had to work to move past all that. To get where you are today."

"Thank you."

"So, here's what we're going to do."

I twisted my mouth. "Ummm, I think that's the same line you used when you talked me into moving in."

"Yeah, and hasn't it been the best month of your life?"

She wasn't wrong.

"You're going to put your books away tonight, and you're going to come to the bonfire with us. Then you and I will study like mad tomorrow."

I leaned back and grabbed my backpack, as reality was setting back in.

"I don't know, Ellie."

"Brooke, it's okay to have some fun. It doesn't take away from your determination. You're smart. You've got this. Give yourself a break."

I wanted to go, but the habits and extreme focus I had used to escape Chatwin were so deeply ingrained, that I had to force myself to say yes. A third fighter entered my battle. The part of my mind that told fear and fortitude to chill for the night.

"Okay, but tomorrow."

"Tomorrow, we'll study all day," Ellie said. "Unless something more fun comes up."

I paused and stared at her.

"Just kidding. All day. No breaks."

"All right, let's go."

The Sunburn was a Grand Mesa tradition to celebrate the end of September and the transition to Fall. Although, it seemed more like an excuse to drink and build a gratuitous bonfire.

I waited in the line to get in with Ellie and two of my other roommates, Jessie and Taylor. We watched as a group of future arsonists ran past us, gleefully carrying canisters of lighter fluid. I gave Ellie a questioning look, but she blew right past it.

When I got to the front of the line, a man stamped my hand.

"How much?"

He pointed to Ellie. "That girl already covered you."

While I had tried to hide my cash-strapped existence from my roommates, Ellie seemed to have caught on quick. I don't think she saw me as a charity case, but she had paid for me more than a few times. Never overtly, she always had an excuse. Just a week earlier a group of us went to a movie, and she handed me a ticket before I could pay. "I thought it might sell out," she said. "So, I bought one for you just in case."

I tried to pay her back the next morning, but she refused. "That's what friends do for each other."

I quickly caught up to her at the entrance of the bonfire. "Ellie, you didn't need to pay for me."

"It's only fair. I dragged you out here."

"Thank you, but I'll pay you back tomorrow."

"We'll square up, don't worry about it."

We entered an open field and were met by a pile of mangled wood that towered in the center. Ten wooden posts stood against each other in a circle, tied tightly together at the top. Stuffed in every open crevice were gnarled tree branches, loose lumber, and in one spot, a random school desk.

"No way. They're going to burn down the town."

"Welcome to Carlson," Ellie laughed.

Jessie walked toward us balancing four plastic cups in her hands. Her fingers tightly curled around the lip of each cup. She handed one to each of us.

"Here you go, ladies. Let's get this night started."

The cups were overflowing with beer. In the slight breeze, I caught a whiff of heavy yeast and nearly gagged. It was the same smell that so often lingered on my father's breath, and those were his sober days. If it had been scotch, my stomach would have turned, and I would have likely ended up on the ground in the fetal position.

I took one of the cups, its cheap rim bowing between my fingers. I wanted to refuse, but my roommates already thought I was boring. I frowned and handed the cup back.

"Sorry, Jess," the words escaped my mouth. "None for me."

"Cool, more for the rest of us," she said and took the cup from my hand.

"Someone can have mine as well," Ellie said. "Party beer is kinda nasty."

A couple of guys ran up and held notebooks out to each of us. "Do any of you want a book?"

"A book?" I asked.

"Yeah, for the book burn," one of the guys said.

I turned to Ellie. "We're burning books now—what have you gotten me into?"

She laughed and grabbed two of the notebooks from the boys.

"The book burn is part of the tradition," she said. "You write down all the things you're holding on to. All your hurts, insecurities, fears. Anything you want to let go of. Then you toss it into the fire. You rid yourself of everything that's holding you back."

"Can I have two?" I asked. The guys looked confused. "I'm just joking."

"I didn't know you were funny, Brooke," Taylor said. "I like you. Why don't you hang out with us more?"

"That's what I keep asking her," said Ellie.

We sat down next to a tree and began writing. I thought about my mom, my dad, and our little house in Chatwin. I thought about the people there. Those who never got tired of dragging my family's name through the mud just to make themselves feel better. I thought about how scared I had been, there were so many lonely nights, and how sad I had felt. I was ready to be done with all of it forever. I left Chatwin to escape its painful memories. What I didn't expect was the freedom that came from creating a new life. No one knew me in Carlson. They didn't know how my mom died. My father wasn't famous for all the wrong reasons. I realized that I could be anyone I wanted to be. I could change my story. I began writing feverishly, ridding myself of my past life.

As the sun disappeared and dusk invaded the field, the lighter fluid boys ceremoniously carried a lit torch and dropped it into the kindling. Flames instantly engulfed the tower. The heat raged against my face, and a collective scream rose from the crowd. Ellie and I ran away from the inferno, laughing. We watched from a distance as the pile burned. Orange flames leapt high in the air, seeming to kiss the stars above. The fire quickly filled itself on the dry fuel, leaving only a trail of embers behind. One of the boys yelled, "Book burn!"

Ellie and I walked toward the fire, its flames settling to a slow burn, its heat lost to the cool night air. I held my notebook in my hands and stared at it. It contained my old life, one that needed to be forgotten; that deserved to be burned. I threw it into the hot coals and watched as the corners blackened and curled. A flame sprang up through the middle.

Brooklyn Blair was gone forever.

CHAPTER 12

I leaned against the kitchen countertop, waiting for a pot of water to boil. I held a package of Ramen Noodles in my hands and stared at the picture on the front. They made it look so appetizing, but I knew what I was getting. Cheap food that would fill me up.

A musty, thick odor permeated the air. I wrinkled my nose.

"What is that?" I whispered out loud.

I stepped toward the trash can in the corner and sniffed. Despite the mound of garbage balancing precariously above the rim, it was not the culprit.

I crept around the kitchen, following the trail of stench. It led me to the sink, where a haphazard stack of dirty bowls, cups, and plates had been abandoned.

I lifted the top plate then paused momentarily as the stack teetered, then settled. I recoiled at what I found in the bowl underneath. At one time it had likely been pasta or some type of cheese, but it had since been consumed by a blueish-green mold.

I gagged and dropped the plate back onto the bowl. "Jessie," I yelled, even though I knew I was the only one home. Based on the chaotic condition of her room, she was the most likely culprit.

The doorbell rang, followed by a quick knock. I wiped my hands on my T-shirt, fearing the foul goo was somehow on me, and checked the pot of water. Small bubbles were forming along the sides, but it hadn't started boiling.

I walked to the door and peeked through one of the sidelight windows. A woman was standing outside. She was beautiful, with perfect golden-brown hair and sleek manicured nails. She wore a carefully coordinated outfit, with a complimenting flap bag in her hand. I looked at my oversized T-shirt and worn leggings and felt completely out of place. I instinctively smoothed my hair, pushed down my messy ponytail, and opened the door.

The woman smiled. I instantly knew it was Ellie's mom. She had the same warm, welcoming countenance.

"You must be Brooke," she said.

"Yes, ma'am."

"I'm Nicole, Ellie's mom."

Without hesitation, she put an arm around me and pulled me in for a tight hug. My body stiffened. Hugging was a rare event in my world. I wasn't sure what to do, but I awkwardly wrapped one arm around her.

"I've heard so much about you," she said. "It's nice to finally meet you."

"You, too, ma'am." I patted her shoulder blade.

This is ridiculous. How do I not know how to give a hug?

She pulled back, and we stood in silence for an uncomfortable moment. Her eyes stayed on me. She was probably wondering why her daughter invited some white trash girl into their home. A girl so unloved, she doesn't even know how to give a proper hug.

I patted my hair again, my mind racing for something to talk about. Anything to end the silence. I caught her stare and saw her eyes shift, looking past me. I was blocking the door.

"Oh, I'm sorry. Come in, come in. Ellie's not here, but you can wait."

What a stupid comment, it's her house.

"I mean, of course you can, ma'am," I stammered. "This is your house."

She put a hand on my shoulder.

"Brooke, first of all, call me Nicole. Second, my husband and I may own this house, but when you're living here, it's your home. I hope you feel that way. We're so happy Ellie found a sweet girl like you to move in."

I smiled and felt my body relax.

"I'm just dropping off a package for Ellie, and I bought some groceries for you all. Would you mind giving me a hand?"

"Sure." I quickly looked for my shoes.

Nicole surveyed the house. I watched her, hoping she wouldn't look in the kitchen.

"So, Ellie told us that you're not from the Carlson area. What part of Colorado are you from?"

"The southern part. Kinda way down at the bottom."

"And you came all the way up to attend Grand Mesa?"

A flash of heat rose up the back of my neck. I knew she was trying to get to know me, but the pointed question had a hint of interrogation to it. I fumbled with a pair of flip-flops, embarrassingly trying to put them on the wrong feet, and finally got them situated. I looked up.

"Grand Mesa just felt like a good fit."

She stepped into the family room and straightened a pillow dangling on the edge of the L-shaped sectional.

"We don't get many out-of-towners. Do you have family close by?"

"No, ma'am…I mean, Nicole, it's just me."

"Huh, interesting."

Interesting? Was that good or bad?

"How have you liked it here?"

"I love it. Better than I could ever have hoped for."

She picked up a crumpled blanket off the floor, folded it neatly, and draped it over the back of the couch. "Good for you. College is such a special time, make the most of it. And thank you for being such a good friend to my daughter."

The comment caught me off guard. I thought I was on the winning end of me and Ellie's friendship. I never considered that she felt lucky to have me as well. I liked that feeling.

"Ellie seems to be enjoying her newfound freedom so much, we hardly see her. I'm glad she has you."

"It's nice to have a good friend."

"She's coming over on Saturday, you should come with her. We're having a barbecue."

The thought of being included excited me, but I was sure she was just being nice.

"Thank you, but I don't want to invade your family time."

"Brooke, our house is always open to our friends. Besides, it will give you a chance to meet everyone, and it'll give me a chance to see my daughter."

"Okay, sounds fun. Thank you. I'll ask Ellie about it."

"She'll be happy to have you there. She always feels more comfortable with her friends than her family."

I felt light on my feet as I helped Nicole with the groceries. I had passed her test. An entirely new emotion rose in me.

I was accepted.

CHAPTER 13

The wide road fell, then rose sharply, weightlessly carrying us higher. Ellie's white coupe hugged the edge of a sharp turn. The reflection from its chrome wheels danced against a metal guardrail, the only protection between us and the deep ravine that bordered the road. I gripped the side of the passenger door and sunk deep into the leather seat as Ellie sped along. Suddenly the low valley unveiled itself to our view. The city of Carlson and its neighboring towns spread out like an endless sea. Infinite trees filled the landscape below. It was as if we had been transported to another world.

"Your parents live *here?*"

"Yes, we're almost there."

Wow!

She slowed the car and turned off the main road. Two opposing stones towered aside a wide entrance. Written in rustic bronze letters, *The Views.*

We pulled up to a small, green booth, and Ellie lowered her window.

I wasn't sure what I was looking at. "Is this a toll road?"

She laughed. "No, it's a guard shack."

"Your parents have a guard shack?"

An older man with a round face casually leaned out the window of the booth. He wore a crisp, white shirt with a badge on the sleeve that said, *The Views Community Security.*

"If it isn't my favorite Foster," he said.

"Hi, Mr. Vaughn."

"How are you, Ellie? It's been a minute."

"I know, I'm sorry. I've just been so busy with school and stuff."

"That's right, you're a college girl now. How are you liking it?"

"It's good. I mean it's GMCC, so you get what you pay for I guess."

The man laughed. "Hey, college is college. If it were easy, everyone would do it. I know your dad's sure proud of you."

"Thanks, Mr. Vaughn."

"Any other cars coming with you today?"

"No, just me."

"Well, it's nice to see you."

Ellie briefly waved. "You, too."

He lowered his head, looked past Ellie, waved, and said to me, "Have a nice day."

I smiled and returned the gesture.

He sat back in his booth. A moment later there was a low hum, and the entrance gate slowly swung open.

"Are you kidding me?"

"What?"

"Your parents have someone just to open a gate for them?"

She laughed. "No, it's not just my parents' place. He works for the HOA. There's lots of homes up here. You act like you've never seen a gated community before."

"I didn't even know there was such a thing."

"Be serious."

As was often the case, I was in danger of revealing too much of my past. It was a delicate game of unmasking just enough to connect, but not enough to elicit follow-up questions.

"I mean, of course I know what they are." I lied. "We just didn't have any where I grew up, but it was an older town."

"How small was your hometown?"

"Small enough we didn't need gates."

Ellie laughed.

We continued down the narrow road passing long driveways that weaved between perfectly manicured yards. Each one seemed to lead to large homes that appeared to be built less for functionality, and with their immense windows, more to capture the views of the valley below.

Ellie pulled into one of the driveways. A gray bricked mailbox stood at its edge, with Foster stamped into an address stone. We continued up a hill that leveled off in front of four garage doors.

The house was stunning; a modern ranch style, with a variety of pitches and peaks, large pillars, and a massive wood alcove leading to the front door.

We got out of the car, and I just stood still, staring. "Woah."

"Yeah, my parents definitely like to go big."

"You grew up here?"

"Kind of. We moved here when I was fourteen."

"You could fit like five of my houses in here."

"Now you're exaggerating."

Actually, if anything, my estimate was low.

Ellie led me through one of the garages and into the house. We walked through a large mudroom and entered the kitchen. The inside was as grand as the outside. It looked like the luxury dream homes I had envied on television. I ran my fingers along the white granite of a large island countertop which dropped weightlessly into a waterfall edge. Stainless steel appliances popped against white cabinets.

The room opened along a high vaulted ceiling, and I looked up toward a series of dark gray beams forming an artistic pattern. Can lights were positioned impossibly high.

Off to the side of the kitchen was a large family room. A man sat alone on one of two deep couches. He had his back to us, watching a football game.

Ellie approached the man. "Hi, Dad!"

He stood and pulled her into a hug. "Ellie girl."

"Dad, this is my roommate, Brooke."

"Hi, sir."

He smiled wide and extended his hand. I grabbed it, his palm dwarfing mine.

"Hi, Brooke, it's nice to finally meet you. I'm Jack Foster."

"It's nice to meet you, too."

Nicole walked into the room. "Girls! You made it."

She gave both of us a hug.

To me, she smelled perfect. Not just a few random sprays of perfume, but an orchestra of scents perfectly matching a lazy Saturday in the fall.

"How are you, sweetheart?" she asked me.

"Doing good, ma'am, thank you."

"Remember, call me Nicole."

"Yes, ma'am…I mean, Nicole."

We followed Jack into the kitchen. "Make yourself at home," he continued. "Everyone's out back, and the barbecue will be ready in about half an hour."

"What are we having?" Ellie took a handful of baby carrots from a vegetable platter in the kitchen. She bit into one, the fresh snap echoing as she chewed.

"Barbeque chicken and smoked brisket," he said. "Plus, your mom's making potato salad and her famous Texas sheet cake. It's going to be a feast."

"Sounds delicious," I said.

"My dad's famous for his barbeque chicken," Ellie said.

"Really?"

Nicole laughed. "Don't encourage him, girls, he's a legend in his own mind."

"My third-place trophy from the Carlson Town Days Cook-Off would beg to differ," Jack countered.

"Oh, please." Nicole rolled her eyes. "If Jack had his way, that trophy would be sitting out here on the mantel."

I laughed. The nervousness I had been carrying since the invite melted away. I eased my guarded personality and grabbed a few carrots and a celery stick.

"Thank you again for inviting me. Can I help with anything?" I asked Jack.

"Nope. You're our guest, so just enjoy yourself."

With that, Ellie led me through a set of sliding glass doors to the backyard. We stepped out onto a large deck. There was a sitting area on one side and an outdoor kitchen on the other. The aroma of Jack's meats cooking in the afternoon air smelled so good.

The yard stretched in front of us, wondrously opening up to the expansive valley, and bordered by large pine and cottonwood trees. Tucked in a corner, a group of aspens rustled in the slight breeze, reminding me of those behind my home in Chatwin.

Blue water danced in the sun in a rectangular pool that ran along one side of the yard. Four sets of double chaise lounge chairs with thick blue padding sat on the deck along the pool's edge, each accompanied by a shade umbrella.

Ellie pointed to the trampoline. "So that's my little sister Morgan. She just turned fourteen, and that's her best friend Maddie jumping with her."

I watched the girls practicing backflips, laughing at each other with each failed landing. I looked to the other side of the yard, where a group of older boys were throwing a football. A couple of them had their shirts off, and their sweat glistened in the afternoon sun.

"Who's that?"

Ellie followed my gaze. "That's just my older brother Brad and his friends."

"Hmm."

"No."

"What?"

"They're gross, you can do better."

"I didn't say anything."

"You didn't have to."

Ellie started across the backyard. I followed, stealing one more peek at the boys along the way. We stopped against a bronze iron fence. Just feet away, the edge of the backyard dropped off to a steep, sloping cliff. I gripped the top railing of the fence as the emptiness engulfed me. Vertigo briefly seized me. It was terrifying and awe-inspiring at the same time. "You can see everything from up here."

"Yeah, this is my happy place," Ellie said. "Sometimes I'll hop over the fence and just sit with my feet hanging over the edge."

"Are you crazy?"

"No, it's magical. I can let my mind be completely free."

I looked at the narrow space between the fence and the edge and wondered how she had found enough space to stand, let alone sit.

"Do you want to try?"

"No. No way."

She laughed.

We stepped away from the fence and walked back toward the house. As we stepped onto the grass, a football came spiraling toward us. I cowered in fear only to watch Ellie snag the ball out of the air. A perfect catch.

"Nice pass, Harrison," Ellie shouted. "You only missed by a few feet."

"The sun was in my eyes," yelled the boy.

Everyone looked confused for a moment and then started to laugh.

"You mean the sun that's behind you?"

The laughs grew louder.

"Shut up." Harrison looked embarrassed.

I noticed that all six boys were now standing, staring at us. One of them moved forward and approached Ellie.

"Hey, sis," he said and reached for a hug.

"Ooh, gross. I'm not hugging you when you're all covered in sweat."

"Whatever." He backed away.

"Hi, I'm Brad," he said and extended his hand.

"Brooke." I took his hand.

Brad was perfect. He had well-defined arms and tight, photoshopped abs. He towered over Ellie but was the perfect height for me if I wanted to rest my head against his chest.

Where did that come from?

His sandy blond hair was messy yet chic.

"This is my older brother," Ellie said. "My much older brother," she added, looking at our prolonged handshake.

I smiled and let go.

Brad tightened his gaze and shook his head at Ellie. "I'm not that old."

"And this is his band of directionless misfits." Ellie pointed to the rest of the boys.

"Carl, Mike, Harrison, Aaron, and Randy."

They all gave a slight wave but continued to stare at us.

"Mike's still in school, but they finally kicked the other ones out after…how many years did it take you guys to graduate? Was it six or seven?"

"Five," they all shouted in unison.

Ellie laughed.

"Now they just hang around my parents' house with nothing to do."

Ellie threw the ball back to Harrison, a tight spiral that caught him right at his sternum. He doubled over the ball as a deep breath escaped him. The other boys started to laugh.

Ellie just laughed and walked away. I followed her and then turned back to watch Brad as he rejoined the group.

They were all watching us.

"Dude, stop checking out my sister," I heard Brad say.

I noticed he looked back at me. I quickly looked away.

In Chatwin, a barbeque was throwing a package of hot dogs on a worn-out grill, with the only technique being not to burn them.

Jack's barbeque chicken was unlike anything I had tasted before. Tender and full of flavor. If it wasn't the best in Carlson, I don't know what secret sauce the first and second place winners were using.

I sat at an outdoor table on the Foster's back deck and listened as Ellie and Brad argued over the details of a childhood memory.

"Here's your problem, Brad," Ellie was saying.

"Oh, please, El, please diagnose all my troubles," Brad fired back. "Psychoanalyze me now that you've taken one psychology class."

"Hold on, if you would let me speak. Your problem is you love the game more than the actual relationship. You love the excitement of it. The unpredictability. You love one-upping yourself with the most creative gift you can give or most exciting adventure you can take a girl on."

Brad scowled. "What's wrong with that?"

"Nothing. There isn't a kinder person I know. But once you get there, right at the point of committing, you pull back. When the chase is over, it loses its excitement, and you move onto the next girl."

While the conversation had started as playful banter, I could see that Ellie's words hit Brad a bit harder than she intended. He stared at her quietly.

"But, Brad." Ellie softened. "When you find the one, she is going to be the luckiest girl in the world. She will be treated like a princess for the rest of her life. I just hope you don't let *the one* pass you by."

He stared at her for a moment, then smiled. Suddenly he flicked a potato chip at her, catching her just above her eyes.

"Brad!" she said, and they both started laughing.

The October days were getting shorter and shorter, and the evening sun had set. A combination of ambient light and four large spotlights kept the night sky from overtaking the backyard. The games had stopped; everyone slowing down after the afternoon activities and heavy meal. Morgan and Maddie swung slowly in a hammock, their faces buried in their phones, and Brad's friends drifted lazily around the pool.

Jack and Nicole stepped out from the kitchen and onto the deck. He gently put his hand on her back and caressed it as they walked over to where I was sitting. I quickly moved from my slouched position and sat up straight.

I should have helped them clean up.

They sat across from me. "Well, what did you think, Brooke? Did you enjoy dinner?"

"Yes, it was amazing. The best chicken I've ever had."

Jack playfully nudged Nicole. "Another satisfied customer."

"I never said your chicken wasn't good. I just think the fame is going to your head."

They both laughed.

Jack turned his attention back to me. "So, what's your story, Brooke?"

A familiar pit grew in my stomach. It would be just like my life to have something great happen, like meeting Ellie and her family, and then have the mask torn off and my true identity exposed.

You can take the girl out of Chatwin, but you can't take Chatwin out of the girl.

"My story?"

"Yeah, where are you and your folks from?"

"I grew up in southern Colorado."

"Oh really, I have a couple of clients down there. What city are you from?"

"It's a place called Chatwin."

"Chatwin?" Jack's forehead folded into fine lines as if he were thinking. "Chatwin? Sorry, I don't think I've heard of it."

"You wouldn't know it's there unless you were looking for it. It's close to Mayfield."

"Okay, I know Mayfield. Wow, you're really far down there. What are you doing all the way up here in Carlson?"

I looked down toward my hands and began stroking my fingers back and forth along the palms.

"Jack," Nicole said softly.

"What?"

"You don't have to answer all these questions," she said to me. "It's okay."

"Sorry, Brooke, I didn't mean anything by that," Jack said. "It's just unusual for someone outside of the area to come to GMCC."

"Honestly, I didn't even know GMCC existed. It's just hard in small towns with small town mentalities, to get into the big schools."

"Really?" said Nicole.

"Yeah, like I felt most of the teachers and counselors almost didn't want to see the students succeed. I mean, that sounds bad, but it was almost like, 'Hey, we can't escape this town, and you're not going to either.'"

Jack arched his back slightly, stretching his shoulders, and let out a deep sigh. He shook his head. "That's such a sad attitude to have."

"You must have worked hard to get here then," Nicole said.

I sighed then looked directly at her. "I've never wanted anything more."

"Your parents must be proud," said Jack.

"Yeah."

"I'd love to meet them sometime, if they ever come up to visit," said Nicole.

"It's just my dad. My mom died when I was little."

Their expressions changed into that familiar look of pity. I immediately wished I hadn't said anything.

"Oh, I'm sorry to hear that. How old were you?"

"Nine."

Nicole raised a hand to her cheek and shook her head. "My goodness," she murmured.

I was surprised by her response. Something about it felt more genuine than most I received. She reached over and placed her hands on mine.

"I lost my father when I was ten."

I could feel a connection run through our hands. An understanding that only those who have lost a parent so young can share. I stared deep into her eyes. Our hearts hurt for each other.

"He died in a car accident on his way to work one morning. Wrong way driver."

Although I hardly knew Nicole, my eyes clouded with tears. "I'm sorry."

"My entire world shattered in that moment." She looked down and then back to me. "But you know that feeling, don't you? The pain, the emptiness, the longing for one more hug, one more kiss, one more *I love you.*"

She had reached inside of me and pulled out feelings that I didn't know anyone else shared. Feelings I could never put into words.

"Every day."

"We move forward, don't we? Put on a brave face, take one step at a time, but in the quiet moments, the emptiness never really leaves."

"It's like a hole that can't be filled."

We stood up at the same moment and met at the edge of the table. We held each other. A real hug this time, full of love.

"Your mom would be very proud of you," she whispered in my ear.

"Thank you."

"If you need anything, our home is open to you."

"Thank you."

Brad joined us. "Mom, what are you doing to this poor girl?"

Nicole and I broke our hug, laughed, and wiped our eyes.

Ellie shook her head. "This is why I don't bring my friends over."

Nicole looked at her son. "It turns out that Brooke and I have a lot in common. That's all."

My heart soared. It had been a long time since I felt loved.

CHAPTER 14

"Brooklyn."

The word echoed, low and steady, wrapping around me like a fog.

I know that voice.

"Brooklyn."

I willed my mind to work, to pull me from sleep, but I was drawn back toward my hibernation. My eyes stayed closed, and I left my head on my pillow.

"Brooklyn."

This time I shot up into a sitting position and searched the darkness.

"Mom?"

For a moment I thought I saw her sitting at the foot of my bed. Her golden-blonde hair pulled back into a crisscrossed ponytail. Her blue eyes swimming in the dark room. I scrambled across the blankets toward her—but she was gone.

"Mom," I pleaded.

"Brooklyn, come quick, sweetie."

Her voice held a steady, calm tempo.

"Come and see."

Suddenly I was on a dirt road. The world awoke to the warmth of the sun that towered on the horizon. Both sides of the road were surrounded by fields of tall, yellow grass. The soles of my feet pressed against the road, tiny pebbles pushing hard against my bare skin.

"Brooklyn." My mother's silhouette appeared at the end of the road, outlined by the blinding sun. "Brooklyn, come and see."

"Mom," I shouted and began running to her. My feet couldn't keep up as I pushed forward, toward a long overdue embrace. "Mom."

"Come and see, baby girl."

My heart pounded, the excitement carrying me along. I was closing the gap; forty yards, thirty yards, twenty yards, ten yards. I held my arms out, ready to leap into hers, and then she was gone. The road fell away, and I skidded to a stop. My heart burst.

"Mom…Mom, please no. Please don't leave me."

"Brooklyn, do you see?" she asked.

"Mom, where are you? Please don't leave me again."

"Brooklyn, it's okay, sweetie. Do you see?"

I took a deep breath and tried to look through my clouded eyes. "Do you see?"

I was standing atop a cliff overlooking a large valley. The landscape was layered with fields of lilies running endlessly toward the horizon.

"Isn't it beautiful?" she asked, her voice growing more distant.

"Mom, where are you?"

"I'm here, sweetie, but you need to see. Isn't it beautiful? You created this."

⌖

I woke with a start and sat up in my bed. I searched the darkness, but it was all gone.

The road, the lilies, and my mom. It was only a dream.

CHAPTER 15

The library was quiet. Too quiet. Only the soft rustle of papers and the occasional whisper cut through the stillness. The warmth of the room pressed in around me, and I tugged at my sweatshirt. The sleeves bunched at my elbows. I moved the top of a pen along my lips; its once smooth body pitted with my bite marks. I stared at the words in front of me. Heavy paragraphs explored the Ming Dynasty. I had been stuck on the same page for the past ten minutes. I read the words repeatedly, but they weren't registering. My sleep-deprived mind refused to be complicit to my feeble attempt at studying.

A series of unrelated thoughts had connected to each other, captivating my attention. I started out thinking about the sticky notes I needed for my weekly journaling assignment in English and ended up thinking about my father. Maybe it was the dream about my mom, but for the first time since I moved to Carlson, I wondered what he was doing. Was he happier without me? Although I seemed to be only a slight obligation when I was there, had he found the freedom to drink himself to death? Maybe he would just give up and join my mom in suicide.

In the back recesses of my mind, I carried with me the fear of receiving a phone call telling me he was dead. When I was young, it was the thought of being an orphan that petrified me. I would lie awake at night worrying about where I would go if he died. A girl in the grade above me at Chatwin Elementary was taken by the state of Colorado when her mom was sent to prison. Her dad was long gone, and she had nowhere else to go. I never saw her again. I had no family, except my Uncle TJ in Mesquite, Nevada. I had only seen him a couple of times and even then, he never said a word to me. I worried that I would be given to strangers and sent to a world I didn't know.

As I got older, it was the fear of being alone that began to haunt me more. There was no one to catch me if I fell. Not that I expected my father to be there for me, but there was solace in knowing I wasn't the lone survivor of my family, that my life wouldn't be condensed to blank lines left on emergency contact forms. Whether good or bad, someone might remember my existence.

I wondered, if he died, who would call me? What if he died in his sleep or in a pool of his own vomit? How long would it take before someone noticed? If he didn't show up for work, would the men at Chatwin Fabrication even bother to check on him? And if they found him, who would find me? Would I walk out of class one day to find Sheriff Holiday leaning up against his old Chatwin patrol car to tell me my daddy was dead?

I bit down on the end of the pen, adding another mark. I leaned forward, hovering over my textbook, and cut the thoughts off. This was not a rabbit hole I was willing to go down; I had left that part of my life behind.

I rubbed my eyes and scrolled across the words again. My mind pleaded for focus, but a twist of anger tugged at my conscience… or was it regret?

This thought was unsettling. I didn't have any regrets. It was his fault how we ended things, not mine. He got what he always wanted, which was to be alone.

I leaned back in my chair and sighed, my mind relenting again to ghosts of the past. The memory of my last weeks in Chatwin were still fresh in my heart. I had sat with our small graduating class on the run-down, makeshift risers in the middle of the Chatwin High football field. Each step or wrong move threatened to topple the archaic structure. The sun was beating down with endless strength, reflecting against the small cluster of metal bleachers in the stadium. I shielded my eyes from the glare and scanned the small audience of families and well-wishers. As always, and expected, my father wasn't there.

When my name was called, the only people to cheer for me was Mrs. Timmons and a few students who clapped for everyone. I walked toward Principal Anderson, held my diploma, paused for the customary photo, then headed for the other side of the risers and kept on walking.

If I could have left home right then, I would have. At least at that point, the end was in sight. I had envisioned a grand exit. With my bags packed, I would just leave one day while he was at work. I'd leave a note, of course. *Have a good life,* or *I'm leaving, so you don't have to pretend to care about me anymore.* Maybe something longer, where I could share all my feelings about him. What a horrible person he was and how disappointed my mom would be in him. A letter that he could read over and over for years to come, as he drowned himself in his beer and his tears.

Yet, when it was finally time, I couldn't do it. I couldn't just leave. I needed there to be an end. A chance for us to peacefully go our separate ways and move on.

One night after he'd come home from work, I mustered the courage and entered the front room where he was watching television.

"Dad?"

He quickly folded in the leg rest of his recliner and fumbled with the remote, turning the television off. He looked at me and smiled.

"You didn't have to turn your show off. This will just take a second."

"It's okay," he said. "What's going on?"

I stared at him for a moment. He was a stranger to me. All the years since my mom had passed, living under the same roof, yet we hardly knew each other. His entire aura had changed when she died. It was like the light had gone out of him. The hardness that concealed him had faded over the years, but he looked worn. Grey dusted the sides of his dark brown hair. Creases appeared around the corners of his eyes and fine lines around the lift of his mouth. He looked much older than the forty-three-year-old man he was. He looked tired of being tired.

"I, um, just wanted…or thought you should know…or would want to know that I've been accepted to a college and I'm leaving."

I waited for him to be angry, guarded in case he got really angry, and prepared myself for the inevitable lecture about who I thought I was and why I thought I was so special. Instead, he smiled.

"I'm proud of you, Brooklyn."

I fought hard to keep a steeled expression as a gentle warmth rose through me.

"Your mom would be very proud of you, too. You're everything she hoped you'd be."

My lip quivered, as the mere mention of her brought a flood of emotion. We looked at each other for a moment. A silent acknowledgment of the grief we shared.

I quickly dismissed the tender moment, finding bitterness and anger to be easier.

"Anyway, I'm leaving next week."

"So soon?"

I turned my eyes away from him, not wanting to face his disappointment. I stared at a spot on the carpet. A burn mark from an ember that popped from the fireplace long ago.

"I've already got a bus ticket, so don't try and talk me out of it."

"I wouldn't do that. I want you to go."

"I bet you do."

He leaned forward and sat perched on the edge of his chair.

"No, that's not what I mean. I want you to go because you deserve it. You've worked hard."

I glanced over to him. "Thank you."

"If you're taking the bus, the college must be close by."

"It's just a small community college in northern Colorado."

"Grand Mesa, right?"

I turned from him and stared in the direction of my bedroom. My brow furrowed, and I clenched my teeth.

"You went through my stuff?" I could barely get the words past the seething anger in my throat. "I can't believe you would do that."

"I didn't touch your stuff." He stood and walked over to a pile of letters and papers scattered on the TV stand. "Some loan department or something from the school sent me a letter asking for information."

"I hope you sent it back. I really need that aid."

He quickly searched the pile, disregarding each letter and envelope with an exaggerated thump on the stand until he found what he was looking for.

"Here it is.

Grand Mesa Community College. Dear parent or guardian, please read the following instructions regarding financial aid for Brooklyn C. Blair and return forms two through five. Your prompt attention is appreciated."

He handed the letter to me and moved back toward his chair.

"Of course I sent the forms back. Why wouldn't I?"

I could think of a million reasons, but I kept them to myself.

"Sorry, I just thought maybe you wouldn't…"

"That I wouldn't care?" He stared at me with a knowing grin.

"Yeah, kinda."

He shook his head and looked away. "Despite what you think, Brooklyn, I'm not your enemy. I sent the forms in, just like they asked."

"Thank you."

"You know, I can drive you up if you'd like. I'm sure Marv would give me the day off. Heck, he owes me probably a year's worth of vacation days."

"That's okay, the bus ticket's nonrefundable."

"Well, we should at least have a goodbye party or something, don't you think? Maybe I can take you to dinner."

I smiled and laughed to myself.

"What?"

"Nothing."

"No, if you've got something to say, say it."

"It's just… a party? Like, what? Do you think we can simply bury the last ten years as if they didn't happen?"

He nodded his head and looked away from me.

"I just thought you should get a proper goodbye."

"I think we both know it's a little too late for goodbyes. I just wanted you to know I was leaving."

He looked toward his hands and began to nervously press his thumbs up the palm of each hand.

"I know I haven't been much of a father to you. I guess I can't expect you to need me now, but…"

I looked away and shook my head. Of course he would make himself the victim in all of this.

"You're right. You haven't been a good father. In fact, you've been a horrible one."

I studied his face, waiting for an acknowledgement that what I said had hurt him. I wanted him to feel just an ounce of the pain I felt. Yet, he didn't even flinch. He didn't react at all. He just stared at his hands with his stupid hollow, soulless eyes. He didn't care.

"I've made it this long without you. So don't try and play the hero now. This has nothing to do with you. This was all me. I did this despite you. I don't need you. I've never needed you, so let's not pretend we owe each other anything. Let's call it what it is. This is goodbye. You live your life and I'll live mine. That's what you've always wanted anyway."

My heart raced and silence filled the room. I walked away, pausing around the corner to take a deep breath. I pounded my fist lightly against the wall. I felt stupid for telling him. I didn't need his approval. I didn't need him ruining the one good thing to happen in my life.

My memories were interrupted by the alarm on my phone. It was time to go to class. I blinked hard and returned to the present. I looked again at the countless words in front of me. The same words I had been staring at for the past hour. I let out a deep sigh, frustrated at the time I had wasted.

CHAPTER 16

sat at the small white desk in my bedroom working on a project for my Intro to Digital Imaging class. My used laptop fought valiantly to keep up with the editing software I was running. Its fan wheezing tirelessly in the background.

My mind was completely removed from the world around me. A cheap pair of wired earbuds dangled from my ears as I listened to the steady rhythm of a bass guitar working in wordless negotiation with a set of drums to keep time. The result was perfect.

My assignment was to take a photograph from anything on campus and practice the techniques of cropping, exposure, and saturation. I found the perfect shot of a large oak tree transitioning into autumn. Nature had already provided a spectacular canvas, my job was to make its golden red and yellow leaves pop against the clear, blue October sky.

The beat of the music matched my rhythm as I moved the cursor around the screen and systematically gave life to the photo. I mouthed the lyrics softly to myself.

Suddenly a hand grazed my shoulder. I jolted upright, slamming my knee into the desk. The earbuds ripped from my ears, lifting the edge of the laptop and releasing it hard against the surface. I spun around and became tangled in the legs of the chair. I fell hard against the desk as I searched for balance, knocking over a mason jar filled with highlighters and pens.

Brad stood wide-eyed. He reached out and grabbed my arm, steading me before the chair could pull me over.

"Oh, man, Brooke, I'm so sorry."

I stared back at him in disbelief, my heart pounding. I took a deep breath.

"Geez, Brad, you scared me."

"I knocked, but you didn't answer. The door was open, and I saw you working. I said your name, but I guess you didn't hear me. I'm so sorry."

He spoke quickly, clearly embarrassed. Although, likely not as embarrassed as I was. He let go of my hand and bent down to pick up the chair.

"It's okay," I said, brushing hair from my face. "I just get a little jumpy when people sneak up on me."

I did a quick scan of my bedroom to make sure there wasn't a random bra or some other embarrassing item laying around. I caught a glimpse of myself in the bathroom mirror. While it was late afternoon, I looked like I had just rolled out of bed. I was in my standard studying attire of an old T-shirt and leggings. I nervously straightened the collar.

"Is your knee okay?"

A dull pain echoed up my leg. I could tell it would leave a bruise. I bent down and rubbed it. "Yeah, no harm done."

"I'm so sorry, Brooke."

"It's okay, really."

"It's just, Ellie told me that you've had a long week, and you've got like a big test coming up. She also told me you love apple juice." He pulled out a bottle from a plastic grocery sack and handed it to me.

"Really?" I smiled.

"I also brought you some candy to snack on and some of these squishy ear plug things, because I know how much my sister can talk."

He handed the items to me. I held them in my hands. It was such a random act of kindness, that I wanted to cry, but I wasn't about to embarrass myself any further.

"It's like my own little survival kit," I said. "This is really sweet, Brad. I can't believe you'd even think to do this for me. Thank you."

"I hope it helps. What are you studying anyway?"

I looked over at the laptop. There didn't appear to be any damage. "Right now, I'm working on a project for my digital imaging class, but really I'm just putting off studying for a test in American Heritage."

He tightened his face in disgust. Fine lines appeared along his forehead and around his eyes. Even with the change of expression, he managed to be attractive.

"That sucks," he said. "Those American Heritage tests can be brutal."

"Right? Like, the information is awesome, but I don't get why they feel the need to make the test so hard. I swear every question has three answers that could be right."

"I don't miss those days. I wish I could help you, but history's not my thing. If you ever need help with math or statistics though, hit me up. That's my specialty."

"I might take you up on that."

We stared at each other in silence. I wanted to say more, but my brain froze. I couldn't think of anything to keep the conversation going. I looked down at my hands and twiddled with the box of ear plugs.

He nodded toward the laptop. "Digital imaging sounds cool."

I turned and faced the screen. I moved the mouse around to wake it up, and the image of the oak tree came to life.

"I love it. If I could do this all day, I would."

He leaned close to the screen. "Check that out."

I felt the warmth radiating from his body. He smelled good. Not like the boys in Chatwin, who always seemed to be masking some odor with a cheap splash of cologne. I thought to move, to give him space, but I liked being close to him.

"You did this?"

"Well, technically mother nature did it."

"How long have you been doing photography?"

"Since the semester started."

"Really? That's it?"

"I played around with it when I was younger and took some pictures for the yearbook in high school, but it's always been more of a dream than a reality."

"But you love it?"

"Yeah. Like it's so cool how just a simple change in the settings or angle can completely change how a photo speaks to someone."

"That's cool."

"It's so easy for me to get lost in the creative process. "

He backed away and sat on the edge of my bed. Sheets and blankets were strewn in a twisted pile. I wished I had made it.

"So, what are you going to do to make your dream a reality?"

I laughed.

Who did this guy think he was?

"I don't know. I guess I haven't given it much thought."

"I think you need to chase your dream, Brooke."

"Are you like a motivational speaker or something?"

Now he laughed and laid back on my bed, staring at the ceiling.

"I don't mean to be pushy. I just think people spend too much time doing things they don't like. Why not do what you want?"

"Maybe, someday."

"When will someday be?"

I shrugged. "I don't know…someday."

"That's what everyone says. Then they look back on their life and realize they never did any of the things they truly wanted to do."

"Well, what are you doing? Are you living your dream?"

He turned toward me. A wide smile broke on his face, lifting perfectly to expose dimples tucked away on both cheeks.

"We're not talking about me."

I spun in the chair to face him and gave him a playful shove with my toes.

"No way, you don't get to punk out like that. Come on, Brad Foster, tell me what you really want."

"I haven't figured out my dream yet."

"Yes, you have. No one who talks with the passion you do is still trying to figure out what they really want, so spill it."

"What do I really want?" he asked.

I eyed him for a few seconds before I spoke. "Yeah."

"I want to travel the world."

"Cool."

He sat up and leaned close to me.

"Not just travel though. I want to have epic adventures. I want to bungee jump into a volcano in Pucon, Chile, climb the seven summits, and go on one of those guided hunting trips in Africa."

"Wow. Okay showoff, way to make my dream seem small."

"Are you kidding? My dream is self-serving, but a photograph can change the world."

"I don't think I'll be changing anyone's world. Unless people need a picture of an old oak tree."

"You have to start somewhere."

"So, where are you on your journey of dreams?" I asked.

"Well, let's see. I'm stuck in Carlson working for my father's accounting firm because that's been the expectation since I was born. All my buddies spent the summer backpacking through Europe, while I stayed behind because, as my dad said, 'You're not getting any younger. You have to stay on track if you want to get your CPA.'"

"It's hard to climb mountains from behind a desk," I said.

He smiled again and looked down, apparently studying the carpet.

"I probably sound like I'm complaining. It's a good life, and in a few years, I'll have more freedom to do those things."

"Someday."

"Someday," he said and laughed. "Hey, how did you turn this around on me? We're supposed to be talking about your dreams."

"I just asked a question, you're the one who kept talking."

He reached over to the desk and began picking up the loose pens and putting them back in the jar.

"You don't need to do that. I can get it."

"I got it, it was my fault."

"Thank you."

"What are you listening to?" He plugged the end of the headphones back into the laptop. He held one of the earbuds up to his ear and listened. His brow furrowed, and he looked at me with confusion.

"Who is this?"

"I don't know, what song is it?"

"Listen," he said and held the other earbud to me.

I stood next to him, our heads nearly touching. I looked at him, trying not to stare, but not wanting to look away. I grabbed the other earbud and held it to my ear. A gritty, raw and heavy guitar riff filled the silence.

"Oh, this is my nineties alternative playlist."

"You have a nineties alt playlist?"

"You don't like it?"

"No, because I'm not my grandpa."

"Funny." I pulled the earbud away from him.

"Seriously, who listens to nineties music?"

"Hey, don't…"

His eyes lit up, unable to contain his laughter.

"Who listens to so much nineties music that they need to break their playlists down into categories?"

"Don't make fun of me."

"I'm not making fun, I think it's awesome."

"My dad raised me on a steady diet of seventies rock and nineties alternative when I was young."

"That's a strange combo."

"He's a strange man. Wherever he was, his music wasn't far away. I guess I just got used to it. It helps me focus."

The words came out freely, revealing a part of me that I hadn't realized. It was unsettling. I didn't want to be like my father in any way. I wanted to rebel against every reminder of him.

"You should come to Club Sentinel with us some time, I can introduce you to some real music."

"Real music?" I asked. "You're a punk."

"Just joking, but seriously, we should go."

"Okay," I said and felt a rush of excitement. The feeling rising up, bursting through my immediate smile.

"I'm gone this weekend, but maybe the next. I can get Ellie to come. It'll be fun."

"I can't wait, but the music better be good."

The dimples returned. "It will be, I promise."

We stared at each other for a moment, then I looked away.

"Okay, I think I've taken enough of your time. I don't want to be responsible for you getting a bad grade in American Heritage, so I'm gonna jet."

"I think a bad grade is inevitable."

"You'll do great."

I got up from my desk and followed him down the stairs, toward the front door. Ellie and Jessie were sitting in the small family room off to the side. They eyed us as we passed.

At the door I said, "Thanks again, Brad."

"For sure, and sorry again for scaring you."

"It's fine, I promise."

"See ya, guys," Brad said as he walked out the door.

"Bye, Brad," they said in unison and laughed. They almost sang it.

I closed the door behind him and turned toward the family room. I held up the apple juice.

"That was sweet of him."

Ellie was shaking her head.

"What?"

"Seriously, Brooke, my brother's totally crushing on you. It's so gross."

I fought hard against a smile, my lips curling up slightly. I wanted it to be true, but I felt like an acknowledgment of it would jinx the fantasy somehow.

"No, he's not. He doesn't even know me."

"He wants to know you," Jessie said, and they both laughed.

"Yeah, I'm sure he's totally into the no makeup, baggy T-shirt look."

"Oh, come on, Brooke," Ellie said. "You're like the American dream. You look good in everything. Plus, you're amazing."

I rolled my eyes. "You guys are crazy. He was just being nice."

I walked back to my room, looked at my survival kit, and smiled.

CHAPTER 17

The cold night air mixed with a gentle but steady breeze, enough to numb my cheeks and the tip of my nose. I dug my hands deep into my coat pockets and shifted back and forth from one leg to the other. Anything to try and stay warm. The line to enter Club Sentinel stretched a half-block down the street, nearly rounding the corner onto Coolidge Drive. Our group, which was originally just me, Ellie, and Taylor, had somehow morphed into a friend of a friend crowd.

The people behind us didn't seem pleased to watch others cut in line, increasing their wait in the bitter cold. I avoided their glaring eyes and pretended to be by myself.

The heavy bass coming from inside the club created a subtle vibration in the queue ropes. I was hypnotized by the pulse snaking its way along the velvet lines.

Boom, pause, boom, pause, boom.

"Right, Brooke?"

I had been so lost in my own thoughts that I hadn't heard a word Taylor had said.

"I'm sorry, what?"

"Don't you think Colton was totally cheating on me?"

I searched for a way to answer without hurting her feelings, but it was obvious the boy was using her. He would show up around the townhome every couple of weeks, and if he and Taylor weren't curled up together on the couch, or not so secretly disappearing to her bedroom, they were arguing about something. It always ended with him leaving like he couldn't care less, and Taylor slamming the door behind him, then she collapsed into a puddle of dramatic tears afterward.

"I don't know, maybe."

"Right? Like it's so obvious when one minute he's like, 'Oh, babe, I love you. Babe, I can't live without you. Babe, you're the only one for me.' Then he ignores my texts for a week."

Her eyes were heavy. Weighted tears clung to her long lashes. I stared at her, not sure what to say. This version of her was so different from the girl I lived with and was around every day—when Colton wasn't in her life. That girl was happy. She was smart and she was kind. She seemed unbreakable.

The girl standing in front of me right now, wearing a coral skirt that was too short and displaying the slight tipsiness of a secret pre-club shot or two, seemed totally shattered.

"I don't know Colton well enough to tell you what he's doing or not. But I do know that you deserve better. You're too strong to be shedding tears over some boy who can't see what he's missing."

She laughed and rolled her eyes, gently wiping away the tears caught in the creases below her eyelids. "Thanks, Brooke."

"Let's promise to go inside and just have fun tonight. No punks, just the girls."

"Okay." She linked her arm with mine. "I promise, no sweaty, gross club boys tonight. Just you and me, Brooke."

She rested her head against my shoulder. I could feel a slight tremor pulse through her body, as if she was just now feeling the cold.

It felt good to connect with her. To fit in. My friendship with Ellie came so easily, but that seemed to be Ellie's skill. She made everyone feel like they were her best friend. It was harder with my other roommates. They had years of friendship and stories together. I laughed as they shared memories, but never as hard as they did. When they would finally compose themselves, it seemed every eye would turn to me, as if knowing I was just trying to fit in.

"Sorry, Brooke, I guess you just had to be there."

Like it or not, I was an outsider, just trying to cling to an opening big enough so I didn't get left behind.

My real talent for connection was in situations like this. One-on-one, where we could be vulnerable and real, without an audience to perform for. In these moments, I could slowly plant the seeds of friendship.

"What if Brad's in there?" Taylor asked.

The question caught me off guard. "What do you mean?"

"Come on, Brooke, there's really nothing between you two?"

"No. I thought there might be, but I haven't heard from him since he stopped by the house a couple of weeks ago. Even tonight, Ellie was the one who told me to come, not Brad."

Taylor scowled. "Boys suck."

I laughed and nodded in agreement.

As we reached the front of the line, the bouncer surveyed us intently. I looked down but watched him from the corner of my eye. Despite the cold, he was wearing a T-shirt. His large biceps bulged at the sleeves. He was so stone-faced, for a moment I didn't think he wasn't going to let us in. Finally, he nodded and pointed toward the entrance.

Ellie was waiting for us just inside the doors. The warmth of the club was a welcome relief, but the scent of the crowded room triggered my claustrophobia. A mix of sweat, perfume, and cheap beer. I almost turned and walked out.

Ellie held her phone to her ear. "Brad's supposed to be saving us a table, but he won't answer his stupid phone."

Taylor raised her eyebrows and gave me a playful nudge, but I quickly stepped away.

"He probably can't hear it."

Ellie turned to me. "What?"

"Exactly."

Taylor looked across the room. "Isn't that Harrison over there?"

Ellie followed Taylor's eyes. "Where?"

"The guy trying to look cool in the beer line."

"Harrison!" Ellie yelled.

We weaved our way through a mess of dudes with bad pickup lines and desperate girls who were falling all over them.

"I should have left when I had a chance," I said to Taylor.

"No way. We're in this together, remember?"

Ellie snuck up behind Harrison and gently caressed her hands through his hair until they covered his eyes. "What does a girl have to do to get a drink around here?" she asked.

"I can think of a few things." He spun around to meet his admirer. The excitement on his face melted when he saw Ellie smiling back at him. "Seriously, Ellie?"

"Hey, Har, I didn't know you could talk dirty." She put her hands on his hips, pulling him close. "Maybe there's a side of you I need to get to know better."

"Gross, Ellie." He pushed her away. "You're my best friend's kid sister."

Her laugh cut through the noise.

"How did you guys even get in here? Aren't you like eighteen?"

"Nineteen." Ellie snapped. "And you just gotta know the right people."

"I guess."

"Where's my brother anyway? I've been calling and texting him."

"He's got a table over in the corner. I'll take you over there, this line's not moving anyway."

We followed Harrison through the crowd and bumped into our roommate, Jessie, along the way. She was talking to a couple of guys.

"Roomies!" She gave each one of us a hug and a kiss on the cheek. She was well along the path to being drunk. "How did you guys get Brooke out on a Friday night? Is she finally ready to release her wild side?"

I smiled. I never knew how to respond to a playful comment that was also an indirect shot at my personality.

"Taylor, come meet these guys," Jessie said. "They're not bad for a rebound and a slump buster."

Taylor looked at me. I was sure she would tell Jessie no, but her quick look away told me she was already gone.

"Seriously?"

"Sorry, Brooke."

"You just said we were in this together."

"I need this, Brooke."

Jessie grabbed her arm and pulled her away.

"Come on, Mom. Can't we play for just a little bit?"

Another jab. She laughed, and I watched as they eagerly walked away. The two guys waiting for them smiled and handed each of them a drink.

I looked at Ellie and shook my head. "If I'm ever that desperate."

"Taylor can't be alone," Ellie said. "She's never been able to."

We continued our journey through the club and finally found Brad. He was sitting at a large rectangular table talking with his friend Mike. He was wearing a navy-blue sweater. The collar of a white dress shirt emerged from the top and brushed against a shadow of facial hair.

He was perfect.

He looked over at me and smiled; his entire face lit up. I wanted to act like I hadn't been thinking about him, that I couldn't care less whether he was there or not, but all I really wanted to do was be close to him.

"Hey, Brooke." He stood to give me a hug. My face gently brushed against his. I didn't want to let go, but I didn't want to embarrass myself either and quickly moved away. Then he reached past me and gave Ellie a hug.

"Don't you ever answer your phone?" Ellie asked.

"Did I miss your call?" He reached into his front pocket for his phone.

"Yeah, I called and texted."

"I'm sorry, I can't hear anything in here. I missed a call from Mom, too. I thought they were out of town, what's she calling about?"

"Probably just checking in on her baby boy," Ellie said. "Making sure you're not getting into trouble."

Brad raised his eyebrows and winked at her. "Well, I am her favorite."

Ellie rolled her eyes. "Believe me, I know. Everyone knows."

We all sat around the table. I was hoping to take the open seat by Brad, but Harrison sat there. I ended up across from him, between Ellie and Mike.

"Do you guys want a drink or anything?" asked Brad.

"I'm good."

Ellie looked at him, raised her eyebrows, and smiled. "I'll take a fireball."

Brad shook his head. "Yeah, I don't think so."

"If you won't get one for me, I'll just rub up against any man-whore here, and I can get whatever I want."

"Manwhore?" Mike asked. "What's a manwhore?"

"Pretty much every drunk dude in this club. Just looking for any action they can get."

He laughed, took a drink, and leaned back in his seat.

"That's a sorry opinion to have about the male species," said Brad.

"Ah, yes, let's not forget about Brad," Ellie said. "He's a special kind of manwhore…the sophisticated manwhore."

"A sophisticated manwhore?"

"Yeah, you know, you don't get all sloppy drunk like these other guys, but you're looking to get lucky just as much as any of them."

We all started laughing as Brad shook his head. "How do we come from the same family?"

"I'm sorry about my sister," he said to me.

"I'm just kidding with you, big bro," said Ellie.

Brad leaned across the table to me, and I met him in the middle.

"I'm glad you came tonight."

"Me, too."

"It's never boring with Ellie around."

I laughed. "Nope."

"Hey, I'm sorry I haven't called."

"Oh, you're totally fine. I wasn't expecting you to."

"Things get kind of crazy around the accounting firm toward the end of the year. All of our clients are starting to close out their year and want to work around all the tax stuff."

I felt dumb for thinking he had been avoiding me. Even more dumb for thinking he would put effort into avoiding me, given how little we actually knew each other.

"You look really good tonight," he said.

Warmth spread through my body, and a shy smile crossed my face.

"Do you want to dance?"

"Uh, no, I don't dance."

"Come on, everyone can dance."

"No, seriously, where I grew up, dancing was lining up in a straight line, moving one foot forward and one foot back, then spinning around and clapping."

"I think you just described the hokey, pokey."

"That's about what it was. Even then, I wasn't good at it."

"Come on, if nothing else, at least I can spend time with you."

I smiled and gave in.

He took my hand, and I followed him onto the dance floor.

I tried to move to the beat but couldn't figure out whether I should move my hips, my head, or my arms. I looked around, hoping to copy what others were doing, but it was obvious they had more rhythm than I did.

My eyes met Brad's. "I told you I couldn't dance."

"You're doing great. Don't worry about everyone else, it's just you and me." He moved close and slid his hands around my waist, his fingers meeting at my lower back. I placed my arms around his neck and followed his movement.

"This is better."

"This is perfect," he said.

I looked at him, wondering what he meant, but it didn't matter. There was nowhere else I wanted to be.

After a few songs, the crowd and the confined air got to me. "I need a drink."

"Yeah, me, too. I'll go get us a couple of waters."

"Thanks." I walked back to our table. Ellie was there with a couple of her Carlson friends.

"What was that about?" she asked.

"What?"

"You know what."

I stumbled for the right words. "I don't even know what I'm doing."

She placed her hand on my knee. "It's okay, Brooke, my brother's a great guy."

Suddenly Taylor fell onto the seat next to me. "There you are, Brooke. I've been looking all over for you."

"Sorry, I was dancing."

"Well look at you, letting loose."

"Yeah, I guess."

She leaned against my shoulder, the full weight of her body pressing against me. I didn't need to be the daughter of an alcoholic to know she was completely wasted.

"Are you okay?"

"I'm so much better. Thanks for helping me forget about Colton."

"You're welcome."

"I won't need a ride home. Jessie and I are going to bounce with these guys."

Ellie looked concerned. "Tay, I don't know if that's such a good idea, babe. You don't want to rebound this hard."

"Yeah, let's just go. We can get some food or something."

"Guys, I'm good."

"Taylor, you coming?" Jessie asked from the edge of the dance floor.

Ellie glared at Jessie and shook her head no, but Jessie just laughed.

"Thanks for looking out for me though." Taylor left as quickly as she had arrived.

I looked at Ellie. "Is she going to be okay?"

"She'll be fine."

"How is that the same girl we live with?"

"I've known her since junior high. She's always had a flair for the dramatic."

"It's funny. I get labeled as the boring one who needs to lighten up, but is this the alternative? Getting stupid drunk and making a fool of yourself?"

"I don't think you're boring. And don't listen to them. We're all just stupid and young, trying to figure out life and have some fun along the way."

"Is this supposed to be fun? Hooking up with random guys so she can forget the jerk who dumps her every other week?"

I knew I sounded judgmental, and I was getting angry, although, I wasn't sure at what. The walls were closing in on me, and I needed to get out.

"I'm sorry. I didn't mean to get mad."

"That's why I love you, Brooke. Even when you think you're mad, you're nice."

"I think I'm actually going to head home. I'm not feeling so great."

"Are you okay?"

"Yeah, I'm fine. It's just super stuffy in here."

"I'll go with you."

"No, stay. Have fun. I'm totally fine, I promise. Will you say goodbye to Brad for me?"

"He'll be sad you're gone."

"I don't know about that."

"Trust me, I know my brother. He likes you."

I felt my face flush. "Love you," I said and gave her a hug.

When I finally made it outside, I welcomed the fresh air. After a few deep breaths, my head stopped spinning. Compared to the noise inside, the quietness of the night was striking. Peaceful.

"Brooke," I heard Brad ask as he quickly made his way toward me. "Are you okay?"

A rush of embarrassment rose through me. I turned and faced him.

"I'm sorry," I said. "I didn't mean to leave so quick."

"Why are you going? Was it my dancing?"

I chuckled. "No, it was just getting too crowded in there."

"Are you okay?"

I looked up at the night sky. The moonlight peaked around drifts of milky white clouds. "Yeah, it's just…"

"It's just what?"

"I hate this."

"What?"

I turned and faced the entrance of the club. I thrust my hands toward it.

"All of this. I hate this scene. I hate that people can't just be real."

I turned back to him. "Taylor is an awesome girl. She's got so much going for her. Yet, she's making a fool of herself over some dumb guy."

I looked away again. I could feel Brad step closer to me.

"I'm sorry," I said. "I sound like I'm judging everyone."

"No. I'm sorry. I don't know why I thought Club Sentinel was a good place to hang. I didn't want a crowd; I really just wanted to be with you."

Another burst of warmth rose through me, opposing the winter air. I looked at him from the corner of my eye. He was watching me.

"I'm glad you invited me tonight. Sorry I left without saying goodbye."

"It's okay. I didn't realize you and Taylor were so close. It's hard to see friends make stupid choices."

"That's the thing, we're not even that close. I mean, I like Tay, but it's not really about her."

"What'd you mean?"

I looked away, then looked back at him. "Can I tell you something?"

"Anything."

"My dad was an alcoholic…is an alcoholic."

I heard the words leave my mouth and couldn't believe I let them escape.

Brad stared at me in silence. I caught a subtle shift in his eyes as if he were searching for the right words. It was the same look I had been given for a decade. A look of pity. I hated that look, but the words wouldn't stop.

"He was a good man once, but then he started spending all his days drinking, trying to avoid life. And he left me every night in that stupid old house with no one around. Every night, a scared little girl sleeping with a baseball bat next to me."

"Brooke," Brad said quietly.

I was saying the words to him but talking to myself. I felt like he wanted to come closer to me, but I stayed just far enough away.

I continued, "And I would call him. I would beg him every night, 'Dad, please come home.' And you know what?"

"What?"

"He never did. Not once."

I took a deep breath and let out a muffled laugh. I shook my head.

"Who does that to a child? Even when he was nice to me, he was fake. Like he felt guilty about never being there for me."

Suddenly Brad was next to me, and then I was in his arms. They were strong, and he held me close. My body relaxed when I rested my head against his chest. We stayed like that for a long time. Eventually I pulled back and wiped my eyes. Embarrassment was setting in. I laughed again.

"I'm sorry."

"No, I'm sorry," he said. "I didn't know that about your dad or about your childhood. I would have never invited you here and put you in this situation."

"No one here knows. I try and keep that part of my life hidden, but I guess the past always comes back."

I stared up at the night sky again and released the air from my lungs; I could see my breath. It occurred to me that this would likely be the last moment Brad and I shared together. My past was now visible, and this fairytale would come to an end. I didn't belong in this world. I was broken beyond repair.

"Hey, it's freezing, do you want to get out of here?" He took my hand not waiting for an answer.

We drove to the Foster's house. They were out of town, just as Brad had thought. As we walked in, all the indoor lights were off. Brad disabled the alarm and pushed a light switch next to it. The family room and kitchen lit up.

He walked toward the fridge. "Do you want something to eat, or a drink?"

"I'll just have water, thanks."

I walked to the back door and looked through the glass. It had started to snow. It was dark, but I could see a fresh layer beginning to cover the ground. I stepped close and peered out. The window was cold, and my breath left a layer of fog, momentarily obscuring my view. I had always found the snow to be magical and peaceful. It could take barren land and transform it into a beautiful wonderland.

"I love watching the snowfall."

Brad walked up behind me. "Do you know what we should do?"

"What," I said, skeptical of his enthusiasm.

"Our neighbors have this amazing hot tub. Like seriously unreal. We should totally go sit in it."

"Now?"

"Yeah, why not? Have you ever sat in a hot tub with the snow falling all around you? It's incredible."

"We can't just use your neighbor's hot tub."

"Sure, we can. They'll never know."

"I don't have a swimsuit."

"Just borrow one of Ellie's."

I laughed and shook my head.

"That's cute that you think I could fit into your sister's swimsuit. I'm like the Jolly Green Giant next to her."

"Borrow one of my mom's."

"Seriously? I'm not wearing your mom's swimsuit. What would she think if she found out I took one of hers?"

"You're not taking it, you're borrowing it. Brooke, you're way over thinking this. Live life uninhibited." He shouted and quickly left the room.

I couldn't help but laugh. Standing in the Foster's family room, a huge smile on my face. Nervous and excited by Brad's spontaneity. I looked around at the house. Every detail of it was immaculate. I wondered how a poor girl like me had fallen into a world with such good people. Maybe it was karma. Maybe the universe was saying,

Hey, sorry for crapping all over you for the past nineteen years. Let's do you a solid and drop you in a fairytale.

More than anything, I knew at that moment that I was falling for Brad. I knew it was crazy to think that, but all I wanted to do was be with him.

He came back into the room holding up a yellow and green floral swimsuit.

"No way," I scoffed. "I've never seen your mom look anything but amazing. There is no way that's her swimsuit."

"It was in her room."

I reluctantly took the swimsuit and walked to the bathroom to change. A few minutes later, we met back up in the family room. Brad was in a T-shirt and a brown knee length swimsuit with a silhouette of a palm tree on the side. My borrowed suit seemed to sag and be tight all at the same time. He brought a couple of towels with him, and I quickly grabbed one and wrapped it around myself.

"You ready?" he asked.

I looked out the back windows at the increasingly falling snow.

"So, your neighbors are cool with you using their hot tub?"

"Sure!" He ran out the back door.

I called after him, "What does sure mean?"

He was already cutting across the grass toward the neighbor's backyard. I quickly followed, the snow on my feet unbearably cold. I saw him slip between two pine trees and disappear.

"Brad?" I whispered and picked up my pace.

I cut through the same two trees and saw his silhouette lifting the cover off the hot tub. I wanted to protest. I didn't like breaking and entering, but my feet were too cold to turn back. I tiptoed over and dropped my towel by his. He reached for my hand and led me in. The heat hit my feet like a thousand tiny needles. Out of the corner of my eye, I watched him take off his shirt. Even in the dark I could make out the shape of his body with his well-defined biceps and chest.

I pulled a hairband from my hair and let my long blonde curls fall. I wrapped the band around my fingers and pulled my hair back up, to keep it out of the water.

"You should wear your hair down more," he said. "It looks pretty."

I smiled. "Maybe another time."

I lowered myself into the water up to my chin. I stared up at the pinkish-orange winter sky and watched a million tiny snowflakes fall. He was right, this was amazing.

We sat silently in the water for a while, lost in our own thoughts. I worried that maybe I had shared too much with him about my father, but it felt good to tell someone. I needed to. It was nice to trust enough to share.

Brad was sitting on the edge of the hot tub, his legs in the water. When I looked over at him, he was staring at me.

"What?" I asked curiously.

"Just wondering what you're thinking about."

"Too much."

He lowered himself back in the water until he was at the same level as me. Our faces were only inches apart. I felt his hands grab mine, and we interlocked fingers. We sat like that for a moment, and then he pulled me closer. Our lips met. I hadn't realized how much I had been longing for this moment. I didn't want it to stop.

Suddenly a gust of wind blew and a cloud of snow swirled around the yard. In that instant, it seemed every spotlight in the backyard came on. The world was flooded with light. We stopped mid-kiss; I screamed and quickly pushed Brad away. I was out of the hot tub and running toward the Foster's house before Brad had even thought of leaving the water.

I stood just inside the door, freezing and dripping water all over Nicole's travertine tile. I couldn't see Brad. I worried that he might be dealing with an upset neighbor. I debated going back out to help him, when I finally saw him run through the trees.

"Are you okay?"

He reached the doorway and bent over with his hands on his knees. He was breathing hard and laughing.

"What's so funny? I thought your neighbor was going to kill you."

He laughed harder. "Stop, I can't breathe."

"Seriously, this isn't funny."

He kept laughing.

"Can I at least have my towel?"

He handed it to me and tried to compose himself. The towel had fallen in the snow and was wet and cold. I did my best to dry off.

When I thought he could finally answer without laughing, I asked, "So, how mad is your neighbor?"

"Our neighbor isn't home."

"Who turned the lights on then?"

"The wind. They come on when they detect motion close to the house."

"Seriously? I thought they were coming out with a shotgun or something."

"Yeah, I probably should have mentioned that we're good friends. They let us use their hot tub anytime, and we let them use our pool."

I looked at him and let the smile fade from my face, pretending to be mad. "Seriously? That would have been good to know when I was screaming and running toward the house."

"And since we're being honest, that's not my mom's swimsuit, it's my grandma's."

He collapsed to the floor in another fit of laughter. I threw my towel at him but couldn't stop laughing. I wasn't falling in love with Brad; I was already there.

CHAPTER 18

The Grand Mesa Fine Arts Building was silent. Its hallways dim and empty, classrooms locked for the night. At its heart, a gold pendulum hung from the ceiling three stories above, suspended in the vast open core of the building. It swayed in a slow, deliberate arc, stretching from the highest floor to the polished tile of the basement below. Calm, constant, and strangely mesmerizing in the stillness.

Surrounding the wide circle of the pendulum sat a series of tables and easels. Paintings, sculptures, and other forms of art filled the space. Bright lights beamed down from the rafters creating a halo against the shadows of the empty building. A set of double doors led to a lit sidewalk that was dusted with a layer of snow. The frigid February air crystalizing the outside world. At the entrance of the doors was a small, backlit marquee. *Grand Mesa Winter Art Show.*

I stood alone, next to one of the many easels, and listened to hushed conversations. Family and friends of the participants spoke softly so as not to disturb others in the appreciation of creativity.

I fidgeted with my hands and fought the urge to bite my nails. "A nasty habit," my Grandma Belle had always said. I looked at the photo I had chosen to present for the show. It was a picture I had taken of Brad and Ellie's sister, Morgan, back in December when I had been invited to go ice skating with their family over the holiday break. I used a new, high-resolution camera Brad had surprised me with for Christmas. "Your someday starts today," he had written on the tag.

"I can't accept this," I told him.

"Why not? Don't you like it?"

"No, I love it, but it's too expensive. I can't let you spend this much on me."

He had laughed and kissed the top of my head. "You deserve everything I can give you. We're going to get years of use out of it."

Years?

The word still lingered in my thoughts. I wondered what had he meant? Was it an innocent phrase or did he dream of our future together like I did?

The camera became my constant companion, and the scene around Morgan was so perfect, it was as if it had been staged. She was gathering a handful of snow in her turquoise gloves and bringing it to her smiling face. Her blue eyes sparkled against her pink beanie. A full moon rose over her shoulder, twinkling against the tiny ice crystals that danced around her. I knew when I captured it that it would be my piece for the art show.

Now, staring at it, pasted against a 16 x 20 white mat and resting gently against the easel, it looked childish to me. The submissions by the other photography students seemed to ooze with talent and emotion. They perfectly captured light and dark and had a depth to them that spoke to the viewer. Mine was a glorified Christmas card. I felt the heat of embarrassment rush through my body.

I pulled my phone from my back pocket to distract myself from my fragile thoughts and to see if Brad had texted. He said he would try and come after work, but my phone showed no new messages. Another busy day at the accounting office.

Hey, where are you? Do you think you'll be able to make it?

I opened my Instagram feed and began pointlessly scrolling through the new posts. I came across one that Brad had posted earlier in the day. It was a selfie of the two of us from the night before, after he got a late-night cookie craving.

Nothing better than making midnight cookies with the love of my life.

Love of his life?

I had to pinch myself every time I thought about it. How had I become the love of anyone's life?

I clicked on his Instagram profile. His recent posts were filled with pictures of us. I scrolled passed and came to one from a month earlier of him, Mike, and Harrison. The three were covered in a heavy layer of white snow.

A January blizzard creates the perfect opportunity to tie a rope and a tube behind an SUV and go street sledding with the boys.

I laughed. The post failed to mention anything about Mike's dislocated shoulder.

I gave the phone two more long swipes and landed on a series of photos from the previous spring. I clicked on one of them. It was of Brad, weighed down by hiking gear, with his arms stretched high above his head.

We reached the summit of Mount Elbert just before sunrise! This is only the beginning. Reaching for my goals. #sevensummits.

I swiped back and clicked on another photo. He was wearing a tank top and had a towel draped around his neck.

7 days, 14 workouts. Gotta stay fit for the ladies.

I smiled and shook my head. Sometimes I wondered why he was with me. We were different in so many ways. I was an introvert. I liked isolation and time by myself. He liked to squeeze the most out of every day and could not sit still. He always wanted to be doing something with someone, and they were never small ideas. I wondered if I could keep up with him or if he could slow down for me.

I put the phone back in my pocket and looked at the crowd. The attendance was sparse. I had a few passersby, but they simply looked at my picture, gave a kind smile, and walked on.

"Hello, Brooke," my professor said as she approached from across the exhibit.

"Hi," I said and made a small sidestep between her and my photograph.

"Are you enjoying the evening?" she asked.

"Yes, ma'am."

"It's always a little intimidating to share your talents with the world, isn't it?"

"Yes, ma'am, it is."

"Brooke, I love what you've presented here tonight."

Her validation surged through my body. I sidestepped again, clearing her view of my photograph.

"Really? I was just thinking how amateur it seems compared to the others."

"No," she said. "I've been doing this for a long time, and I can tell when someone has talent and when they don't. Just because a photograph seems beautiful, doesn't mean it captured the moment. With the technology we have today, you can make any picture from your phone look amazing."

She gently placed a hand on my shoulder and moved me close to the photo, next to her.

"But with your photograph, I feel like I am living the scene. The colors pop, but what sets it apart is that you are presenting pure joy on a canvas. People see this, and they can actually feel the happiness this young girl is feeling. They can experience it."

She saw what I saw in that moment with Morgan. Something that couldn't be expressed in words. It had to be tangible, protected from becoming just another dissolving memory.

"Brooke, you have talent. You lack training and technique, but you've got it."

I couldn't believe she was talking about me. She stepped closer.

"Honestly, you're better than many of my Advanced Photography students," she whispered.

"Thank you." I wasn't sure how to respond to the praise.

"I know we're a bit late to the game here, but I would like you to consider joining our summer internship."

"Really? I didn't think I qualified."

"Well, normally I hold the spots for my advanced students, but I keep one or two open for students just like you."

"I don't know what to say, that's amazing."

"So, is that a yes?"

I nodded my head in agreement. "Yes, of course. I would be honored."

"Were you planning to be around this summer?"

I thought about Ellie and Brad and the new life I had created.

"Yes, ma'am, I'm not going anywhere. I'll be here all summer."

"Perfect. I'm sure you have a lot of questions. I'll send you an email detailing the internship and what I require. There are some forms I need you to fill out and send back as soon as possible. I'll also get you added to our group chat."

"Okay, thank you. I'll get everything back to you right away."

She stole another look at my photo. "Good job, Brooke. You're going to do great things this summer."

"Thanks, Dr. Brown, and thank you for the opportunity."

As she walked away, I spun around and shared a silent, excited scream with my photo. I pulled my phone back out. Still nothing from Brad, but I found Ellie's name and began to type.

Oh my gosh! Just got offered a summer internship from my photography professor.

I turned back around and found Brad walking toward me. He was holding a bouquet of flowers and smiled when he saw me.

"Hey, babe."

I ran to him and wrapped my arms around his neck, followed by a quick kiss.

"I'm sorry I'm so late."

"It's okay, I'm just happy you're here. You'll never guess what just happened."

"What?"

"My professor came over, and she loved my photograph."

"Of course she did. I keep telling you, you've got mad skills, Brooke Blair."

"And then she offered me a spot in her summer internship program."

"Seriously?"

"I know, right?"

"Brooke, that's awesome."

He wrapped me in his arms.

"You did say yes, right?"

"Of course, I said yes."

"See, babe, I told you, there are no more somedays. You're already there."

"Thank you."

He handed the flowers to me, and I held them up to my nose. Their aroma surrounded me. He gently held my hand and stepped close to my photograph. I rested my head against his shoulder.

"When is the internship, do you know?"

"I don't. She's supposed to send me a bunch of information."

"Maybe it will line up with Harrison's climbing trip."

"What climbing trip?"

"Harrison and Mike and a couple of other guys are going to Australia to climb Kosciuszko this summer."

"Really? Why aren't you going?"

He slightly shrugged his shoulders, looked off into the distance, and then at me.

"It's the same week I was planning to take you to Yellowstone. But maybe if it lines up right, you can do your thing and I'll go with them."

"What do you mean, maybe? Brad, internship or not, you have to go."

"I just don't want to break my promise to you."

"I appreciate that, babe, but Yellowstone will always be there. I never want to stop you from doing the things you love."

"I know."

"I hope you do. Brad, I'm not like other girls. I want you to live your dreams. I want you to live your someday. You need to go on this trip."

He nodded, and I could see the excitement in his eyes. The reality of going, beginning to race through his mind.

"I hope we always push each other toward our dreams," I said. "Let's promise that to each other, okay?"

He smiled and wrapped his hands around my waist. He kissed me again.

"I don't deserve you."

"That's funny, because I don't deserve you. We must be perfect for each other."

"I never want to let you go, Brooke. I want to be with you forever."

Forever?

I studied his face. His eyes told me he meant it. Genuine and full of love.

I smiled, moved in close to his embrace, and held him tight.

"I love you," I said.

"I love you, too."

CHAPTER 19

The room was dark, the shadows of night long since settled in, broken only by the orange glow of a streetlight peeking around the edges of the blinds. I tiptoed through my bathroom and gave my teeth a final brush. I let the sink run just long enough to rinse my toothbrush. I carefully twisted the cap back onto the tube, its ribbed edges pressing hard against my fingertips as it fought against the built-up remnants of dried toothpaste.

I moved toward my bed. My arms stretched out in front of me in the darkness. I relied on short, careful steps and my memory to guide me. My shin grazed the corner of the bed frame, stopping me in my tracks. I moved my hands along a heap of blankets and slid onto the mattress. The cold sheets sent a shiver through me, and I quickly pulled the blankets to my chin.

I took a deep breath. A sense of relief flowed through my body. It was the first time all evening that I had been able to truly relax. No more forced laughs and endless conversations where every word was carefully crafted to impress and not embarrass myself.

I reached for my phone and remembered carelessly tossing it onto my bed as I had rushed in to use the bathroom. I sat up and patted my hands along the blankets, hoping I hadn't lost it when I moved them. I stretched toward the end of the bed and methodically swiped my hands back and forth. Finally, my fingers brushed across the screen, and the phone came to life. It was one thirty-seven a.m.

How was it so late?

There was a text from Brad.

Thanks for coming tonight, beautiful. I had a great time!

I bit my lower lip, grinning at the screen.

Thanks for the invite, it was amazing! Your parents are awesome!

I turned the phone off and stared into the darkness, waiting for sleep to arrive. The magical evening replayed in my mind. Jack and Nicole had invited me and Brad to the Broadway production of *Les Miserable* in Denver. I had never been to a real theater before. Brad bought me a new dress, and Jack treated us to dinner before the show at a high-end Italian restaurant just off Sixteenth Street.

I panicked when I searched the restaurant's menu, realizing I couldn't pronounce the names of the entrées. I settled on spaghetti Bolognese, since it was the only word I recognized. It was also the least expensive.

"I'll have the spaghetti," I said when it was my turn to order.

"Brooke, I can't let you order that," Jack said.

I looked from the waiter, to Jack, and then to Brad. I wasn't sure what I had done wrong, but it felt like the heat in the restaurant had doubled and every eye was on me. I looked back at the menu.

Had I mispronounced spaghetti?

"I appreciate your concern for my wallet," said Jack. "But I didn't invite you to Denver to have you order something I can make for you at home." He looked at the waiter. "No offense, I'm sure the spaghetti is fantastic."

"None taken, sir."

Jack grinned. "Do you trust me?"

I looked at him, and he flashed his infectious smile. The same one he had passed on to his son. My nerves eased and I smiled back. I looked at Brad and Nicole, who seemed to be enjoying Jack's performance, and then back to him.

"Okay," I said and laughed.

"Good." He clapped his hands together. He turned again to the waiter.

"The lovely Brooke will start with the wedge salad."

"Excellent choice," the waiter said and smiled at me.

"And for her entrée, she would like the Pasta con Pesto di Brontë."

He looked at me and winked. "You're going to love it."

He was right. It was the best food I had ever eaten. It would have been the highlight of the night, if it hadn't been outdone by the musical. When we walked in the doors of the Buell Theatre, it was as if we had entered another world. Brad pushed aside a velvet curtain, and we stepped into the auditorium. It was alive with conversation and the sounds of the orchestra warming up. I stared along the cascading walls to the layers of balcony seating rising high above us. They seemed to go on forever. Every seat was carefully positioned to take in the massive stage that spanned the theater and towered from floor to ceiling.

A few hours later, after a standing ovation and endless applause, I stood transfixed as others began to file out. I had lost myself in the story of Jean Valjean. Of love, grief, repentance, forgiveness, and starting over. Brad gave me a gentle nudge, and I realized I was holding up our row.

"How did you like the show, Brooke?" Jack asked as he merged his car onto I-25, and we headed back to Carlson.

"It was so amazing. I didn't want it to end."

Nicole turned from the front passenger seat and smiled. Maybe I imagined it, but when she saw I was resting my head on Brad's shoulder, her eyes shifted slightly and her smile seemed to fade. I lifted my head and settled back into my seat.

"I know what you mean. Nicole and I saw it for the first time years ago in London."

"Oh, wow, I bet that was awesome."

"It was. I mean, the performance tonight was great, but seeing it in the West End was unreal."

"That would be amazing."

"I remember being so emotionally moved by it, that I didn't want to leave."

"Exactly. That's how I felt tonight."

"Actually, he couldn't have left even if he wanted to," Nicole said.

Brad laughed.

"What?"

"Jack was not just emotionally moved, he was sobbing."

"Oh, that's sweet."

"No, we're talking big, ugly tears."

"Ugly?" Jack raised his eyebrows.

"He was such a wreck, that the ushers were worried about him. They thought he was having an emotional breakdown."

Brad and Nicole began laughing, and I joined in. Nicole's laugh was loud and sharp, identical to Ellie's.

"It wasn't *that* bad."

"No, it was." Nicole was still laughing.

The laughs slowly faded, and we settled into our own thoughts as the lights along the freeway rolled by. The eighties played quietly on the radio, Jack's music of choice.

He broke our silence. "You know what I was just thinking?"

"What?" asked Nicole.

"We should invite Brooke to go with us down to Florida in May."

In the light dimly shining from the control panel of the car, I saw Nicole turn to him, and it looked like she was scolding him with her eyes.

What was that look?

Jacked turned to her, and his expression changed. His forehead tightened as his eyes seemed to searched for answers.

"You should totally come," Brad said. "There's so much to do there. Warm water, jet skis, paddle boarding, and just chilling on the beach. It's the best."

I barely heard him as I continued to watch the silent interplay between Nicole and Jack.

It was the look she gave him, her initial reaction, that had me lying awake in my bed. I wanted to ignore it, to pretend it had nothing to do with me, but it felt personal. Because it wasn't just the look, it was several little things. Like the fact that she never hugged me anymore, or that she no longer invited me to be part of their family events. The invitation to the theater came from Jack, not her. Maybe she felt it should be Brad's choice to invite me or not. That made sense, but why did I feel like she was ignoring me? Maybe she had finally seen past my facade, to the imposter that I truly was. Maybe I didn't belong in their world. Maybe I just had some deep seeded mommy issues.

"Good night, Brooke."

"I'm sorry, El, did I wake you?"

"No, I crawled into bed just a few minutes before you did."

"Okay, good, I was trying to be quiet."

"How was the play?"

"It was so amazing. I loved it, the whole night, everything was just magical."

"I knew you'd like it."

I heard her turn over in her bed and give a gentle fluff to her pillow. My cue that she was settling in for sleep. I silently stared into the darkness. After a few minutes, it was clear that my thoughts weren't going to release me that easily.

"El," I whispered, checking if she was still awake.

"Yeah," she responded, a bit groggier now.

"This will sound weird, but do you think your mom likes me?"

Another turn in her bed, I could feel she was facing me now. "Uh oh, what did she say to you?"

"Nothing, really. I guess that's the problem. She never says much of anything to me anymore."

"My mom loves you, Brooke. She's told me that a number of times."

"It just feels like she doesn't want me around as much anymore."

"She's hard to read sometimes."

"Hmm," I sighed. "I guess I haven't noticed that before."

"For better or worse, if my mom doesn't like someone, she'll let them know."

We were both quiet again, going back to our own thoughts. Sleep began to wash over me, my eyes suddenly heavy from the day.

"You have to understand something about my family, Brooke." Ellie snapped me back to attention.

The anxiety within me began to fire all at once, feeding off the validation it expected to receive. I turned in my bed and leaned closer to her. I didn't want to miss a word.

"My parents have big dreams for Brad. He's got a lot going for him, you already know that. He's smart, he's always done well in school, he's a natural leader and hugely charismatic. He's the oldest, and he's always been my mom's favorite. No one can measure up to the great Brad Foster in her eyes."

She stopped herself. The dynamic had shifted when I began dating Brad. She couldn't speak as freely about him as she once had. I could sense she was searching for the right way to continue.

"Don't get me wrong, Brad is amazing," she went on. "We're the best of friends. He's always included me in everything and always has my back. But he also casts a big shadow, you know?"

"I can see that." I chose my words carefully.

"He has a huge personality," Ellie said. "Because of this, I think my parents have always expected big things from him. Especially my mom. But what makes Brad so great, also drives my parents crazy. I think my dad's idea of big is Brad taking over his accounting firm someday. He can't see why Brad wouldn't want that and the success it brings."

I thought about the Foster's home, their cars, their lifestyle, and the vacations they went on. It was all materialistic, but I envied it. I enjoyed living the good life vicariously through them. I enjoyed that Brad spoiled me.

"But I don't think Brad's idea of big is being an accountant," Ellie continued, as if reading my thoughts. "Big to Brad is climbing the highest mountains, traveling the country on foot, and doing something that no one has ever thought of before. He hates to be restricted."

I twiddled with a frayed thread from my blanket, wrapping and unwrapping it around my fingers. "Do you think I'm holding him back?"

She laughed. "No, that's the great thing. You give him the freedom to dream. I've never seen him more alive. You're perfect for him."

Her words brought a smile to my face. I felt an unconscious burden lift from my mind. The fear that I had simply been playing a childlike game of house was replaced by a future that suddenly seemed tangible.

"But my mom likes to control Brad's life, so you need to give her time to get used to the idea of you and Brad."

"Does she not want me in Brad's life?"

"She doesn't want anyone in his life."

"What do you mean?"

"I mean it's not personal. She wants the best for him, but *her* version of the best. She feels like he's wasting his time and he needs to get serious. She hates all of the 'Brad Stories' because in her mind, it says he hasn't changed at all since he was five. It was cute then, but now I think she finds it embarrassing."

I held the frayed thread in my hand and smoothed out its length. I curled it again around my index finger and let the tightness throb for a moment.

"So, how do I get your mom to accept me?"

"Brooke, the reality is you could be the absolute perfect person for Brad and still fall short in my mother's eyes. She loves having you as a friend for me, because you're a nice, sweet girl who can only be a good influence on me. You're not a threat. She doesn't expect much from me anyway."

"Ellie," I interjected. "That's not true."

"Listen, I love my mom for many reasons, so I'm not going to sit here and cry to you about how horrible my amazing parents are. Especially to you. You've made me realize how lucky I am. I have a mom and dad who have loved me and hugged me and always been there for me. But at the same time, my mom takes zero pride in me. She never tells anyone I'm going to college because she doesn't view Grand Mesa as a real college. I think it embarrasses her. And that's okay. I've learned to live in Brad's extremely large shadow, and I like who I am. So, for me, in my mom's eyes, you can only add to my life. But to Brad, she sees you as a threat. You're nineteen years old and just one more example, to her, of him not wanting to grow up. She wants him to get married and start having her grandkids. She views you as a little girl, just like she does me, not a wife."

"She told you that." My anxiety rising again.

"No, but I know my mom. What I'm saying is, no one will be good enough for Brad at the start. Just keep being you and don't worry about trying to earn her love. She already likes you, so you have a head start. She just needs time."

We were quiet again, and within a few minutes, I heard Ellie gently begin to snore. I laid there as my thoughts continued to swirl. My mind began picking at the insecurities of my past. I could leave Chatwin behind and pretend it wasn't a part of me, but I was still that little poor girl with the worn clothes, an alcoholic father, and a mother I wasn't enough for. What would Nicole think if she found out her baby boy was risking all his dreams on a girl with a lineage of failure? She was never going to accept me. The best I could hope for was that she wouldn't hate me. I had enough people in my life who hated me.

CHAPTER 20

started to worry on day five and was in a complete panic by day eight. Something was wrong, and I knew I was in trouble. My period hadn't come, and I was way late. My cycle varied from time to time, but nothing like this.

I sat on the edge of the bathtub and stared at the pregnancy test sitting on the countertop. The test instructions said to wait three minutes for the results. I held the edge of my fingertips to my mouth and then pulled them away, searching for a nail to bite. Nothing, just the nubs I had already worn down days earlier. My stomach hurt.

Maybe it's morning sickness.

The twist of worry was unrelenting.

I had watched enough television to see this exact scenario play out numerous times. Now that it was my real-life drama, it wasn't nearly as entertaining.

A thousand thoughts filled my mind.

What will Brad think? What will he do?

Will he marry me?

What if this was just a fling?

Will he feel trapped, forced into something he never wanted?

"Brad hates to feel restricted," isn't that what Ellie said?

What will Jack and Nicole think?

Nicole's going to hate this… hate me.

What if it's too much for Brad? What if he leaves?

I could lose everything I've spent the last year building.

I'd have nowhere to go.

Would I crawl back to Chatwin and beg my father to take me in?

I bet the town would line up to see that.

Brooklyn Blair, the girl who thought she was so much better than good ol' Chatwin.

You're not special. Now, take your rightful place here in the land of the miserable.

The alarm on my phone went off, silencing the voices in my head. I didn't want to look. I needed more time. Just five more minutes. Maybe a little more. I just needed a couple of more days and surely my body would do what it's supposed to do.

Please don't let this be real.

I reached over and grabbed the test off the countertop.

Positive.

No.

I slid off the edge of the bathtub onto our turquoise bathmat.

No.

I wrapped my arms around my abdomen and doubled over, my forehead pressing against the cold, tile floor.

No.

The tears I had been holding back for days, refusing to release, mounted a final assault, pounding in my head.

One, two, three, four, five. Breathe.

But I couldn't breathe. Instead, a sound escaped from my mouth that somehow perfectly matched the anguish I was in. I collapsed to the floor and pulled my knees tight against me. All I could do was lay there and sob.

CHAPTER 21

"Brooklyn."

"Mom?"

I was on the dirt road again. Everything was the same as before. The sun, the fields of grass, and my mother's silhouette in the horizon.

"Brooklyn, come quick, sweetie. Come and see."

"Mom, where are you?"

"Come and see, sweetie."

I began running toward her, faster this time. I was not going to lose her again.

"Mom, I'm coming. Wait for me. Don't leave me again."

"I'm here, sweetheart. Come and see."

I was getting closer. Her face, obscured by the glare of the sun, was almost within my view. And then she was gone again.

"Mom."

I collapsed to my knees, out of breath. A familiar sadness fell over me.

"Mom, please. Please don't leave me again. I need you."

"It's okay, baby girl. I'm here. Look."

I opened my eyes and blinked away a kaleidoscope of tears. I was atop the cliff again. The valley of lilies spread out before me again.

"Do you see them?" she asked.

"Yes."

"You created this," she said. "Isn't it beautiful?"

I awoke to the gentle sound of my bedroom door opening and the slow whine of its hinges. Ellie was getting back from her early morning class, which she had every Thursday.

I watched her from my sleep-worn eyes. My brain, just waking up, was trying to decipher dreams from reality. She quietly placed her bag on her desk and pulled her laptop out.

It had been five days since I had taken the pregnancy test. I hadn't told anyone yet. I didn't know how, and the secret was crushing me.

I was living in a fog, going through the motions of my regular day, but every thought was consumed by my new reality. With final exams just days away, the timing couldn't have been worse. I tried to focus, but found it easier to lay in my bed, mindlessly scrolling through my phone.

"Brooke," Ellie said, waving a hand in front of my face. "Where are you?"

I blinked hard and smiled at her.

"What?"

"I asked you a question."

"Sorry."

"Are you doing okay?"

"Yeah, just tired I guess."

"Are you sure? You seem kind of distracted lately."

"Do I? I'm sorry, I think I'm just feeling the pressure of finals coming up."

"Tell me about it. I've got two huge papers due before I can even think about studying. It's so stupid that they pile all of this on at the end of the year."

I sat up and arched my back, stretching away the tightness of sleep. I looked at her and for a moment, thought of telling her about the pregnancy. She was always honest with me. An open book. My best friend. I wanted to tell her, I needed to tell her, but I needed to tell Brad first, and that was something I couldn't do.

"Let's not psych ourselves out," she said. "We're going to rock finals and then have the best summer of our lives."

I knew my secret would change everything—ruin everything. "Deal."

"Awesome. Now get up and get to class, you're going to be late."

"I know, I know. I'm moving."

I rubbed my face and shuffled into the bathroom, forcing my body to wake up for the day. I closed the door and stared at my reflection in the mirror. My eyes looked hollow, like I was there but not there. Exactly how I felt.

I heard Ellie leave the bedroom. Her words turned in my mind. *The best summer of our lives.*

That's what I wanted, to be carefree and have fun. I had spent so many years worried and alone, caring for other people and their mistakes. This was my time to be young. To live life without thinking. To wake up with a smile on my face every morning. Instead, I screwed it up again. The universe decided to make me a statistic and prove that actions have consequences.

My eyes burned with a mix of anger and sadness.

Why does it always have to be so hard? What's wrong with me? I ruin everything I touch. My dad, my mom, my friendships, and now this.

I placed a hand on my stomach. There was, of course, nothing to feel yet.

"The worst thing is," I whispered, then held what I wanted to say next, but it rolled out anyway. "I don't want you."

The words hurt leaving my lips and hung heavy in the air. I hated myself for saying it. I knew the pain of not being wanted.

"I'm sorry. I know that makes me a horrible person. A horrible mother. I'm so sorry."

I heard a light tap on the door.

"Brooke, are you okay?" Ellie asked from the other side.

I took a deep breath and wiped my eyes. "Yeah," my voice cracked. "I'll be out in just a minute."

"Brooke, what's going on, babe?"

"I'm good, El, I promise. I'll be done in just a minute."

I heard her step away from the door. I turned the shower on and sat on the edge of the toilet. The secret wasn't crushing me. It was killing me.

When I came downstairs, I found Ellie and Brad sitting at the kitchen table.

What was he doing here?

I wanted to run to him, to fall into his arms, but I wasn't ready to see him. To face him. To tell him.

"Hey, babe," I said, trying to feign excitement. "I didn't know you were coming over?"

I walked toward him, and he stood to give me a hug. I gave him a quick squeeze and moved away.

I looked over at Ellie, who stared at me intently. I gave her a quizzical look with a half smile.

I walked into the kitchen and began to make a bowl of oatmeal. I could feel them staring at me, their silence deafening. I started the microwave and looked back at them.

"What's up, guys?"

"What's up with you?" Brad asked.

I looked at him like he had just asked me the most obvious question. "I'm making oatmeal," I said, pointing to the box.

"Is everything okay?"

I rolled my eyes and shook my head, turning back toward the microwave.

"Why does everyone keep asking me that? It's the end of the semester, I'm sorry that it's stressing me out a little."

"Come on, Brooke," Ellie said. "What's really going on?"

"Nothing." I shrugged my shoulders. I reached for the cabinet next to the microwave and got a bowl out, closing the door with emphasis.

"It's like you haven't been here the past few days," she continued. "I haven't even seen you studying or doing much of anything really."

I shook my head and gave her a dismissive look. "Thanks, Mom."

"See, that's what I'm talking about. I've lived with you for eight months, and I've never known you to be a callous person."

Brad stood and walked toward me. I straightened and turned back to the microwave.

"Brooke, why were you crying in the bathroom?" he asked.

I slowly turned around again, looked past him, and stared directly at Ellie. My lips pursed and I shook my head.

"Why did you tell him that?"

Brad stepped closer to me. "She's only worried about you."

"I'm fine, you guys don't need to worry about me."

"I want to believe you," Ellie said. "But I can tell something's wrong."

I looked toward the floor and let out a heavy sigh. The pressure of the past week began to crumble around me.

"Babe, what's going on?" Brad asked.

I stared at him and bit my upper lip. A tear rolled down my cheek as he inched closer.

"I'm pregnant."

Except for the sound of the microwave, the kitchen was silent. For a long moment, the three of us simply stared at each other.

"What?" Brad asked, more to himself than to me.

Ellie stood and walked toward me, wrapping her arms around my neck. I hugged her back but stared at Brad. His eyes were wide, and his mouth hung open. He looked down at the floor and seemed to be racing with thoughts.

Our eyes met, and he smiled, though he seemed to be searching for answers. Maybe, in a perfect world, he was thinking about us. Maybe he shared my hopeful fantasy of him coming home from work and picking up our baby in his arms. He would smile and play, and then he'd lean over and give me a kiss. We would be together. A family. Who says you have to wait on love? But that wasn't real life.

"I'm sorry."

He let out a half laugh. "You're sorry?"

He walked toward me and wrapped me in his arms.

"You don't need to be sorry, Brooke. I love you." He pushed me back just enough to look into my eyes. "I love you," he said again. "We'll figure this out."

I felt like I could breathe again. I held him tight and leaned my head against his shoulder.

"What are we going to do?"

"We'll figure it out."

"But what does that mean?"

He released his hug and grabbed my hand, leading me to the kitchen table. He motioned for Ellie to come over, and she sat down next to us.

"It means that we're going to push pause," he said. "You're going to focus on your finals, because you can't lose an entire semester of hard work in the last week."

"How can I focus? School doesn't even seem important anymore."

"Maybe not now, but it will. Once the shock wears off, you'll regret not finishing the year."

I held his hand in mine and stroked his fingers with the edge of my thumb. I knew he was right, but I couldn't imagine thinking about anything else.

"Nothing is going to change in a week."

"Okay. You're right."

"And you can't let Mom know," Ellie said, looking at Brad.

"Yeah, totally," Brad agreed. "We can't say anything yet. She's going to lose her mind."

I saw the look they gave each other, as if they were both running scenarios through their minds of how Nicole would react. Their anxious expressions told me none of them would be good.

"I'm sorry."

"Babe, stop apologizing. Why do you think this is your fault?"

"Because I'm the baby mama taking down Nicole's golden boy."

I looked at Ellie, and when our eyes met, she looked away. I was right.

"Don't worry about my mom. Let's push pause. You take a week and finish your finals. I'm going to take a week, clear my head, and figure out what we should do next."

"Will I see you?"

"Babe, I love you, don't worry. I just need some time to process this."

"Brad, I don't think that's such a good idea," Ellie said. "This is a lot to take; you shouldn't be alone."

"I won't be by myself. I'll grab Mike or Harrison. I just need to get on top of a mountain or somewhere and clear my mind. Sitting here stressing while Brooke needs to finish school isn't going to do any good."

I looked at Ellie, furrowed my eyebrows, and silently pleaded with her to disagree. She raised her hand slightly and nodded her head. "He'll be fine," she mouthed to me without speaking.

"Okay."

"And when you finish your last test. I'm going to pick you up, and we're going to Denver to celebrate, just like we planned to."

I took a deep breath and squeezed his hand. "Okay."

He stood and kissed my forehead.

"We're going to figure this out. I promise."

He walked out the door, and despite his reassurances, I wondered if I would ever see him again.

CHAPTER 22

The house was a disaster. The countertops cluttered with worn notebooks, half-empty coffee mugs, and the remnants of many, hurried meals. The aftermath of finals week. Of studying, late nights, and bleary-eyed celebrations.

I tiptoed around a tower of mismatched storage bins and a bulging laundry basket, its woven seams tearing at the top, and finally found my way to the couch. I stared at the mess and felt a sadness wash over me. I had entered this home as a stranger, the girl from nowhere, without a friend in the world. Now the school year was over, and two of our roommates were moving out and on to new adventures. Everything was changing.

I didn't even know where I'd be in the fall. Just one more panic humming in the background of my thoughts. I should be here with Ellie, welcoming new roommates and a new year, but everything was different now.

I checked my phone; five fifty-eight. Brad said he would pick me up at six.

When he told me he was going to take a week to clear his head, he meant it. I didn't hear anything from him for six days. I didn't like it. I needed to talk to him, to know he was okay. To know that we were okay.

As I left campus after taking my second to last final, he finally texted me.

We need to talk. Denver tomorrow? I'll pick you up at six.

I stared at my phone and reread the words, scrolling back to see if I had missed an earlier text. We don't talk for a week after sharing the biggest news of both of our lives, and all I get is twelve stupid words. No, *I love you* or *I miss you* or *I hope you're doing good?*

We need to talk.

The words kept rolling around in my head. What does that even mean? Is it good or bad? It sounds bad.

There was a knock at the door, and I weaved my way back through the maze to open it. Brad stood in the doorway, his smile melting away any anger I was holding on to. He held a bouquet of flowers in his hand, a spring mix with splashes of red, white, and purple.

"Hi, beautiful."

I stepped toward him and wrapped my arms around his neck. "I've missed you."

"I've missed you, too."

<hr>

We headed south toward Denver. Brad's sports car cruised effortlessly in and around the slower traffic as we sang along to the radio. It felt as if real life was taking a break, if just for a moment.

We worked our way through the streets of downtown Denver and pulled up to the valet at Ruth's Chris Steakhouse. Two men in red shirts quickly approached the car and opened our doors for us. We were led inside to a small waiting area.

We sat silently and watched the other patrons in the room. A group of perfectly groomed men walked by with an unspoken arrogance and were quickly joined by an equally beautiful group of women. Their golden skin worked in perfect unison with their hair, their outfits, and their jewelry. I envied their carefree smiles. I turned and looked at Brad. He was watching them as well. I wondered what was going through his mind. Did he share my fear that our life would never be carefree again?

He looked at me and placed a hand on my leg. He gave it a gentle squeeze. "You okay?"

"Yeah. Sorry, I guess my brain's just tired from studying and everything."

The hostess turned toward us. "Foster."

Brad and I stood and followed her through the restaurant. She led us to a quiet booth, with rose petals sprinkled across the table.

"Here you go." She placed a set of menus on the table.

"Thank you," Brad and I said at the same time.

"Is this your first time dining with us?"

Brad looked to me and then to the hostess. "I've been here before. Have you ever been, Brooke?"

I smiled, thinking he was joking, then saw that he was serious. "No, this is my first time."

"Well, we're happy to have you. I hope you have an amazing evening."

"Thank you," Brad said again.

I picked up the menu and began to look through it. The prices for a single item matched my monthly food budget. I searched for the cheapest option.

A man approached our table. "Good evening. My name is Joseph, and I will be taking care of you tonight."

Brad nodded. "Hi, Joseph."

"I see the rose petals on the table. What are we celebrating tonight?"

Brad and I looked at each other, not sure how to answer the question. We had planned to celebrate the end of the school year, but now it felt like we were simply trying to avoid reality.

"We're celebrating the journey that is life," said Brad.

Joseph smiled. "Excellent, sir. Then let's make it a memorable night."

<hr>

The food was beyond comparison. Despite its price tag, Brad talked me into the filet mignon just to see the presentation as it was served, sizzling in butter.

For a moment, we were free. We laughed, we ate, and nothing else seemed to matter. But as we stared at our empty plates, we could no longer put off the inevitable.

"What are we going to do, Brooke?" Brad asked.

I wish he hadn't. I didn't want the evening to end. I didn't want life to begin. I stared at him for a long moment and then down at my plate. I held my fork and moved a small piece of asparagus around.

"We're going to have a baby."

I looked at him, to see his reaction. He stared back with a slight smile.

"I've thought about a lot of things over the past week," he said. "There aren't really any easy choices here. We're still young, and we're just trying to get to know each other. How do you add a baby on top of that?"

I suddenly felt sick. I wanted him to have the answers, to tell me everything would be okay, but he seemed as confused as I was. I shook my head. "I don't know."

"But we made choices, and it's on us to own it," he continued. "My duty is to…"

I put my hand on his and stopped him.

"Slow down," I said. "I feel like you're treating me like a client instead of your girlfriend. Life and love aren't decided in board rooms."

"I'm sorry. I'm not saying it right."

"Brad, I would expect nothing less from you than to do the honorable thing. That's who you are, and that's why I love you. And yeah, I'm freaking out about the future and what's going to happen. And I know you would stand by my side for years to come, because you think it's the right thing to do, but we can't do this simply out of obligation. Eventually we'll end up resenting each other, or worse, the baby."

His eyes were fixed on mine, taking in every word.

"What are you saying?" he asked. "What choice do we have?"

"What I'm saying is, this is our baby, you and me, but it's not fair to bring her…"

"Her?"

"What, I don't know, it feels like a girl." I smiled at him. "But it's not fair to bring her, or him, into a forced family where mom and dad don't love each other. Kids see through that. It would be better to give her…" I caught myself again. "Or him, to a family who will fill their life with love."

He shook his head and leaned back against his seat. He stretched his hands behind his head, letting out a deep sigh, and placing them back on the table.

"Brooke, I can't do that. I won't do that. I'm not giving our baby away. I'm not going to have some kid knock on my door in twenty years and say 'Hey, Dad, I'm the son you didn't want. Surprise.'"

"You're missing my point."

"No, I get it. I know what you're saying, but you want a guarantee that we'll live happily ever after. No one can guarantee that, no matter the situation. Every couple is acting on faith to some degree. They're together because they took a leap."

I brushed a pile of crumbs off the tablecloth, into my hand, and dropped them onto my plate. I looked up. Brad held his steady gaze.

"Do you want to have this baby?"

There it was—the question I hadn't dared ask myself. The answer stirred quietly, like something already rooted inside me. I wanted this baby. I didn't know how it would work or what came next, but I knew, I wanted this baby.

"Yes." I smiled with an odd sense of relief.

"I mean, I wouldn't have chosen this path. I always thought I'd be like thirty before I had kids."

He smiled and let out a soft laugh. "Me, too."

"But whether I want the baby or not, it doesn't change the fact that we can't do this out of obligation. If we're not in love now, we're certainly not going to fall in love while trying to raise a child."

I looked back down at my plate and went back to moving the asparagus around. We sat in silence.

"Brooke, I don't know if it's possible, but I feel like I've loved you since the moment I met you. I remember you walking through my parents' backyard with Ellie, and all I could do was look at you. I felt this strange connection to you. All I've wanted to do since that moment, is to be with you. Every time we're together, I fall in love with you even more."

A memory of my parents popped into my mind. The three of us at the Chatwin Fourth of July celebration when I was six. My father held one of my hands and my mom held the other as we ended the day and walked back home. Slowly, they began swinging me with their arms. Each swing a little farther, and a little higher. They laughed as I laughed. That kind of pure happiness had escaped my life until this moment.

"I think I'd be a pretty good husband," Brad continued. "I have no clue how to be a dad, but I'll be pretty good at it. I want to take this leap, and I want to take it with you."

My hands trembled. My heart was ready to burst. He slipped out of his side of the booth, lowering to one knee beside me. He steadied my hands with his and then pulled away, holding a diamond ring.

"The question is, do you want to take it with me?"

Our corner of the restaurant had gone quiet. Every eye seemingly on us. I wiped a finger underneath each of my eyes and laughed. "Yes."

Brad placed the ring on my finger and applause broke out from those around us. He held my hands and sat back on his side of the table.

"I will never leave your side," he said. "I promise."

CHAPTER 23

On the days when my mom's depression would cast its evil thoughts upon her, seizing her in a wave of unrelenting sadness, I learned to be still. If she could sleep, she seemed to bounce back sooner. I would tiptoe around the house after school, quietly make a snack, and then slip outside. It's amazing how much one can notice when your senses aren't distracted.

I thought of this as I sat in the Foster's family room. No one said a word; the silence was deafening. I detected the faint hum of the refrigerator coming from the kitchen.

Has it always made that sound?

I watched as two birds landed on opposite sides of the back patio, playfully singing to each other. A reminder that summer had arrived.

I shifted on the couch, moving my body from the deep nook next to Brad. His arm rested gently behind my shoulders. We needed to do this together, but I wanted to run. The plan had been to tell Jack and Nicole about the baby and our engagement right away, but Brad kept putting it off.

"Trust me. You have to find the right time to tell my mom certain things."

I was beginning to think what he really meant was if we waited long enough, maybe Nicole would like me again, and it would be easier to break the news. I didn't share his fantasy, and the mounting pressure of hiding our secret was becoming too much. The time was now.

I stared down at my hands, then carefully raised my eyes to survey the room. Nicole had her back to us, slowly pacing in front of the fireplace. She pulled a picture frame off one of the long white cabinets that mirrored both sides of the open, stone hearth. It was a picture of Brad wearing his Carlson High football uniform. She stared at it longingly, and I wondered if this was more for show or if I had really corrupted the image of her perfect little boy.

I looked over to Jack. He stared directly at us, his face void of emotion. My eyes quickly darted back to my hands.

"Mom, say something," Brad finally said.

Nicole let out a quiet breath and returned the frame to its original spot.

"You know, it's funny," she said. "When you were around seventeen, one of the Callahan girls started coming around here all the time. Which one was it?"

"Who, Kylie?" Brad asked.

"That's right, Kylie. Anyway, she started coming over all the time to see you, and I swear, her clothes got skimpier every time. I don't know how Tiffany ever let her daughter out of the house like that."

Brad let out a sigh and moved his arm from around me, leaning forward. He pressed the palms of his hands to his face and rubbed his eyes.

"Mom, what does Kylie Callahan have to do with any of this?"

"Because your dad and I had a serious talk back then about what we would do or say if you came to us one day and told us that you got Kylie pregnant."

"What?" Brad asked, with a laugh. "She was my friend. I didn't even like her like that."

"Well, she liked you, and I know she wanted to get into your pants."

The comment caught me off guard and a laugh rose through me before I could stop it. I bit my upper lip, but the sound released in a quiet snort. Jack gave me a sideways glance then looked back at Nicole.

"Mom, gross," Brad said. "Please, if I never have to hear you use that phrase again, I will be forever grateful."

"The point is, Brad, I thought this conversation might have happened when you were seventeen, but you're an adult now. What do you want me to say?"

"I just told you that we're engaged. Maybe be excited or say congratulations."

Now it was Jack's turn to laugh. "You're missing a bit of context there, don't you think? You told us you're getting married because you got your nineteen-year-old, kind of girlfriend, pregnant."

I shifted and straightened my back. The first shot fired at me.

"Maybe you haven't noticed, Dad," Brad said. "But we've been dating for six months."

"Oh, wow, an entire six months, huh? My apologies, that changes everything. That seems like plenty of time to start a family."

Nicole raised a hand to him and walked over to one of the two opposing armchairs, taking a seat.

"We just need a little time to process this. This is big. This is life changing."

"Believe me, I know," Brad said. "No one was more surprised than me."

I looked at him and raised an eyebrow. His analysis was debatable.

"Are you angry?" Brad asked.

Jack and Nicole looked at each other and then back to us.

"Not angry," said Jack.

"We're not angry, dear," Nicole said. "I've prayed for the day that you would come home and tell me you've found the love of your life. The person you want to spend forever with."

"I have…I am. It's Brooke."

He squeezed my hand and smiled at me. I smiled back, then looked at Jack and Nicole. Nicole gave me a dismissive grin, which disappeared as fast as it arrived. She turned back to Brad.

"I'm not going to sugarcoat things," she said. "This is going to be a lot harder than you think."

"I know that."

"No, I don't think you do. Marriage is hard enough, but you throw a baby on top of it…let's just say you have a lot working against you."

"Of course, but doesn't every marriage have to face that eventually?" Brad asked.

"Sure, but you're starting with the baby. You won't have the time to get to know each other, to drive each other crazy and learn how to compromise through that and love each other more. All your time and energy will be spent taking care of a baby. So, when those bumps in the road come along, and they will come, they just got a lot more difficult."

Brad nodded his head and seemed to be contemplating her words. I kept my eyes down but could feel Jack's stare directed at me. I looked at him, he didn't flinch. He had a bent smile on his face, as if he was enjoying this in some way.

"Brooke, you've been quiet. What do you think about all of this?"

Panic rushed through me, my throat tightening. I stared down at my hands and then back up at Jack.

"It's definitely a surprise," I said and laughed. No one responded. "Um…you know, I get what you're saying Nicole about how difficult this will be."

I looked at Brad.

"And we've talked about that. We know it will be hard, but we love each other, and we're completely dedicated to this."

"You're so young though," said Jack. "If Ellie was in the same situation, I can't even imagine what she would do."

Nicole rolled her eyes and shook her head. "Heaven help us if Ellie had a baby this young," Nicole said. "She can barely take care of herself."

I wanted to defend my friend, but I wasn't about to add another layer to the conflict.

"What are you going to do about school?" Jack asked.

"I don't know yet."

"Well, are you going to drop out? You can't take a baby to class, right?"

"No."

"That's something you need to consider. What about your friends and roommates? Are you ready to give up the college life?"

I felt as if I were shrinking into the couch. We were no longer having a conversation; we were being interrogated. Well, at least I was.

"Yes, sir."

"What about Ellie?" Jack asked. "Does she know about this? And what about your contract at the townhouse? You signed up for another year. That's legally binding, meaning it's your responsibility to find someone to fill it if you can't."

"I know."

"Dad, stop."

"It's fine."

"What?" Jack asked. "I'm not trying to be mean. I'm just trying to be the voice of reason. Brooke said you guys were dedicated to this. I don't think you've thought this through."

Of all the things Jack and Nicole were telling us, none of it was shaking my love for Brad or my belief that we could raise a child together. The biggest reality check revealing itself was that when we did get married, Brad's family would become my family. They would be my only family, and I was starting to realize I would never be good enough in their eyes.

A fire began burning within me. An anger seeping from wounds I thought had healed long ago. Too many people had taken it upon themselves to tell me what I couldn't do and what I couldn't be. To set my sights low and just survive.

"You know we didn't plan this," I said, surprised to hear the words leaving my mouth. "So yeah, I don't have all the answers. But I didn't have all the answers when my mom died. No one told me how to survive that. No one told me how to help my father, who was a complete mess. I didn't know how to raise myself, but I did. I didn't know how to get into college, because no one believed I could, but I'm here."

The room was silent again. I took a deep breath and lowered my voice.

"My Grandma Belle told me that we can't let ourselves get frozen by fear. Sometimes you have to move forward with faith. I've tried to live my life that way. I didn't picture myself having a baby this young. I honestly didn't picture myself ever falling in love, but I love your son, and I want to spend the rest of my life with him."

I looked away from Jack's steady gaze, back to my hands. I worried I had said too much.

"Okay."

"Okay?" Brad asked. "What does that mean?"

"Brad, we love you," Nicole said. "It doesn't matter how old your children get, it makes a mother nervous when they have to make big, life-altering decisions."

She walked over and sat next to me on the couch. The scent of her perfume danced in the air.

"I don't think any of us imagined this," she said. "But I can see you're both in love. If this is what you want, then of course, we're going to support you."

She put an arm around me and gave me a squeeze. I felt relieved by the long-awaited affection. Maybe we could finally be friends again.

"Dad?" Brad asked.

Jack uncrossed his legs and leaned forward. He surveyed his hands.

"I agree with your mother. If this is what you want, then we'll support you."

Brad and Jack stood up at the same time. They shook hands and then pulled each other into an embrace.

"I love you, Dad."

"I love you, too."

Brad sat back down, and I curled up next to him. The dread I had felt on the car ride over relinquished its grip.

"So, I guess the next step is planning a wedding," said Nicole.

A smile crept across my face. These were words I could have never imagined hearing a year ago.

"Have you given it any thought yet?" she asked.

Brad smiled and let out a heavy sigh. "Not much, I guess."

"I have," I said. "I think with the baby coming and the cost involved in that, we'll just keep it simple."

I was deflecting. I didn't know what it cost to have a baby, I hadn't even thought about it yet. What I did know, but didn't want to reveal, is that my father wouldn't contribute a dime to my wedding day.

Jack must have read my mind because he dismissed me with a wave of his hand. "I don't know much about your family, Brooke," he said. "But I know you've had a tough go."

How much did he know?

"We want to make this a special day for our son. We'll cover things."

Brad squeezed my hand again and smiled at me.

"That's really nice of you," I said. "Thank you."

"So, what's your idea?" Nicole asked.

"Well, I know it's kind of silly and sentimental, but Brad and I met in October, and I've always loved that time of year. If we do it early enough, it won't be too hot. Shouldn't be cold either. We'd have the fall colors everywhere. It's just a beautiful time of year."

"Wait, I can't believe I didn't ask this already," Nicole said. "How far along are you?"

"The baby?" Brad asked.

We looked at each other. "I think about ten weeks."

"So, in October, you're going to be what? Maybe about eight months pregnant?"

"Maybe, I guess." I laughed. "I can't count that fast."

Nicole pursed her lips. "That's not going to work."

My daydreams had already gone so far down the path of an October wedding that her words caught me off guard. Maybe she wasn't catching my vision.

"Are you worried that the weather's too unpredictable in October?" I asked. "Because I thought about that, too, but I think if we do it early enough, we'll be okay."

"No, I'm worried that all my friends and family and extended family are going to come to a wedding where the bride is the center of attention, but for all the wrong reasons."

Silence, again.

"You can't be pregnant on your wedding day. It's tacky, it's… white trash."

My heart pounded, and my eyes burned. Like a scolded child, her words hurt and embarrassed me.

"No offense," she said. "It's a fun idea. There's just a certain perception that we have to maintain. I'm willing to go along with this whole baby idea, but you've got to give me something."

Baby idea?

Brad placed his hand on my leg and gave it a squeeze. I looked to him for support but saw the resignation in his eyes.

"She's right, Brooke," he said. "It shouldn't matter, but it does to some people."

"Exactly," Nicole said. "It's sad that people judge others like that, but they do. You don't want people gossiping at your wedding, you want them to be talking about how beautiful you look. You want it to be a celebration of your new life together."

"I don't really care what people say about me."

"Why don't we do it earlier?" offered Brad.

Nicole scrunched her eyes and looked up at the ceiling, as if she were thinking. She nodded her head back and forth.

"The problem with that is there just isn't enough time to throw a wedding together that quickly," she said. "And Brooke's so skinny, she'll be showing sooner than you think."

I sat back on the couch, my will to speak up was slowly fading. "I don't really see what the big deal is. Who cares what people think. It's our wedding, not theirs."

"It's not about you, Brooke," said Nicole.

She was right, it wasn't about me. It was about her and the perfect family she wanted to show off. She shared a sideways glance with Brad. An unspoken understanding between the two of them. I suppressed the urge to yell at him. The man with a thousand ideas and a million opinions, was suddenly too afraid to talk.

Nicole laughed nonchalantly. "I know we probably seem a bit old-fashioned here in Carlson, especially in a progressive state like Colorado, but while it has its downsides, I think it's also what makes it a great place to live."

I didn't look at her. I couldn't look at her. How could I complain about a wedding they were paying for, even if it was my own. I stared past her, into the backyard.

"I'm fine with whatever you think is best."

Brad turned to me. "I feel like you're upset."

"Nope, I'm good. I understand."

"Here's a cute idea," Nicole said. "You could wait until the baby is a year old or so and have a wedding then. A lot of people live together these days and start a family before they ever get married. It's kind of fun to be at a wedding where a little family comes together as one."

I laughed and shook my head.

"What?" Brad asked.

"Nothing."

"No, go ahead, Brooke," Nicole said.

"I'm just so confused by this. So, it's acceptable by the town of Carlson to live together, unmarried, have sex, and have a baby. All of that is better than a pregnant bride?"

Jack laughed. "She has a point."

"Maybe," Nicole said. "But yeah, it does make a difference. Because the moment they see a pregnant bride, it changes what they think of you and of Brad…and our family."

I tried to hide my disappointment. I didn't want to look like I was pouting, but I was done. This was a fight I couldn't win alone.

"Like I said, I'm good with whatever you think is best."

Nicole looked at Brad. "What do you want, Brad, because you're not saying anything."

He looked to me and then to Nicole. "Why don't we plan for next October?" he asked. "I think that would be a good compromise."

"I like that," Nicole said. "What do you think, Jack?"

"Works for me," Jack said.

"Brooke, what about you?"

"Okay."

"Perfect," she said and smiled. The smile of the victor. A smile she must wear often in her unrelenting pursuit to have things her way. She owned me now.

CHAPTER 24

The GMCC student center was unusually crowded, even for lunchtime. The beginning of a new semester brought excitement and uncertainty, motivating students enough to be there, if only to gauge which classes they could skip and which ones would require attendance.

I stood off to the side, next to a row of tinted, floor to ceiling windows and held my lunch close to me. A never-ending stream of students filed past as I searched for Ellie in the madness.

"Brooke!"

I looked around, every table was occupied. Her voice was directionless among the commotion.

"Brooke!"

I scanned the rows of tables but couldn't see her. A group of girls standing next to me began to move, one of them catching my small camera bag with the corner of her backpack. It dragged across my body until finally releasing, falling hard against my hip.

"Sorry," the girl said.

I pushed the bag behind me to keep it protected and continued my search.

"Brooke Blair!" I heard Ellie say.

I held my hands up in confusion, helpless in my inability to spot a face in a crowd. Finally, I saw her standing on top of a table in the corner, waving both arms in my direction. I smiled and zigzagged my way over to her.

"Sorry," I said. "I'm an idiot."

"You're totally fine."

"What's up today?" I asked. "I've never seen it this crowded."

"First week of fall semester, everyone is here."

I placed my camera bag on the table and opened a premade salad I had bought at the Grand Mesa cafeteria. I regretted my choice as soon as I saw it. I picked out wilted pieces of romaine lettuce and a strawberry that looked like it was left over from the previous year. I held it up to Ellie in disgust.

"GMCC catering at its finest."

"Right? Why do we keep eating here?"

I drizzled a small cup of poppy seed dressing over the salad and took a bite. The cold dressing combined with the warm, sagging lettuce, caused my stomach to turn.

"Can you believe summer's over?" Ellie asked, scrolling through her phone and pulling small bites off a super pretzel. "I'm not ready for life to start again."

"I know," I said. "I don't know how I'm going to make it through this year."

"You're gonna rock it like you always do."

"I just feel like I'm in a race against time. I thought the semester ended on December fifteenth, but it ends on the seventeenth."

"Your due date."

"Yep. Two days probably won't matter, but you watch, I'm going to be right in the middle of class and my water will break. How embarrassing will that be?"

I took my fork and speared a piece of chicken. I examined its quality before taking a bite, hoping for a better result.

"Do you worry about that?" Ellie asked. "That the baby will just come at any time?"

"I've started to. I have dreams about it, where everything happens so fast and Brad's not there, so I just completely panic."

She looked up from her phone and placed her hand on my arm.

"That's not going to happen, Brooke. You've got a lot of people who love you and are looking out for you."

"Thanks."

She pulled my bag close to her and took the camera out. "How come you're carrying this with you?" she asked, holding the viewfinder up to her eye.

"Advanced photography. We're supposed to bring it with us everywhere we go."

"Everywhere?"

"Everywhere. She wants us to capture life's unexpected moments."

Ellie pointed the camera toward me. "Smile," she said, but took the picture before I had time to react.

"Now we'll have proof of how bad the food is here."

She laughed and carefully placed the camera back in the bag.

"I saw the monster-in-law was over at you and Brad's place last night."

"Seriously? You knew your mom was there, and you didn't walk over and say hi?"

"Hey, I told Brad when you guys moved in next to me, there was no way I was going to be involved in any daily family reunions."

"That was your mom's choice for us to move there."

"That doesn't surprise me."

"You could have at least come over and rescued me."

"That bad, huh?"

"No, I shouldn't say that. Your mom's actually been really nice to me lately."

Ellie smiled and continued scrolling through her phone.

"What?"

"Nothing."

"No, really."

She put her phone down and looked at me.

"My mom's always so quick to judge. She was so against the idea of you and Brad, but now that it's kind of been forced on her, she's seeing how great you are."

A small light of validation rose through me. The hope of moving from outsider to the inner circle.

"You really think so?"

"She's always liked you, but now she's also seeing the benefit of having you in Brad's life."

"What do you mean?"

"You're getting Brad to settle down. He's around more often, he's working toward becoming a CPA, and he's going to be a dad. You're turning him into the version my mom has always dreamed of."

"I hope that's a good thing."

"It is, he has to grow up sometime."

I looked down at my salad and stared at the brown edges of the lettuce. I scrunched my nose and pushed the carton aside.

"There is a downside to the new Brad."

"What's that?"

"I shouldn't say this…but sometimes I don't want him around all the time. Is that bad?"

Ellie laughed. "I guess it depends on the reason."

"I love him, obviously, but have you ever noticed that he can't sit still?"

She laughed again and wiped her hands. Small flecks of salt weightlessly fell to the floor, disappearing on the dark gray laminate flooring.

"Are you just noticing that?"

"No. I know he's always on the go. But like, I get to Saturday morning and want to sleep in and slowly start my day. He wants to go on a ten-mile hike…for fun."

"Yep. Brad's like a dog."

"Did you just compare my future husband to a dog?"

"I did and he is. You have to let him out so he can run and get all of his energy out. If not, he'll just sit and stare at you all day."

I sat back in my chair and laughed. I loved the man, but Ellie's analogy was perfect.

"I think now that we live together, he feels like he has to be around all the time. He hasn't fully grasped how much of an introvert I truly am."

"You guys will get into a nice flow once you've had time to settle in."

"I think so, too. I've been pushing him to do more things with Harrison, which seems good for his sanity. They'll go climb a mountain together, and he'll come back totally refreshed and chill."

"Just like a dog." Ellie let out a loud, high-pitched laugh. She quickly covered her mouth, and we both started laughing. Each laugh seeming to send us into a deeper fit of laughter. I turned away, trying to compose myself, but when I looked back, we started up again.

Ellie took a deep breath and checked her phone. She wiped her eyes and wadded up the brown paper sleeve her pretzel came in. She pulled her caramel-colored satchel bag onto the table and placed her phone in the side pocket.

"Are you guys nervous about the appointment tomorrow?"

"Not really nervous. More excited, you know? I can't believe I'm already at eighteen weeks."

"So, what's your final guess?" she asked. "Am I going to have a niece or a nephew?"

"It's totally a girl."

She laughed. "That's funny because I asked Brad the same question, and he said it's totally a boy."

I shook my head and smiled.

"Well, we'll know soon enough."

"Is my mom still insisting on going?"

"Yep."

"And you're okay with that?"

"It's fine. I have to pick my battles."

"You better pick one soon, or she'll walk all over you."

"I know." I looked down and played with the zipper on the camera bag.

"Sorry," Ellie said. "That sounded condescending. I shouldn't let my issues with my mom spread to you."

"No, you're right. Sometimes I feel like I'm in a relationship with Brad and your mom. I need to speak up more."

"But, so does Brad."

She looked at her phone again and gathered the last of her stuff. "I've got to get to my stats class."

I sat up in my chair and grabbed the camera bag. "I need to get going, too."

"Promise you'll call me tomorrow as soon as you find out?"

"You'll be my first call."

She leaned over, and we hugged.

"I love you," she said. "Good luck tomorrow."

"I love you, too."

CHAPTER 25

The waiting room of the Carlson Summit OB/GYN was crowded as usual. Five doctors shared the space and had a perpetual stream of patients. I walked in with Brad and Nicole and stared at the rows of blue padded chairs lining the walls and filling the open space in the center. A series of side tables and three round coffee tables were strategically placed to break up the monotony of the room.

Despite the potential for frantic chaos, the office carried an aura of calmness. The other patients sat quietly, scrolling through their phones or reading a magazine as they waited to be seen.

I stepped to the receptionists' desk where a middle-aged woman in burgundy scrubs held a phone to her ear, staring intently at her computer monitor. I studied her red hair, pulled up into a messy bun, and followed faint streaks of gray that wisped from her temples into the loose hold.

I looked over at another woman sitting behind the desk, farther down. She was younger, with dark brown hair, and wore the same burgundy scrubs. She smiled at me.

"How are you?" she asked.

"Good."

"We'll be with you in just a minute."

"Thank you."

The older woman hung up the phone and smiled at me.

"Sorry about that," she said.

"No problem."

"Who are you here to see?"

"Dr. Roberts."

She turned toward her monitor and moved the mouse with her hand. A few rapid clicks of her index finger and she turned back to me.

"Brooklyn Blair?"

"Yes, ma'am."

"Perfect." She glanced back at her screen. "And it looks like you're here for your eighteen-week checkup."

"Yes, ma'am."

"Ooh, this is the fun one. Are you going to find out whether it's a boy or girl, or wait to be surprised?"

"We're definitely going to find out. I don't think I can handle that kind of suspense."

"I'm the same way. Three kids and I couldn't wait for any of them. We even did that 3-D fetal imaging thing with my youngest daughter, just so we could find out early."

"That's a good idea," I said. "We should have done that."

She handed me a tablet with a narrow stylus pen.

"I just need a signature from you, right at the bottom."

I held the tablet, scrolled past pages of information I hoped wasn't important, and signed.

"Well, whatever it is, congratulations. Take a seat anywhere, and the nurse will call you back when they're ready."

"Thank you." I handed the tablet back to her.

Brad and Nicole found a few open chairs next to one of the round coffee tables. I put my phone in my back pocket and sat down next to Brad. I watched him thumb through a scattered pile of magazines on the table. He pulled one out and looked at the title, *Pregnancy Today*. He put it down and reached for another, ending up with *Maternity Life*. He quickly set it down as well and dug deeper into the stack, finding one called *The First Year*. He opened to a random spot; an article titled *10 Tips to Make Breastfeeding a Breeze*. He flipped the magazine out of his hand, back onto the pile, and shook his head.

I grabbed his hand and gave him a reassuring smile. I had never seen him so uncomfortable.

"Are you okay?"

He sighed. "Yeah."

"Nervous?"

"Not really."

"What's wrong then?"

He rubbed his hands together and looked up from the pile of magazines. He stared across the waiting room to the only other man in there. With a gentle nod to each other, they seemed to share silent acknowledgement of awkwardness.

"Do you feel out of place?"

"Just a little."

"Now you know how I felt at your fantasy football draft party the other night."

He chuckled and leaned back in his chair, shaking his head again. "That was not even close to being as awkward as this is."

"Really? It was me and like twenty dudes there. I was totally out of place."

"So, if I never make you go to another fantasy football draft, can I skip the rest of these appointments?"

Before I had a chance to answer, a female nurse stepped out from behind one of the closed doors. "Brooklyn Blair?" We stood up and followed her into a small exam room.

It was typical of most exam rooms, plain and sterile with only the essential equipment needed. Beige linoleum ran the length of the floor, curving up along the edges where it met the cream-colored walls. I sat down on a large exam table in the center of the room, leaving two empty chairs for Brad and Nicole.

There was a soft knock on the door, and it opened slightly. A woman poked her head in, looked at us, and smiled. "Brooklyn?"

"Yes."

She opened the door all the way and came in, closing it behind her. She brushed a strand of blonde hair from her forehead, tucking it behind her ear, and gently pressed a small amount of sanitizer into her hands from a dispenser by the door.

"My name is Jen, and I'll be performing your ultrasound today."

I nodded. "Hi."

She prepped a few items and turned on a large monitor for us to see and a smaller one for her. She handed me a white towel.

"All right, Brooklyn, are you guys ready for this?"

"You can call me Brooke," I said and caught a sideways glance from Nicole. "We're nervous, but ready."

"No need to be nervous, Brooke, this is the exciting appointment."

She looked over to Brad and smiled. "How about you, Dad? How are you holding up?"

"Oh, I'm not the father," Brad said. "Brooke got knocked up by one of her professors. I'm just here to support her as a friend."

"Brad!" Nicole and I shouted at the same time.

Jen stopped what she was doing and stared at Brad. Her body began to shake with laughter.

I glared at Brad. "Don't listen to him."

"That was funny," she said. "Thank you, I needed that today."

Brad smiled, clearly enjoying the successful impact.

"I apologize for my son," Nicole said. Jen waved her off.

"Okay, Brooke, I'm going to have you lift up your shirt, just above your stomach."

Of all the reasons I didn't want Nicole there, this was at the top. I felt awkward enough, I didn't need an audience. I hesitantly pulled my shirt up. Jen grabbed a plastic bottle and swung it gently through the air a couple of times, hitting it hard against the palm of her hand.

"This is going to be a little cold, so I apologize."

She squeezed a large amount of clear gel out of the bottle and onto my stomach, just above my navel.

"Are you doing okay?"

"Yes, thank you."

She held what looked like a wand in her hand and pressed it against the gel and my stomach. The monitors came alive with a grainy black-and-white image.

"Okay, so what I'm looking for here guys is to see how the baby's growing inside of you. I'll be capturing a number of measurements, but I'll point out different features along the way."

I expected to see a clear outline of the baby, but it was hard to distinguish what was what. Patches of gray faded to black. The images flashed across the screen quickly, then Jen would point, click, and measure. Adding a note to each still shot.

"So, right here you can just make out the top of the baby's head. And if we follow it down, you can see the spine."

"Wow," breathed Nicole.

I looked over at her.

How can she see it, and I can't?

Everything looked like a cheap night camera to me. I felt like I was missing out on the most important moment of my baby's life. I craned my neck to get a better view.

"Now, if I can get the baby to move just a bit this way, I can get a good look at the heart. Come on sweetie, move that arm and turn just a little more this way. There we go."

A flutter appeared on the screen, clearer than anything we had looked at so far. I could see it. My breath escaped me.

Jen pointed out the chambers of the heart, but I already saw it pumping and working its magic.

"Oh my gosh," I said. "There is a life inside of me."

"What did you think it was?" Brad asked.

I gave him a playful shove.

"No, I guess it just seems…real now. I don't know how to explain it."

I looked over at Brad and smiled. I turned back to the monitor and shook my head in awe.

"Do Mom and Dad want to know the sex of the baby?" Jen asked.

Brad and I looked at each other again and smiled. Our long-standing debate would finally be answered.

"Yes," I said.

"If you look right here." Jen clicked to capture another screenshot. "You'll see that you're having a baby girl."

I cupped my hands around my face and laughed. Nicole let out a soft, excited scream. We both looked at Brad, who pretended to be disappointed, then smiled.

"Congratulations, you guys." Jen wiped the gel off my stomach with the towel. "I'll print off a few pictures so you can show off your beautiful daughter."

"Thank you," Nicole said.

"Brooke, when you're ready, I'll let the nurse know, and she'll take you to one of Dr. Roberts' exam rooms."

I gave Brad a questioning look.

"Oh, I was told we wouldn't be seeing the doctor today."

"He likes to go over the ultrasound images with some of his patients."

"Do you have time?" I asked Brad.

"Of course."

I looked at Jen, who was now standing by the door, holding the handle.

I nodded.

"Perfect," she said. "I'll let the nurse know."

"Thank you, again."

"You bet. Congratulations, you guys."

The nurse led us to a different room. Brad and Nicole sat in the chairs, and I climbed onto the table. I stared at my hands, following their creases with my fingers. Our excited conversation celebrating the reveal of our baby girl faded, and the new exam room was quiet now except for the faint sound of voices as they passed on the other side of the door. Brad and Nicole silently scrolled through their phones.

My legs dangled off the side of the exam table, heavy from waiting longer than expected. I lifted them up and tucked them underneath me, the crinkle of the exam table paper momentarily pulling Brad and Nicole from their digital trance.

I looked around the room, a mirror image of the first one, minus the ultrasound equipment. There was a chart on the wall showing the monthly stages of a fetal growth from beginning to end. I held our printed ultrasound photos and smiled at the tiny life captured in the images.

"Should I go see what's taking so long?" Brad asked.

"I'm sure they're just busy. You can leave if you need to."

"No, I want to be here for you, babe. I just wasn't expecting it to take so long."

"I'm sorry."

He turned to Nicole. "Mom, you can go if you want."

"Yeah, Nicole, you don't need to wait."

She looked at me without expression but still managed to convey that she knew I didn't want her there, which I knew was exactly why she was going to stay.

"Kris is a family friend," she said. "I'd like to say hello."

She said this as if I didn't know Dr. Roberts was a friend of theirs. As if she hadn't chosen him for me, even though I said I was more comfortable with a female doctor. She had dismissed that opinion as being silly.

Finally, there was a tap on the door, and Dr. Roberts came in.

"Brooke, how are you? I'm so sorry to keep you waiting."

"It's no problem."

"Nicole, Brad," he gave Nicole a hug, "It's so nice to see you again. What an exciting time for your family."

He sat down on a short, circular chair and turned to face a computer monitor hanging on the wall.

"Thanks, Kris, for taking such good care of my granddaughter," Nicole said.

He looked up at her and smiled.

"That's what I heard. A baby girl. Congratulations, guys."

He pulled the ultrasound images up on the screen and studied them. He zoomed in on certain areas and jotted down a few notes into a yellow file folder. He turned to face us.

"So, guys, the reason I wanted to meet with you is that we noticed some possible abnormalities during the ultrasound."

My heart dropped.

"Abnormalities?" Brad and Nicole asked simultaneously.

"Is the baby okay?" I asked.

He held his hands out in front of him and lowered them, trying to calm us.

"Yes, the baby is healthy, and she's strong."

"But there's something wrong?" said Brad.

"Possibly."

"What is it?" I asked.

"The abnormalities seem consistent with Trisomy 21."

"What's that?" Nicole asked.

"Better known as Down syndrome," said Dr. Roberts.

For a moment, time stood still. The room fell silent. My breathing stopped; the air pulled from my lungs. My mind frantically tried to make sense of his words. I suddenly felt sick.

"No…" I looked at Brad. His eyes were wide, and his mouth hung open slightly. He looked at me, but his stare was distant and hollow.

"It can't be because we tested for that earlier," I said. "Remember, Brad? What appointment was that? Like week twelve or something. Didn't your nurse tell you that? I'm sure it's in the file."

I moved to get off the exam table. To grab the yellow folder and hand it to Dr. Roberts. He gently placed his hand on my arm. I looked at him, his eyes swimming with compassion.

"You're right, that was at your twelve-week appointment," he said. "And yes, we did check for early signs."

Brad's face was heavy with worry. "And you said everything looked good. I remember, because the nurse called and said that nothing showed up on the tests, and we didn't need any additional testing."

My hands were shaking. Nicole gently caressed my shoulder, and I looked at her.

"The nurse said everything was okay."

Nicole nodded. "I know, sweetie."

Dr. Roberts sat back in his chair and held his hands in front of his face as if he were praying. Then he brought them down.

"I'm going to be honest with you, it's extremely rare to see Down syndrome when the mother is so young. The earlier tests take in a number of factors, including a blood test, but also including your age. There was nothing there that we saw which would indicate your daughter had a higher chance of this."

"How can you be certain now?" asked Nicole.

"We're not, and that's important to remember. This isn't a diagnosis. What we're seeing, though, are potential soft markers on the heart and some of her measurements are small."

"But those aren't definitive?" Brad asked. "They could be wrong?"

"Yes, that's why I think we should do an amniocentesis."

I sat back on the exam table and looked at Brad. I shook my head. "No, I don't want to do that. I've heard those are dangerous."

"Brooke, let the doctor speak," Nicole said and held a hand out to pause me.

Dr. Roberts leaned forward and looked directly at me. Again, I saw compassion rather than condemnation.

"You're right, there are risks, but they are very minimal. However, they do exist, and it's smart to acknowledge them and weigh that."

"What if I were your daughter, would you recommend it?" I asked.

"Brooke." Nicole stopped me.

Dr. Roberts looked over at her and then back to me.

"That's a good question," he said. "I happen to have a daughter who's seventeen, and if she was in your shoes, I would not want her or my grandbaby to be hurt. But I would recommend the test, because I would want her to know for sure. There are choices and decisions that can be made but should be considered carefully and not made in the depths of extreme emotion. We can do the test today. We'll be very careful, and you'll be able to know for sure in three days."

I looked at Brad and then back at Dr. Roberts.

"Okay, let's do the test."

He gave me a nod and turned to Brad and Nicole.

"So, doc, there's a good chance that the ultrasound results are wrong?" Brad asked.

"Don't be mistaken, I don't want to give you false hope here. I wouldn't be having this conversation with you if I didn't think the potential was high, but it's not conclusive. I think it would be much better going forward if we know definitively what we're dealing with."

Nicole placed her arm around Brad's shoulder and gave him a squeeze. "Thank you, Kris."

Dr. Roberts stood, and the circular chair slowly rolled away from him. He held out his hand and shook Brad's.

"You're welcome. I wish we were having a different conversation."

Nicole stepped toward him, and they hugged. "Jack and I will have to get together with you and Becky soon," she said.

I slid off the exam table and stood close to Brad. He reached his fingers out to me, and we held hands.

"Brooke," Dr. Roberts said as he approached me. "My nurse will take you over to the testing lab. It will be quick and painless, and we'll have some better answers in just a few days."

We walked out of the exam room and through the waiting room. The excitement when I had checked in seemed so long ago. A reminder that life can change in an instant.

<h1 style="text-align:center">CHAPTER 26</h1>

I sat on the couch in the Foster's family room, my head tilted back, staring up at the vaulted ceiling. A spiderweb dangled loosely from one of the beams, gently swaying to the rhythm of the slow turning ceiling fan below it. I smiled at the slight imperfection in Nicole's flawless home.

She's going to go crazy if she ever sees that.

My smile was fleeting as the knot in my stomach clenched and reality settled back in. It had been three days since we left the hospital, and we still hadn't heard anything back. The wait was killing me.

I lifted my phone. I had missed a text from Ellie:

"Any word this morning?"

I felt for my friend. More than once over the past couple of days I had seen her crying.

"Not yet. Brad's gonna call if we don't hear something soon."

I turned my head toward the kitchen and saw Brad and Nicole talking at the table. They had been doing a lot of that. Quiet conversations that always seemed to stop once I entered the room.

Ellie and Brad's little sister, Morgan, sat down next to me. "Hi, Brooke."

"Hey, Mo," I said and wrapped my arms around her.

"Can I get you anything?" she asked.

"That's sweet, but I think I'm good right now."

"Okay."

She curled her legs underneath herself and rested her head on my shoulder. I could feel her slow, steady breaths.

"Are you scared?" she asked.

The question surprised me. I wondered how a fourteen-year-old could be so observant. I turned toward her, and she lifted her head from my shoulder. I looked into her dark brown eyes.

"A little," I said.

"I would be, too. I'm sorry."

"Thank you."

"I know my opinion probably doesn't matter much. But I think the baby's going to be okay. I just feel it."

I pressed my head against her forehead. "What do you mean your opinion doesn't matter much? You know I always love to hear what you think."

Brad came in from the kitchen. "Hey, Brooke, can I talk to you?"

I looked at him and then back at Morgan, raising my eyebrows. "Sure."

I stretched my back and followed Brad into the mudroom, just off the kitchen.

"Is everything okay?" I asked.

"My mom wants to go with us," he said.

"When we get the results?"

"Yeah."

I looked down and sighed. I walked farther into the mudroom, then turned around to look at him.

"No, Brad, I don't want her there. I don't want anyone there. If it's bad news…"

"It's not going to be bad news."

"Okay, but this one needs to be just you and me."

"It's really important to her, babe."

I stared at him, pleading with my eyes that he would tell her no, but I knew I had already lost.

"Does she know that we're not meeting with Dr. Roberts? That we're just meeting with some lab tech who's going to give us the news that might completely change our lives?"

He stepped toward me to give his patented comfort hug, which I had come to learn was his victory action. His "I know you can't say no to me" hug.

"She knows all that. She just wants to be there for us."

"Fine, it won't matter what I say anyway. If she wants to go, she's gonna go."

"Babe."

"Just invite her, because the last thing I need right now is a fight."

He kissed my forehead. "Thank you."

Nicole stepped into the mudroom. "The hospital just called. The results are in."

We waited outside the elevator in the lobby of the Carlson Valley Hospital. Its wide doors rolled open, revealing the large, empty compartment. We stepped inside, and Brad pushed the button for the sixth floor. The doors slowly rolled closed.

My breathing was short, and my heart pounded in my chest. I felt like I was going to faint and held tight to Brad's hand.

Nicole stood in the opposite corner, emotionless, staring straight ahead. She hadn't said a word since we left the house.

"If it's good news, I wish they would just tell us over the phone," I said.

"They can't," Brad said. "Because then if you were asked to come in, you'd already know the results are bad."

The elevator chimed, and a recorded voice played over a speaker. "Sixth floor." The doors rolled open, and we stepped into another large lobby. Two hallways spurred off, going in opposite directions. One had a sign above it that read, *Out-Patient Surgery.* The other had a sign with a matching design, but said, *X-Rays, Scans, Radiology.*

There was a small reception desk in front of us with an older man sitting behind it. Nicole walked over to him.

"Hi, we're here to get lab results."

"Well, you're in the right place," the man said and smiled at Nicole. "You just step down this hallway behind me, and it will be your first door on the left. You can't miss it."

"Thank you," Nicole said and waved us over.

We walked past the desk, and Brad gave the man a slight nod and a smile. "Thank you."

"You're very welcome."

By the time we caught up to Nicole, she was already talking to the lab receptionist.

"It's for Brooklyn Blair," I heard her say.

The woman behind the desk said, "Okay, give us just a minute, and we'll bring you back."

Nicole turned to us. "They said it would be just a minute."

"Thanks, Mom," Brad said, but she had already turned away and was walking toward a large, built-in aquarium.

When my name was called, we were led to an office, rather than an exam room. This felt more inviting than our usual appointments. There was a large desk with a black executive chair on one side and two matching seats on the opposite side. I sat down in one and was surprised when Nicole sat in the other. My emotions were raw, and I was getting upset. I needed the father of my child next to me. I needed him to hold my hand through this. I turned around to Brad and nodded for him to take Nicole's seat. He shook his head no.

"Brooklyn Blair?" a woman said as she walked in.

"Yes."

She took the seat behind the desk.

"I'm Cindy. I'm the lab specialist here. It looks like your baby was tested for Trisomy 21, is that correct?" she asked.

"Yes."

"Do you understand what this is?"

"Yes, Down syndrome."

"Okay, good."

She opened a folder and scanned a printed page with her finger.

"So, the lab results show that your baby did test positive for the disorder."

The room was silent. I was surprised at how quickly she had given us the news. I wondered how many times she had done this before to be able to deliver such misery so nonchalantly.

I put my hands together and cupped them around my nose and mouth. I could hear sniffles coming from Nicole. I turned around and looked at Brad. He was pacing and holding his hands behind his head. Our eyes met, then he looked away. I wanted to hold him…I wanted him to hold me. Anything that would take away the agony that was beginning to crush me. I leaned forward, ready to stand, but Nicole was already stepping toward him. She wrapped her arms around him, and he melted into his mother's embrace. After a minute, he pulled away, wiping his eyes.

"I'm sorry for the bad news," Cindy said. "It is never pleasant. I just have a few questions for you and things we need to go over."

"Go ahead," said Nicole.

"Do you understand what your baby has?"

"Yes," I said.

She handed me a pamphlet. It had a sketch drawing of a child with Down syndrome on the cover, with the title, *Understanding Down Syndrome.* Cindy began reading from a form she had, her tone mechanical.

"It's important to understand that children with Down syndrome often face a lifetime of medical complications. Some parents find their children never speak, never walk. They require care into adulthood. This can be incredibly hard—not just on you, but on your marriage, your finances, and your other children."

I stared at her in silence.

"Mrs. Blair, do you understand?"

"I understand, those are possibilities, yes," I said. "And he's not my husband."

"Excuse me?" Cindy looked surprised.

"Brad's not my husband, he's my fiancé."

"Thank you for clarifying," Cindy said. "I need to inform you that, if you so choose, there is no gestational limit on abortions in the state of Colorado. You must be over the age of eighteen to have an abortion without parental notification. There is no waiting period required. Abortions can be performed by any health-care practitioner as long as they follow the strict protection laws set forth by the state of Colorado."

She looked up from the form and stared at Nicole, then me.

"How old are you, Ms. Blair?"

"Nineteen, almost twenty."

"Just a tip, public funding is available. With you being so young, you could argue pretty easily that there is significant potential for this pregnancy to impact and even endanger your life." She turned toward Nicole. "I've seen a couple of young girls end up getting funding for their abortions that way."

My head was spinning. I couldn't believe that in three short days we had gone from finding out we were having a baby girl, to learning there were potential abnormalities, to confirming Down syndrome, to now discussing terminating the pregnancy. I wanted to vomit.

She slid a form over for me to sign. "This just says that you understand everything we've discussed here. If you have further questions, the hospital has a counselor on staff. She can provide more information and help you through whatever you decide to do. The number is on the back of the pamphlet."

I signed the form and pushed it back toward her. She placed it in the folder, closed it, and stood.

"Well, again, I'm sorry. It's never easy to deliver bad news. I wish you the best of luck. You can have the room for as long as you'd like."

"Thank you," Nicole said.

The three of us sat in the silence. I couldn't speak. I felt broken.

CHAPTER 27

We exited through the sliding glass doors of the hospital into a life that I knew would never be the same. I attempted to take a deep breath of the outside air, but it got caught in the tightness of my chest. It hurt to breathe. My lungs were in a battle of wanting to scream in agony and desperately seeking the oxygen, the lifeblood, needed to sustain them.

I stepped past the awning that sheltered the main entrance. The sun flooded over me like a thousand tiny fires. I squinted and could feel my pulse throbbing in my temples.

"You guys don't have to decide anything right now," I heard Nicole say from behind me. "Let's take a breath, let this sink in, and then we'll lay all the facts out."

I heard her talking, but her voice was distant, as if I were observing the conversation from afar and not a part of it. I couldn't think. I had nothing to say. I stood in silence.

"Brooke, why don't you go home and rest," Brad said. "I have to run and help Harrison move some stuff into his new place."

It took a moment for his words to register, then all at once the sounds and movements around me came back to life.

"Wait, what?" I asked.

"I need to go help Harrison move into his new place."

"No, Brad, not today. Not now."

"I know the timing sucks."

"Do you though?" I asked. "Because I don't understand you sometimes. You're so busy wanting to please everyone else, I think you forget about me."

A middle-aged couple looked over at us as they walked toward the hospital. Brad gave them a half smile and stepped closer to me, reaching for my arm.

"Babe, you need to calm down. It's okay."

"No, it's not. We just learned that our entire lives are going to change forever, or that our lives are over or whatever that woman was telling us in there. I don't want to be alone right now."

"I'll text Ellie and tell her to come over," Brad said.

I looked away and stared at a small pond that greeted visitors along the path to the entrance. A fountain towered from its center. The water dancing and gleaming in the sunlight as it tumbled back to the surface. I shook my head and gently bit my upper lip, turning back to him.

"I don't want Ellie there," I said. "I want you there."

"Babe, I committed, I can't…"

"Brooke, I think everyone just needs a bit of time to process this," Nicole said. "I can drop Brad at Harrison's. You head home, soak in the tub, and rest a bit."

I laughed and looked back at the fountain.

"What?" Brad asked.

"Nothing."

"No, Brooke, if you have something to say, then say it," Nicole said.

"It's just, I thought my family was bad at communicating, but your family, if something big comes up, you all want to run to your different corners and think about it for days."

"Well, you can criticize our family…"

"I'm not criticizing, I love your family."

She rolled her eyes. "Well, in our family we feel it's smart to think things through so we can have an intelligent conversation instead of a pointless argument. You might want to try that instead of always saying the first thing that comes to your mind."

I felt something pass between us, unspoken but undeniable, laced within her words. She hated me, and I was tired of trying to earn her love.

"Okay, do whatever you need to do," I said.

He stepped toward me. "I promise it'll go super-fast."

I backed up a step. I didn't want his hug now. He paused and gently leaned toward me, kissing my forehead.

"I love you, Brooke."

I looked away. "I love you, too."

I turned back and watched the two of them walk away. I was all alone.

I walked over and sat on a bench by the pond. Its green paint was faded, and a light dusting of pollen clung to its cast iron ends. All of this felt familiar. The silence, the grief, the wondering, just like the long days after my mom died. A heavy sadness cast itself over me, and my thoughts began to spiral. All the dreams I had dared to dream for my daughter had suddenly been taken away. Every milestone we had secretly smiled in anticipation of, had been robbed from her. Robbed from us. Her first steps, first birthday, first day of school, first friends, first school dance, first date, first love, first breakup, first car. Her high school graduation, college graduation, marriage, and babies. We had it all planned.

I looked up at a thread of white clouds that moved undetected above. "Why?" I whispered. "Why do you keep doing this to me? This was my time to be happy. Time for my dreams to come true. Why can't I be happy? Is it so hard? Can you not give me just one thing in my life that is good? One thing that isn't a struggle?

Why can't I have the life that everyone else has? And now you've brought my daughter into this? A poor, sweet, defenseless little girl. You're going to make her suffer, too? You're going to ruin her life, too? Why would you do that? What about her dreams? What about the life she deserves? I'm not going to let you do that to her. I'm not going to let her suffer like I've suffered. You can hate me all you want, but I'm not going to let you hate her."

One, two, three, four, five. Breathe.

"Excuse me."

I lowered my head to a silhouette of a person standing in front me, the figure glowing against the sun. I held a hand over my eyes and could see it was a woman. She moved and sat down next to me. My eyes adjusted from the brightness. She was smiling at me. She was young, maybe in her late twenties or early thirties, with shoulder-length brown hair pulled back into a ponytail. She wore a loose fitting, gray cardigan sweater, which seemed odd given the early September heat.

"I'm sorry, I don't mean to bother you," she said. "It's just, I couldn't help noticing you sitting here all alone. Is everything okay?"

I sat up straight and nodded my head. I coughed gently into my hand and cleared my throat.

"Yeah, um, just a hard day I guess."

"Are you a patient here or visiting someone?"

"I'm a patient…well, I guess actually my daughter is the patient."

"Oh, how old is she?"

I placed a hand on my stomach and massaged the area. "It's actually my baby."

"Your first?"

"Yes."

"I'm Paige by the way."

"Brooke."

"It's nice to meet you, Brooke. Is there anything I can do for you?"

I gave her a smile. "No, I'm good, but thank you."

"Are you sure? I don't mean to be nosy, but usually when people around here look as sad as you do, it means they're dealing with something terrible. I just wanted to make sure you were okay."

My mind pleaded with me to dismiss her question, to not burden her, to tell her everything was okay, but I wanted to share it. I needed to tell someone. I looked at her, met her gaze, and then looked down.

"We just learned that our baby is going to be born with Down syndrome."

One, two, three, four, five. Breathe.

Paige was silent. I looked up to find her staring at me. The heat of embarrassment rose through me, and I looked away.

Why did I share this with a complete stranger?

She placed a hand on mine. "I'm so sorry to hear that. It must be really difficult to get that kind of news."

I nodded my head but couldn't talk.

"Are you here with someone?"

"He had to leave."

She nodded her head and took a quick glance at my ring finger. "Your husband?"

"Fiancé."

"I bet it was hard for him to hear as well, huh?"

I hadn't thought about what Brad must be going through. My heart hurt for him as well. I nodded my head again.

"It's sad when you feel your dreams are being stolen from you."

I looked at her again. Her eyes were filled with compassion and a sense of understanding.

"How did you know that?"

"I've been there; still there I guess."

"You have a child with Down syndrome?"

"No, my little guy has his own set of struggles. He was born thirty-three days ago at twenty-six weeks."

"Twenty-six weeks. I didn't even know that was possible."

"Honestly, I didn't either. He was just over one and a half pounds when he came. I thought for sure we had lost him. No way he could survive. In fact, they told us he wasn't going to make it, but he's still fighting. Getting stronger every day."

I shook my head slowly and stared at her clear eyes and fresh smile. She looked normal, unlike me. My eyes were puffy and red, the weight of the last few days taking its toll. How could someone survive such heartbreak?

"So, your son's here?"

"Yep, he's up in the NICU. Basically, intensive care for newborns."

"Why don't you look sad?" I asked.

She smiled briefly and looked down.

"I'm sorry, I shouldn't have asked that."

"It's okay, it just means I'm doing a good job of lying to other people or lying to myself. I'm not sure which one is worse."

She turned toward me; her eyes glazed with tears.

"How sad do you feel right now?" she asked.

"Devastated."

"Don't let my outward appearance fool you. There's a lot of sadness behind the mask I put on. I've sat where you're sitting, and I've cried the tears you're crying. Too many to count. It's really, really hard sometimes."

"How do you do it? My heart hurts so much right now, I don't know how I can possibly go on."

"I don't know. I'm only a month into this journey, and I fear every day that I won't know what to do tomorrow, but I don't have a choice. I try and stay in the moment and not worry about the what ifs."

A man walked past us carrying a toddler in his arms. We watched as they walked to the edge of the pond. He gently dropped the girl down onto her two unsteady feet and dipped her tiny hands in the cold water.

Paige added, "I also let the daily miracles carry me."

"Daily miracles?"

"That's what I call them. Right when I start losing hope or when the worry consumes me, it seems like something happens to carry me through. Luke, that's my son, will show some small measure of improvement, or someone will do something nice for me and my family, or I'll hear how Luke has touched someone's life. Small things like that always seem to happen just when I need them, and it gives me that little bit of hope to keep moving forward."

My head turned at what she said. I looked at her, my brow furrowed, my mind searching for understanding.

"How is he able to touch someone's life?"

Her face lit up.

"Sounds crazy, doesn't it? How can a little baby who spends all his days clinging to his own life, change someone else's?"

"It doesn't sound crazy to me."

"Since Luke was born, my husband Ben and I have spent countless hours here. Long days and even longer nights. Bless them, but we were getting asked by family and friends for updates all the time, and it was getting exhausting. About three weeks ago, I was at my breaking point. I was on the night shift here with Luke and decided that I would just send out a mass Facebook post, to update everyone. I began writing it, and the words just came out. I was mad, and I talked about how unfair all of this was and how hard this was on my family."

The sadness hidden behind the mask.

"Luke was really struggling at that time. He had stopped gaining weight, and we're talking minuscule amounts, but he needed to progress. I wasn't in a great spot emotionally, but just as I was writing that, one of the night nurses came in and told me that Luke was gaining. I wrote that in, after all my ranting, as the final paragraph. I left it with, 'Have faith and don't ever give up hope.'"

"That's amazing."

"I almost forgot I posted it and regretted doing it in the morning, but do you know what happened?"

"What?"

"My words connected with people. Not just with my family and friends. I was getting comments from people I didn't even know, thanking me for sharing."

I watched the man playing with the little girl by the pond. She had taken off her pink sandals and was now dipping her toes into the water, squealing with excitement each time they touched the surface.

"Why do you think it connected with people?"

"I'm not sure. I've thought about that a lot, and I think everyone has their struggles, but we're too scared to be vulnerable and share them. We want to bury the pain and wish it away. So now, I just write what we're experiencing. The highs and the lows. I've found it to be therapeutic as well. And I continue to hear from people how Luke has changed their lives, motivated them, and helped them see things differently. Imagine that, a tiny baby changing world. This thought carries me through a lot of my days."

I watched her for a few seconds. "He sounds like a special boy."

"Would you like to meet him?"

"Oh…no. I've taken too much of your time."

Now she stared at me again. "Brooke, I would really like you to meet him if you have the time. Let him change your day."

I followed Paige back into the hospital, and we took the elevator to the fourth floor. As we exited, there was a small waiting area next to a secured door. The room was empty. A small television hanging in the corner quietly showed an afternoon talk show. Above the secured door, a sign read *Carlson Valley Newborn Intensive Care Unit.* Paige pressed a button, and a buzzer rang. She looked up at a camera hidden above the door. A voice came over the intercom. "Come on in, Paige."

We entered an open room with a long reception desk stretching away from the door. The light blue laminate on the desk was faded in spots and peeling away at one of the edges. I looked straight ahead and saw a row of small rooms, each with their door slightly open. The lights were dim. I could hear the faint beeps and noises of the medical equipment.

A nurse at the reception desk said, "Welcome back."

"Thanks, Amber," Paige said. "This is my sister, Brooke."

I looked at her surprised and saw her wink at the nurse.

"She's here to visit Luke, if that's all right?"

The nurse smiled. "Of course, but let's keep it short before people start asking questions."

"They only let immediate family in here," Paige whispered to me as she led me to Luke's room. "The other nurses aren't so keen on the idea, but I knew Amber would let you in."

Luke's room looked like all hospital rooms, except his bed was a miniature version of a normal bed. It left a void in the room, casting an immediate reality to the fight taking place between his tiny life and the death that threatened to take him. The bed was covered with a large, clear plastic protection. There were monitors to the side, displaying numbers I didn't understand.

I stood next to him and looked in. He was smaller than I had imagined, as if he would break if I touched him. I watched him sleep, his lean body sprawled out on the miniature bed; his chest gingerly rising and falling with each breath. I looked closer to see his hands and feet. He had ten fingers and ten toes.

"It's amazing how much he's grown," said Paige.

"Really? He's so small."

"Oh, yeah, if you had only seen him when he was born. Like I said, I thought there was no way he would survive."

"But he is alive. This tiny, little life."

I looked over at her. "Thank you for bringing me here and sharing him with me."

"Brooke, I realize we don't know each other, and I'm sure you've got plenty of people who are supporting you, but I don't want you to lose hope. I haven't walked a day in your shoes. Your challenges are different from mine, but in many ways, we're all the same. I have two older children at home, and I can tell you, children are hard, no matter how perfect they may seem. And as parents we have to make hard choices, even when those choices aren't life and death. My point is, it's difficult either way. This is just a different kind of hard."

I looked back at Luke. The fear and uncertainty returned, rising through my chest and seizing my mind.

"I'm not sure I'm the one to do it."

"If you don't, who will?" she asked. "There are no coincidences. Just realize that the perfect life you had planned for your baby was always going to be filled with challenges. Don't let anyone else define what is normal. Regardless of perceived flaws or limitations, every life is precious."

A nurse walked in, grabbing a handful of sanitizer after closing the door. She rubbed her hands together and walked over to the monitors.

"Hi, Paige," she said.

"Hi, Grace."

"How's our little guy doing this afternoon?"

"Doing better. They were a little worried about his breathing earlier, but he seems to have relaxed."

"Any gains?"

"Not yet."

The nurse put on a pair of rubber gloves and stepped to the edge of Luke's bed. I stepped back, not wanting to interfere.

"All right, little man, let's see how you're doing."

Paige put on her own pair of gloves and walked to the opposite side of the bed. She gently reached her hand in and caressed Luke's arm with the edge of her finger.

The nurse stepped away and began looking through the drawers of a medical cabinet. I watched as Paige rested her head against the plastic shell over Luke's bed. She stared at him with a mix of love and concern.

I quietly pulled my camera from my bag and focused on her and Luke. I smiled, wondering if my mom had looked at me with the same kind of love. I took a picture. Paige looked up and smiled at me.

"Thank you," I whispered.

CHAPTER 28

The shadows of night loomed over the sidewalk, broken only by the faint orange glow of scattered streetlamps. A far-off thunderstorm gently echoed across the evening sky. I quickly moved toward the porch light shining in the distance and could see the windows of our townhouse were dark. "Brad, please tell me your home," I whispered out loud.

I reached the door and pressed hard against the handle. It was locked.

Where are you?

I fumbled with my key, unlocked the door, and stepped inside.

Although it had only been a few days, it felt like a lifetime since I had been here. Since *we* had been here. We had rushed out the door, not wanting to be late to the ultrasound appointment. The excitement of that moment, now lost in a sea of uncertainty.

I turned the lights on, set my keys and phone on the edge of the couch, and walked into the kitchen. I opened the refrigerator door. A cool blue light illuminated scattered items on mostly empty shelves. We needed to go shopping. I grabbed a yogurt, kicked off my shoes, and curled up on the couch. I rubbed my thumb firmly against the soles of my aching feet. The exhaustion of the day suddenly washed over me. I laid my head against the armrest and closed my eyes.

I heard a chime in the distance. My brain fought to recognize the sound, but sleep pulled me in the other direction.

The chime rang again, and my eyes shot open. The yogurt cup rolled away from me, dropped off the edge of the couch, and splattered on the floor. I was still clutching the spoon tightly in my hand.

Someone was at the door. I lifted myself off the couch, stumbled, and quickly steadied myself against the armrest, letting the last haze of sleep dissipate. I unlocked the door and turned the handle.

Ellie stepped in, said nothing, wrapped herself around me, and held me tightly. For a moment I wondered what was wrong, then it all came flooding back. The pain and sadness of the day.

"I'm so sorry," she said.

"I know."

"Are you okay?"

I took in a deep breath, my shoulders pulling tight against her grasp, then released it. "I'm surviving."

She stepped away and wiped her eyes with her sleeve.

"Where have you been? Everyone's worried about you."

"Really? I was at the hospital and then came here."

"Didn't you get my texts?"

"No," I said and pulled my phone off the couch. The screen lit up with a picture of me and Brad at a Rockies game from earlier that summer. I unlocked the phone and remembered I had put it on airplane mode when I had gone into the NICU with Paige.

"Airplane mode." I held the phone up to Ellie. "I completely forgot I did that."

"Brad's been looking for you."

My phone dinged as a series of missed text messages rolled in from Ellie and Brad, along with an email from the Carlson Medical Lab.

"Where is he? We were supposed to meet back here."

"He's at our parents' house."

"Why?"

"I don't know, but he doesn't have a car and needs us to go pick him up."

The Foster's house was the last place I wanted to be. After the last few days, I couldn't stomach any more reassuring words mixed with hugs and sympathetic smiles, but I needed Brad home. We needed to be together.

"I just spilled my yogurt. Let me clean that up and we can go."

"I'll help you."

Ellie pulled into her usual spot in the driveway. I opened my door, but I hesitated for a moment in the passenger seat. I didn't want to go inside. I just needed to get Brad and go, so we could put this day behind us.

"You coming?" Ellie was standing in front of the car. I hadn't even realized she was out.

"Yeah." I stepped out of the car.

The wind blew, coming in waves. The powerful gusts pushing hard against a cluster of aspen trees soaring high above us, their leaves rattling in the heavy sky.

Ellie stepped back toward the car and opened the driver's side door. "Forgot my phone." Another blast of wind blew, showering us in a mist of rain. We both screamed and quickly ran to the front door, laughing as we went.

Was it okay to laugh?

Ellie opened the door, and Brad was standing in the foyer. The smile on my face disappeared as I saw the concern on his face, reality settling back in. I stepped toward him, and he wrapped an arm around me. I snuggled against the warmth of his body.

"You ready to go?"

"Hold on, I just want to talk."

"Babe, we can talk in the car and talk all night if you want to, but let's go home first."

He grabbed my hand and led me into a sitting room just off the front entryway. We sat down on one of the couches as Ellie walked away into the kitchen.

"Can't we please just go home?" I quietly pleaded.

"Brooke, I've been doing a lot of thinking."

"I guess not."

He looked down and tapped his fingers together. He took in a quick breath, as if he were going to say something, then stopped himself.

"What's going on, Brad? You're scaring me."

He looked up at me with clouded eyes.

"Sorry, it's just that this whole thing has really hit me hard. I've tried to be strong for you, but my mind has been racing ever since the ultrasound. And then today—today was just horrible, and I kinda wasn't there for you. I'm sorry about that. Everything hit me at once, ya know?"

"If this didn't rock you to your core, I would be worried about you."

"Right," he responded. "It's crazy, isn't it? I've never had to face something this hard."

"No, I get it. I met this amazing woman today, and she was talking about children being hard, but—"

"Hold on, hold on," he stopped me. "If I don't get this out now, I'll never say it right."

The knot in my stomach tightened as my mind raced with possibilities. He opened his mouth to speak but was interrupted as a bolt of lightning lit up the night sky followed by a crash of thunder. I jumped and looked out the picture window.

"Brooke."

I turned back to him. He stared at me intently. Something was wrong. I could see it in his eyes. Something was missing. His effortless smile was gone. The light that surrounded him, somehow extinguished. My heart raced as a slow burning began to build around my eyes.

"Sorry. Go ahead."

"Like I was saying, I've never faced something this hard before. And I've been trying to figure out what I'm supposed to do, because I have no idea. I want to be there for you and do what's best for the baby."

"Okay."

"I think we have three options. We can have the baby and raise it, knowing that it will—"

"She. Not it, anymore, *it* is *she*."

"Right, she. We can have her and raise her knowing that she will never enjoy a full quality of life."

My heart held onto the word *we*. He said we, as in all of us. Still together. He wasn't leaving me.

"Option two," he continued. "We can have her and give her up for adoption."

"Adoption? We already—"

He didn't let me finish.

"Or three, and what I think is our best option and the best for the baby, is we can end the pregnancy and start over."

I heard the words, but my mind refused to process them. All at once the man sitting next to me, the love of my life, became a stranger. I realized it wasn't his light that had been extinguished, it was his love for me and our baby.

"End the pregnancy and start over? What are you talking about?"

"Brooke, the reality is, I'm young and you're even younger. We've been trying to do the right thing here, we've been trying to do that all along, but we both know we're not ready to be parents yet. We were careless, and we've had to make some hard decisions, but we've stepped up and tried to deal with the consequences."

"Carelessness and consequences? Did you rehearse this? Because you might want to practice it again and restart."

"Don't get offended, you're missing what I'm saying."

"No, I'm not. But, Brad, I specifically told you when we were in Denver that I didn't want you to go down this path with me simply because you felt it was your obligation."

"And I told you I loved you, and I meant it."

Loved.

Past tense. There it was. Another heart shattered by the simple addition of the letter *D* to the most coveted word in the English language.

He hurried on. "But let's not kid ourselves. We wouldn't be engaged and talking about babies right now if it hadn't been forced upon us. That's the consequence I'm talking about. I didn't say it was bad, I'm just saying we've tried to do all the right things. We need to do the right thing here."

"What is the right thing?"

"You know and I know that we're not in a position to be raising a child with disabilities. We can barely take care of ourselves."

"I think it will be really hard." I choked on my words. A tidal wave of sadness was building behind them, as I tried to stave off a reality that suddenly seemed inevitable.

"But I have no doubt we can do it together."

"Brooke, I know you've fought through a lot in your life, and I think you're trying to talk yourself into grinding through this, but this is a lifetime sentence. This is all day, every day. You told me the only way you got through your childhood was by believing there was an end in sight. You always knew you were going to leave. That was your carrot. There's no carrot here. There's no end."

"That's what you do for your kids. You take it for granted because you have good parents. I'm going to fight for her because no one ever fought for me. What else can we do?"

"That's just it, and you have to get past the stigma, so just listen before reacting."

"What are you talking about?"

"I was listening to the lady at the lab today, and then randomly, I was talking to Harrison's friend Lisa this afternoon. She was telling me that people have this horrible perception of abortion, but it's not the 1900s anymore. Like people don't have to go down a back alley and pay some shady dude. The technique has improved a ton, it's safe, and it's surprisingly common."

I blinked hard and shook my head, staring at him in disbelief. My breath came in small bursts, like the wind had been knocked out of me.

"Brad, do you know what you're saying? I have a life inside of me. We both saw her. Remember when her foot moved and you thought that was freaking awesome?"

"Oh, come on, Brooke," Nicole interrupted. "I know you're a little girl, but stop being so naive."

She had been listening, the entire time. Of course, she would need to have her say. I noticed for the first time that I couldn't hear the television in the other room.

"Nicole, this doesn't involve you."

She stepped into the room; her eyes fixated on me. Ellie followed behind her, wide eyed.

"How dare you walk into my house and tell me it doesn't involve me. Who do you think you are?"

"Guys, stop," Ellie said.

"You mooch off my family for the past year and then have the gall to tell me to butt out."

"I never took anything that wasn't given to me."

"But you never refused it either. Face it, Brooke, everything you have, came from us. The townhouse you live in, that's ours. The car you're driving, that's Brad's. Your phone, it's on our plan. When was the last time you bought a meal for yourself? Everything you think is yours, came from us. So, don't tell me I don't have a say."

Of all the things people had said to me in my life, nothing cut as deep as these words. She was right. I hadn't realized it, but this new world I had created for myself, my dream world, was nothing but a mirage. None of it was mine, and I suddenly realized how quickly it could all be taken away.

Nicole didn't stop talking. "There's nothing left to discuss. We've decided the best thing to do is have the pregnancy terminated."

"What?" Ellie asked.

"Ellie, stay out of it," Nicole shot back.

"We decided? That's funny because no one asked me. So, it's more like you decided. You can't force me to do that."

Nicole stepped toward the window and stared outside. Large drops of rain fell heavy against the glass, gliding slowly down the pane. She let out a deep sigh.

"Please understand, Brooke, I'm not trying to be insensitive. I know these are hard choices, but you need to rely on my life experience here. You're a child yourself. You don't need to repeat the mistakes of your parents."

My eyes shot to her and then to Brad.

Had he told her about my family?

He didn't react.

"You know nothing about my parents."

She turned around to face me, a wry smile on her face.

"Really? So, you didn't grow up in poverty, living off the

government? Your mom didn't kill herself, and your dad's not a raging alcoholic? So much so, that you never talk to him anymore? I know your family better than you think."

"Mom, please stop!" Ellie said again.

"Honestly though, I don't need to know any of that," Nicole continued. "I could tell what you were the second I saw you. You're a parent's worst nightmare."

Brad took a step forward. "Mom."

"You come in dressed like the clearance rack at Target, you see all our wealth, you latch onto our son, and remarkably a few months later you're pregnant."

Ellie marched toward me and grabbed my arm. "Come on, Brooke, let's go."

I pushed her hand away.

"Are you kidding me right now?" I demanded.

"I'm not kidding at all. I haven't spent all these years building a life for my son only to have you steal his dreams. The worst thing you could do to him and this family would be to have this baby."

"Wow, that's a great speech grandma. You should put that on her birthday card."

Her lips pursed and she glared at me. I was playing with fire and I knew it.

Ellie whirled on her brother. "Brad, are you going to do something?"

"Ellie." Jack appeared in the room.

She walked over to him. "Dad, do something."

"Your mom's right, this is for the best."

Her mouth dropped as she stared at her father. She slowly turned to Brad, held out her hands, and shrugged.

"What is wrong with you guys? Are you just going to sit there and let this happen?"

Nicole and I stared at each other, absorbed in our mutual hate.

"All I ever wanted was for you to like me. I looked at you as this amazing mother who had raised amazing kids, but you only love them when they reach your impossible standards."

She twisted her mouth—almost a smile and shook her head.

"That's why you were excited about this baby and now you're not. Brad as a father and you as a grandmother, imagine how impressed people would be? But because you think she's flawed, you want nothing to do with her. You think it'll be embarrassing. You should be ashamed, because you saw the same life on the screen that I did."

She sighed again. "Sweetie, you know nothing about me. I'm not going to get into a battle of when life begins. You can't prove it any more than I can disprove it. That's not what we're talking about here."

"That's exactly what we're talking about here. Life. I saw the heartbeat. Brad, you saw it, too."

He looked at me but didn't say anything. He turned his eyes to Nicole and then back to me.

"Brooke, the heartbeat doesn't mean anything," he said. "It's a reflex, just like the leg moving. It's doing what the brain tells it to do."

I stood and wrapped my hands around the back of my head, pulling my elbows forward. I couldn't believe what I was hearing. I wanted to scream. I looked at Ellie. A single tear hung to the corner of her lashes, then it slowly dropped, rolling down her cheek.

"I saw a baby today who was born at twenty-six weeks," I said and turned to Brad. "Do you believe that? Twenty-six weeks, and he's still alive and getting stronger every day. That's only seven weeks older than our baby girl is now. How can you say our daughter's not alive?"

He looked at me and shrugged his shoulders. "It's not that simple, Brooke."

"*Yes, it is!*"

He stood there, indifferent. Nothing I said was making an impact. This was the end of us.

"But I know I'm not going to change your mind. I understand now."

"Understand what?"

"That you already said goodbye to her. That's how you could leave the hospital and go help Harrison as if life were moving on as normal."

"You're seriously going to criticize me for how you think I should act? You have no idea how hard this has been for me."

"I'm not criticizing. My heart broke for you just like it did for me, but I realize now, that's the moment you gave up on her."

Nicole stepped toward Brad and placed a hand on his shoulder. Her eyes rolled to me.

"Well, how much are you willing to sacrifice to save this so-called life?" she asked. "Because if you keep this baby, don't expect anything from us. You might think that Brad's going to be forced to help you financially. He won't. We'll bury you in legal fees. This all ends. You're not getting one more dime from us. You can walk back to the townhome I own, because you're not taking the car I own, and you can pack your stuff, because you'll need to be out of there by morning."

"Stop it, Mom!" Ellie was crying now.

I looked around the room. From Jack, to Nicole, to Brad.

How was this happening?

My head pounded, and I wanted to cry, but not here. Not in front of them. "It doesn't matter. I don't want anything more from you."

"You always think you have all the answers, don't you?" Nicole snapped.

"You're making a mistake, Brooke," Brad said quietly.

Our eyes met. I had spent so many hours looking into those engaging eyes. This man who I never expected to fall in love with. The boy who said he would never leave my side.

"Did you ever really love me?"

"Brooke, don't."

"I think you did once or at least you were good at faking it. So, when did you stop? Did you feel stuck, and this became your loophole? You're willing to kill your daughter to get out of it?"

Nicole stepped in front of me. I thought for a moment she might slap me.

"Get out of my house."

Brad stared at me. "Brooke, that's so unfair."

"You said you loved me. Is this really how you want to say goodbye? You're going to sit here and do nothing."

Nicole began to push me backward toward the door. I swiped at her hand, and she grabbed my wrist. Jack jumped between us, and Ellie let out a scream.

"I can't believe you would do this to me."

"You did it to yourself, Brooke," said Brad. "I was trying to make it easier. I was trying to do the right thing."

Jack took my arm and walked me out the door.

Ellie grabbed her keys. "I'm going with her."

Nicole turned on her daughter. "Ellie, you stay right where you are."

Ellie glared at her mother in disbelief.

"You're going to kick her out and make her walk home in the rain? Have you lost your mind? I'm done with you…with all of you."

She stepped toward the front door, staring at her dad as she walked past.

I followed her out. I didn't look back at Brad, or any of them.

We stood on the porch together as the door slowly closed behind us.

Thunderclouds rolled overhead, and the skies released another unrelenting round of rain. We stood in silence, the storm washing over us, puddles forming around our feet.

"Let's go home, Brooke."

CHAPTER 29

The world was empty around us. Heavy fog and rain-soaked pavement blended with the darkness of night to create a lonesome landscape. The hum of the windshield wipers played in the background, accompanied by the methodical fall of rain as it danced on the windshield.

I hadn't spoken a word on the drive, neither had Ellie. There had been enough talking for one day, enough worlds had been shattered.

She pulled into the parking lot of my townhome, *Nicole's townhome,* her headlights cutting through the gloom. The lights from the community cast a faint orange glow, lost in the misty air. We sat in our silence.

"I'm going to talk to Brad," she finally said. "This doesn't make sense. He's not thinking straight."

I looked over at her. In the cool, blue glow of the dash lights, I could see the sadness in her eyes. The redness of unexpected and unwanted tears. The happy girl I had met a year earlier was gone, another victim of life's drama.

I touched her arm. "Do you know you're the best friend I've ever had?"

She sniffed and a smile appeared on her face. "You're my best friend, too."

I put both of my hands in my lap and laced my fingers. "Earlier tonight I wanted nothing more than to be with Brad. But things have changed. Maybe I was blind to it before, but I saw it clearly in his eyes tonight. He doesn't love me."

"Brooke, I don't think that's true. I know my brother."

"And nobody knows your brother better than you, which is why you know I'm right."

She stared at me and shook her head, then turned to look out her window. I leaned over and rested my head on her shoulder.

"I'm so sorry," she whispered.

"It's not your fault."

For the first time that night, a single tear rolled down my cheek. It fell on her shoulder, and she turned to me, wrapping me in her arms.

"I'm so, so sorry, Brooke."

I wiped my eyes but stayed in her embrace. I think she needed the comfort as much as I did.

"I'll talk to my parents. They can't kick you out now that the semester has started. They wouldn't do that."

"I can't do it."

"Do what?"

"Your mom has spent the last few months controlling my life. She acts as if I owe her for getting pregnant. I can't do it anymore. I won't live in her debt."

"Then come live with me."

"She won't let that happen."

"She doesn't need to know."

"She'll know. She'll make sure of it."

Ellie released her hug and turned toward me. I leaned back into the passenger seat and looked at her.

"Then, where are you going to go?"

"I don't know yet."

"Let me help you."

"I will, for sure. I just need a minute to figure things out."

"Do you want me to stay with you tonight?"

"No. I'm okay. I just need to get some sleep, and then I can think better."

"Then I'll pick you up for breakfast tomorrow."

"Perfect."

"Should we plan on eight?"

"No way. Your mom can kick me out of here, but she better let me sleep in first. Let's say ten."

"Okay." Ellie laughed.

I reached for the door handle, then paused and turned back to her. I wanted to say goodbye, but if I did, she'd never let me go. So, I would do it quietly, for both of us. I hoped she'd understand. I had already pulled her into enough of my chaos. She deserved peace and to be happy.

"I'm sorry, El."

She turned to me, looking confused.

"For what?"

"For all the problems I've caused your family."

"Brooke, this isn't your fault. And our problems go back a lot farther than you. We just never talk about them."

"Thank you for everything you've done for me. I love you."

"I love you, too."

I opened the door and stepped out, the cool air brushing against my skin. I shut it gently behind me. She stayed there, watching, and I gave her a small wave. I would miss her, my one true friend. The girl who had changed everything.

It was three minutes after one in the morning. I held my phone in my hands and hovered my thumb over the call button. The screen timed out and went black. I pressed it again and entered my passcode. This same routine had repeated itself over and over for the past hour.

Just make the call, Brooke.

I hesitantly pressed call, my heart racing. On the fourth ring, he answered.

"Hello." His voice was groggy but familiar.

I couldn't speak. My voice choked, and then I heard the line go dead.

No, no, no. Please don't hang up.

I pressed his phone number again to redial. This time it only took two rings.

"Who is this?" His voice now angry.

"Dad."

"Brooklyn?" he said, his voice softened.

"Dad, I'm in trouble. I need help."

CHAPTER 30

"Brooklyn."

My eyes opened. I was on the dirt road again. The tall grass swayed next to me in a gentle breeze.

"Brooklyn."

"Mom, are you here?" I asked.

"I'm right here, sweetie. I'm always right here."

Her silhouette appeared at the end of the road. I wanted to run to her, but I didn't think my heart could take another rise of hope only to lose her again.

"Come and see, sweetie. It's beautiful."

I began walking toward her, but my steps were heavy. It felt like I was stuck in mud. I looked down. The road was dry. I tried to lift a leg, but my muscles resisted. I looked at my mom and reached out to her.

"Mom, please help me."

I fought one small step forward and then another. A wave of sadness was pulling at me, all the energy seeming to drain from my body. I kept pushing, each step a little farther than the one before, the distance between us narrowing.

"Mom, I'm coming. Wait for me. Don't leave me again."

"I'm here, sweetheart, come and see."

My heart grew hopeful.

Please let her hold me—just for a minute.

Then, all at once, my legs gave out. I stumbled forward, my hands in front of me bracing the fall. I skidded to a stop. My palms burned. I turned them over and brushed away a spray of pebbles pressed into my skin. I sat on my knees and let the sadness overtake me. The tears from a life that had never been fair. The tears of a shattered heart.

I heard the gentle sound of footsteps beside me. I stared at my mother's bare feet, then looked up at her flowing, blonde hair. Her blue eyes sparkled. She was just as I remembered her.

"Mom."

She crouched over me and wrapped her arms around me. My heart leapt at a moment I had hoped for but never thought possible. I felt the warmth of complete love radiate through my body. The sadness and fear I carried with me, my constant companions, disappeared.

"It will all be all right," she whispered into my ear and rested her cheek against mine.

CHAPTER 31

I awoke to the hum of an approaching vehicle. Its headlights splashed through the narrow slits between the blinds, rolling across the wall as it moved along. I leapt off the couch, nearly tripping over my suitcase, and carefully peered out the window. It was still dark outside; there was no way my father could have made it so quickly. It had to be Nicole. She had probably been seething over our argument and was ready for round two. I steadied for another confrontation. One more knockout punch before she chased me away.

I couldn't see the car from the window, but I could make out the faint glow of taillights in the distance. I craned my neck to get a better look, then heard footsteps approaching. I quickly backed away and braced for a knock at the door.

I looked at my suitcase and the worn bankers box next to it. The edges of the box were bowed in and one flap of its lid was torn. I had little to remind me of Carlson except a heart full of memories. I guess there wasn't much to remind Carlson of me either. I would simply be another forgotten face in life's journey.

There was a small tap at the door. I took a deep breath and stepped toward it, unlocking it and slowly turning the handle.

"Dad?"

I was surprised to see him. He looked different, taller somehow. He was wearing a black baseball cap, its shadow covering his eyes, and a heavy, brown jacket. He was clean shaven, his perpetual five o'clock shadow gone, highlighting the narrowness of his face. He lifted his head and stared at me from his piercing brown eyes. They were clear, as if he had spent the last year catching up on a decade of lost sleep.

I stared at him, the past racing between us. The hate inside me, simmering again.

This was a mistake. Why did I call him?

His eyes lingered for a moment on my stomach. He didn't say anything; he simply leaned past me and reached for my suitcase.

"Let's get you home."

I tried to gauge the tone of his voice. It wasn't anger or frustration, it felt more like indifference. Typical. I grabbed the box, gave the house a final look, and closed the door on Carlson.

I followed my father to the parking lot where a white pickup truck was running. Exhaust fumes lifted slowly from the rear of the truck, illuminated against the red taillight. The truck was older; its body rusted in spots. The passenger door had a long, narrow scratch running along it. The outside elements filling the clean metal with a dark orange streak.

With a jerk, my father lifted the suitcase into the bed of the truck and walked back toward me, taking the box.

"I'll put this inside the cab, so it won't blow away," he said.

He opened the driver's door, leaned the seat forward, and placed the box on the second-row bench. I climbed in through the passenger door.

"New truck?" I asked as I settled into the seat.

"New to me, I guess. My car finally gave up the ghost. Threw that rod it had been threatening to for a while."

I pulled the seatbelt across me and leaned close to him to buckle it. I concealed a sniff, a trick I had learned when I was young to smell if he had been drinking or not. I could only detect the faint scent of gas fumes on his jacket.

I leaned back to my side and stared out the passenger window, watching the lights of Carlson dance by as we drove away. Soon we exited the city limits and headed south on I-25. Of all the ways I had dreamed college would go, I never thought I would be dropping out. My escape, the hope I had hung onto for so many lonely years as a child, had been taken from me, just like everything else in my life.

The thought of showing my face in Chatwin twisted inside me. I had believed I was better than the town. I thought I had escaped its miserable grasp. Now, not only was I going back, but I would have to face the scorn of being a failure. Just wait until the town matriarchs found out about the pregnancy. That'll be the cherry on top. I would be the headline in all the gossip circles.

I looked up at the moon looming over us. Its yellow glow shining bright against the clearing night sky. I wished Brad was there to see it with me. I closed my eyes and let the rhythm of the road carry me off to sleep.

I awoke to the cool blue sunrise awakening the world around us. The truck moved along, its engine heavy.

I gave my father a sideways glance, embarrassed that I had fallen asleep. As if I had let my guard down. I looked out the passenger window and tried to reorient myself. A shallow river ran along the side of the road, gently leading to sloping canyon walls. Pine trees grew along the water's edge, multiplying as they rose in elevation.

I looked at my father. "Where are we?"

"Almost home."

I looked all around me and then through the rear window.

Unless the ugly flat land of Chatwin had been transformed into a forest, we were definitely not going home.

"What do you mean?" I asked. "This isn't Chatwin."

He let out a sigh. "I don't live in Chatwin anymore."

His words hit me like a punch to the gut. The knot I had felt in returning home, softened into a twinge of nostalgia. Good or bad, our small, green house was the only home I had ever known. Every memory I had of my mom took place in and around those four small walls. And my father had just up and sold it, without even asking me.

"What are you talking about? That's where our home is."

"Chatwin wasn't a good place for me anymore."

"Were you even going to tell me or were you just going to have me come home one day and find that you were gone?"

"Were you going to come home, Brooklyn? Because you sure seemed to make it clear that you were gone and wanted nothing to do with me or that old town. So, was I just supposed to sit there and twiddle my thumbs in the off chance that someday you would pass through and grace me with your presence?"

It was just like the old days. Whenever we talked, it turned into a fight.

"What'd you do with Mom's stuff? I hope you didn't just throw it away. That's all I had left of her, I…"

"Do you think I'm stupid? I kept everything. I wouldn't do that to you."

I turned and looked out the passenger window. I watched the river roll and turn, disappearing under a narrow bridge.

"I couldn't stay there anymore. Everything was a reminder of all that had gone wrong. I'm trying to change, trying to forgive myself, and I couldn't do it there."

"Forgive yourself? What, did you find Jesus or something?"

"I guess you could say that."

I laughed and shook my head.

"What?" he asked.

"Nothing," I said. "It's just typical of you, thinking you can simply wipe the past away. As if all it takes is to say, 'I accept Jesus, now forgive me and take my sins away.'"

My words hung heavy in the air. The only sound was a small stash of spare change rattling in an empty cup holder and the squeak of the dashboard matching every bump in the road. I turned and looked at him. He stared straight ahead.

"Don't think for a minute that I'm dumb enough to believe I'll ever be forgiven for the choices I have made. My fate is sealed, I know that. I'm just trying to live out my life the best I can."

He slowed the truck and exited the highway onto a two-lane road. A sign read *Welcome to Fall Creek*. We traveled in silence until he turned into a small, u-shaped community. The neighborhood was surrounded by towering trees. The houses were small, not much bigger than our home in Chatwin, and close together. They were newer homes, with modern elevations. My father pulled into the driveway of one and put the truck in park. He paused for a moment.

"I don't know what's going on, and you don't need to tell me now. But you and your baby are welcome to stay here as long as you want."

I placed a hand on my stomach and tried to conceal my relief. Having lost everything just hours before, the security of having a place to stay was one less thing I needed to worry about.

"You've got a bed inside, your old one. I don't have sheets or anything for it. I can get those, I just wasn't expecting you."

"Thank you."

"And I'll try and stay out of your way. I got a job that keeps me busy, and I've been going to these meetings three nights a week, so I won't bother you much."

"Okay."

He opened the door and stepped out of the truck. He leaned the seat forward again and grabbed the box, tucking it under one arm. Then he walked to the side of the bed and lifted my suitcase out with a heavy tug. He closed the door and looked at me.

"Welcome home."

CHAPTER 32

tried to sleep, but it evaded me. The silence of the house rang in my ears. I rolled over in my bed and was met with the familiar pop and squeak of worn-out mattress coils. I stared at the head-board, a spot I had studied on many sleepless nights when I was younger. I had randomly placed a series of scratch-n-sniff stickers along its edge years earlier, a pack I had won at the sixth-grade raf-fle. They were worn and dirty now, but I could still make out their bottle shapes, and I knew the scents by heart. Root beer, orange, cola, grape, and lemon-lime. I reached over and gently scratched the cola one, the outside edges of the C and the A were the only visible letters left. I leaned my nose close to it. I was probably imagining it, but I thought I could still smell the slightest hint of its old scent.

I sat up and rolled my head along my shoulders. My temples pounded, and my eyes ached with exhaustion. I placed a palm against my face and massaged the pain.

I grabbed my phone off the edge of the bed and held my breath, secretly hoping Brad had texted me or maybe Ellie, wondering where I was. The screen came to life, but something was wrong. In the upper corner were the words *No Service*. I quickly unlocked the phone and a message popped up, *No Network Connection*. I slapped the side of the phone. "No, no, no, no, no."

I tried to make a call, but the same message popped up. Nicole's words echoed through my mind. Her list, the things that she told me were hers and not mine. She must have canceled my phone. She couldn't even give me a day. Doubt raced through me again, flooding me with fear. What was I doing? What if Brad changed his mind, how would he find me? My phone was the last connection I had. With it, Carlson was only one apologetic text away. Without it, I was all alone.

I threw the phone to the end of the bed and held my head in my hands. The throbbing pain screamed at me. I sighed and got up, stepping out of the bedroom and into the empty house. My father had left for work soon after we had arrived.

The home was an upgrade from our place in Chatwin. New paint, baseboards, and fixtures, but it was sterile. The walls were bare. The furniture, all of it from Chatwin, was either too big or too small for the spaces my father tried to drop them into.

I walked down a short hallway and peaked through an open door. It was another bedroom. A half-full glass of water and a couple of pill bottles on the nightstand told me it must be my father's.

I tiptoed in and lifted the bottles off the nightstand. Generic ibuprofen and 5mg Melatonin. I exhaled a breath I didn't realize I was holding. I opened the ibuprofen and dumped four of the pills into my hand.

I surveyed the room. It was bigger than my parents' bedroom in Chatwin. Wide enough for a king size bed, so it easily fit my father's old queen.

Their bed. The bed where she went to sleep and never woke up again.

Two long, narrow windows stood on both sides of the bed, and a door just steps away led to an en suite bathroom.

My Grandma Belle's dresser sat at the end of the bed, just like it had in Chatwin. I was surprised my father kept it. Even with a larger bedroom, it was still too big. A nice piece of furniture that wasn't meant for poor people in small houses.

There were two picture frames sitting on top of the dresser, one at each end. The one closest to the door was of my parents, their wedding announcement photo. It had always hung in our house when my mom was alive, but I hadn't seen it in years. Not since one drunken night soon after her death when my father had removed every reminder of her. I stared at the two of them in the photo, so young, so happy, so innocent.

The picture at the other end was of me when I was seven years old. My round face and toothless grin coming out of the Chatwin community pool. I was surprised he had kept it, let alone put it up.

I ran my fingers along the smooth edge of the dresser and let them fall onto one of the drawer pulls. I gave it a gentle tug and pulled the drawer open. It was filled with my mom's T-shirts, as neatly folded as the day she left them. I carefully pulled one out. I remembered it. It was teal and had the words Jackson Hole Wyoming written across the front. I held it up to my nose. Her smell was gone. All that was left was a decade of dust and stale air. I folded the shirt and put it back down.

I opened another drawer. More of her things, leggings and sweatpants. I began opening all the drawers. Everything was just as before, even the drawer full of her keepsakes. My father had kept it all, just like he said.

I left the bedroom and walked into the kitchen. I smiled at the sight of gray, granite countertops. My mom had always wanted granite. "Anything to change this ugly laminate kitchen," I remember her saying. She was ahead of her time, as now it seemed granite was common in most homes. I found an empty glass, filled it with water, and downed the ibuprofen.

I opened the fridge; it was sparse as always. A half-eaten microwave burrito, a carton of orange juice, a gallon of milk, baby carrots, and a loaf of bread. My father always kept bread in the fridge. I opened one of two drawers and found the rest of his time-honored ingredients, mayo, bologna, and cheese. I scrunched my nose and stuck my tongue out in disgust. He hadn't changed. He could somehow afford a nicer house, but he would rather starve than buy real food.

When was the last time you bought a meal for yourself?

Nicole's words played through my head. I had started to take food for granted. Before we had even moved in together, Brad and I made it a weekly tradition to go grocery shopping. It was fun to walk the aisles as a couple and pretend to be adults, but he always paid and there was no limit. I couldn't go back to scrounging for every meal again. How was this going to work? Would my father start giving me twenty dollars again, so I could scrimp and save through the week? What about the baby? I imagined diapers alone would use up that budget.

I stared out the kitchen window and bit the edge of one of my fingernails. My empty stomach turned with anxiety. I took a deep breath and exhaled slowly. I watched as two women walked past on an asphalt path behind my father's house. I leaned toward the glass and looked as far down the narrow passage as I could. It seemed endless. I went back to the bedroom, slipped my shoes on, and grabbed ten dollars I had stuffed into the edge of my suitcase. I reached for my phone, then remembered it was useless to me now. I closed my eyes and sighed, then walked out the back door toward the path.

I didn't know where I was going or what I expected to find, but anything was better than sitting in an empty house with only my thoughts to keep me company. A short distance down the pathway, when my father's house was no longer visible, the asphalt gave way to well-worn gravel. The path curved and followed the banks of a shallow stream. A faded sign had the words *Fall Creek* burned into it. The walkway wound along and over the creek, crossing along detailed wooden bridges. Pine trees towered in all directions, and the leaves of countless aspen trees fluttered in a slight breeze.

I lost myself in the serenity of all of it and continued walking until the trees cleared and a sweeping view of downtown Fall Creek came to life in front of me. The asphalt path returned and weaved through a small park. The edge of the park sat atop a wide street with two-story buildings rising in various heights along both sides. The street gently rolled downhill, giving way to houses and a large lake in the distance. The Rocky Mountains loomed majestically in the background, completing the picture-perfect scene.

The downtown area was quiet as I strolled along one side of the street. The buildings were old, but their exteriors were well maintained. Their style and color differed from one storefront to another and carried with them the nostalgia of small-town America.

My legs ached, something I had never experienced until recently, as each new week of my pregnancy went by. I sat down on one of a series of park benches placed along the sidewalk.

I massaged my calf muscle and gave a friendly smile to the occasional passerby. A younger man walked by, holding the hands of what appeared to be his two young daughters. As I watched them, the nagging voice in my head told me that my daughter would never have such a moment with her father. And men wouldn't be lining up to date a single mother. Chances are, she would never have a hand to hold other than mine.

I turned the thoughts off. Maybe sitting wasn't the best idea. I dropped my leg and adjusted the back of my shoe where one of its edges was forming a subtle blister on my heel. I stood up just as a woman exited the store I was sitting in front of. She was short, with wavy brown hair and a slight streak of gray running from her part toward her right ear. She wore a white apron and had a smile that instantly made me feel her kindness.

"Are you coming inside or what?" she asked. I looked around, but she was clearly talking to me.

"Excuse me?"

"I made a bet ten minutes ago when I saw you sit down on this bench. I said before that girl walks away, she's going to come in and buy something from our bakery."

I hadn't noticed the sign on the window until now. *Essence Bakery.* It was in a tall and narrow building, sandwiched between two others. Easy to miss if you weren't looking for it.

"Now I don't know how you've sat here so long without even looking like you wanted to come in, but I can tell you're getting ready to leave, and I can't let you do that."

I was confused. "Okay."

"Good," the woman said and opened the door for me.

As I walked in, the warm, buttery scent of fresh-baked cookies and glazed pastries surrounded me. A long glass display case dominated the front of the shop, drawing me in with its carefully arranged rows of sugar-dusted donuts, swirled cupcakes crowned with frosting, golden éclairs, and soft-baked cookies still glistening from the oven. The interior was bright and cozy, sunlight filtered through gingham curtains and bounced off the pastel-painted walls. Beneath the cheerful charm, the building's age peeked through, with scuffed floorboards, faded signs, and chipped corners.

"No," another woman said, suddenly appearing from the back of the store. She was taller with golden-blonde hair. She appeared to be in her late fifties. I stepped away from the display case. "No way, Cathy, not a chance. You can't win the bet by dragging this sweet girl in off the street."

complete strangers my life story. Sybil took a step toward me.

"I'm sorry," she said. "I shouldn't be so nosy."

"Don't be sorry. I appreciate you asking, it's just kind of embarrassing, you know?"

"You have nothing to be embarrassed about. I raised two kids on my own, when my oldest was three and my youngest was one. I've been there and I promise you can do this."

"You've also come to the right place," Cathy said. "Because here in Fall Creek, we look out for each other."

I smiled. "You're not hiring, are you?"

They looked at each other and smiled.

"Unfortunately, not right now," Sybil said. "We just ended our busy season, when all the families were here spending the summer at Shadow Lake."

"What other skills do you have though," Cathy asked. "Maybe we can ask around."

"Me? Nothing really, unless you consider bad luck to be a skill."

They both laughed. Sybil walked over to me and put an arm around me.

"Come on, Brooke. You have no hidden talents or hobbies?"

"I'm kind of good at photography."

"Well, there you go," she said. "Cathy, weren't we just talking about how we needed to update the photos on the website?"

"Yeah, just last week," Cathy quickly agreed.

I waved a hand and finished another bite of the cookie. "Sorry, when I said I was kind of good, I mean I don't have any professional experience."

Sybil looked at me and shrugged. "Well, you have to start somewhere, don't you?"

"Yeah, but I would be afraid to mess up your website."

"You're not going to mess it up," Cathy said. "If we don't like them, then we just won't put them on there. No harm done."

"But let's not even talk that way," Sybil said. "You just do the best you can, and we'll go from there."

"Really?"

"Absolutely," Cathy said. "Maybe give us a few days to get things read, and then we'll have you come in and take some pictures of the store and some of the treats we sell."

"Okay." I was excited. "Thank you."

I wanted to cry. I had spent so much time trying to defend myself recently, I had forgotten what kindness felt like. What it felt like to have someone believe in me. For the first time in long time, it felt like the clouds hanging over me parted, if only for a moment.

CHAPTER 33

opened the front door of my father's house and listened to see if he was home. The only sound was the gentle push of cool air circulating from the air conditioning. I walked in and let the door close behind me. It latched with a forceful thud, causing me to pause and listen again. The house was still quiet.

I filled a glass with water from the kitchen faucet and leaned back, resting against the edge of the countertop. I had walked into town each of the past few days, mainly to get away from my thoughts, but also to check in with Sybil and Cathy to see if they were ready for my help. The walk back always felt longer. I took a sip of the water and let out a deep sigh; my body thanked me for the moment of rest.

I stopped at a small café; a hole in the wall place Sybil had recommended.

"Don't let its outward appearance turn you off," she told me. "They have the best soups and sandwiches in town."

I placed the white paper sack on the small kitchen table, pulled out a cup of broccoli cheddar soup and a half chicken pesto panini, wrapped in heavy butcher paper. They both smelled delicious.

I unwrapped the sandwich and carried it out the back door, stepping down the short wooden steps onto a narrow concrete pad.

At one edge was a round charcoal grill with two patio chairs near it.

I sat down on one of the chairs and curled my legs underneath me. Aspen trees chatted gently among the pines. I stared into the warmth of the late summer sun and took a bite of the sandwich. The flavors mixed together in perfect harmony.

"It's peaceful here, isn't it?"

I jumped at my father's voice and quickly wiped the edges of my mouth with the side of my finger.

"I didn't know you were home."

"Just got here." He sat down on the other chair. "I wish you'd told me you were getting food. I bought stuff to make dinner."

I looked at him and shrugged, shaking my head. "I learned long ago to never wait on you making dinner. I'd have starved to death as a child."

My words came out sounding more biting than I intended. I looked at him from the corner of my eye. He was looking down, massaging the palms of his hands.

We sat in silence, like we so often did.

"I've been thinking about what you said the other day," he finally said.

"What'd I say?"

"About me believing that I can just wipe away the past."

"I was just tired. I shouldn't have said anything."

He continued to stare at his hands and slowly nodded.

"No, you were right. Truth is, all I do is think about the past."

I could sense where the conversation was going, and I wanted no part of it. I didn't come here to sit on the other side of his confessional.

"Well, we can't change the past, right?"

"You know, when you were little, you'd look at me with your big blue eyes, and you had all the faith and trust in the world for me."

"Dad, stop…I don't…"

"Something happened to me when your mom died. I blamed myself. Actually, I had been blaming myself for a long time before that. She would be so happy one moment, and then suddenly she would be so sad. And I'd do anything I could to cheer her up, but I don't think any of it made a difference. A day or two later she would suddenly be back to her happy self. It was nothing I did. I just kept thinking though, if only I could give her a better life, the sad days wouldn't come so often."

I looked away, my eyes following the trail as it disappeared in the distance. My nine-year-old heart had shared the same hope for my mom, countless times. When I turned back to him, he was staring at me.

"I tried, Brooklyn. I really did."

I looked at him, my face emotionless. I said nothing, looked away, and took another bite of my sandwich.

"When the baby died and then your Grandma Belle, she just couldn't pull out of it anymore. But I never thought…well, I never thought she would do what she did. And then you were the one who found her. No one should have to go through that, especially a little girl."

I hadn't thought about that day in a long time, but in the stir of memories, the pain was still fresh; hiding just below the surface. Wounded, not healed. I could almost hear my screams again from when they wheeled her out of the house, my mind unable to register what was happening. It wasn't real. It couldn't be real. And it wasn't…until the doctor at the hospital walked toward my father who collapsed to his knees in tears. I knew it was real then.

"I hope you know that she loved you," he said, as if he were reading my thoughts. "You were her whole world."

"Apparently, I wasn't enough."

He shook his head and leaned forward.

"Don't say that. It wasn't you. She just…couldn't escape it. And I shoulda been there for you, but it was like a fog came over me. I was living each day, waking up and going to work, but it's like I wasn't really there. I felt nothing."

He dropped his head and stared at his hands again, tracing the lines on his palm with his finger. The falling sun splashed vibrant shades of orange across his face. His eyes seemed to be swimming with the memories of the past.

He didn't give me a chance to say anything. "Do you know what the worst part is? I knew you needed me. I knew I was failing you, but I couldn't get my body to do what my brain was telling it."

His voice cracked, and he ran a hand behind his head, massaging his neck. Then, he leaned forward and stared at the ground.

My brow furrowed and I shook my head. I wasn't falling for his hat in hand routine again.

"Why are you telling me all of this, Dad? Am I supposed to feel sorry for you now? Am I supposed to tell you it's all okay, so you can feel better about yourself?"

We sat quiet again, lost in our own thoughts. A pair of birds danced in the sky, chasing each other from tree to tree.

"That's not it."

"What's not it?"

"I'm telling you this because I hate myself for what I've done. I think that if you know that, it'll free you somehow."

"Free me?"

"Yes, because it justifies the hate you have for me. So, you don't need to feel guilty about feeling the way you do."

"Guilty," I laughed. "I don't feel guilty. You gave me every reason in the world to hate you. I've barely even thought about you since I left home."

I looked away, my eyes burning. A sickening feeling rose through me. I was using my words to hurt him, I wanted him to hurt, but it didn't feel right. The past had left its scars on him, just like it had me. How much pain does one person deserve in the pursuit of getting even?

"Fair enough. But I've got to say one more thing."

"Dad, please, can we not talk about this anymore?"

"I promise I'll never bring it up again, but if I'm ever going to move on, I've got to say this."

He leaned forward and looked me in the eyes, his gaze piercing.

"Of all the mistakes I've made in my life, nothing comes close to what I did to you. I wish I could say I wasn't in my right mind, but that would be casting the blame somewhere else. I was the one who was a drunk. I was the one who let myself get angry. I was the one who picked you up and threw you across that room. I was the one who hurt you."

I couldn't let my mind go there. I had pushed that night, that pain, deep within me, and I was not going to let it back out. I stood, wanting to run away, but I stopped at the edge of the concrete and stared into the sunset.

"After I left your room, I looked at myself in the bathroom mirror. Rage was coursing through me, but I could hear your cries. I stared into the face of a man I didn't recognize anymore, and I hated him. I sat for a long time that night and listened to you cry until you fell asleep. Then I picked up my pistol and walked out into the field behind our house."

A breath stopped short in my chest. I turned and looked at him, his eyes still fixed on me.

"I held the barrel below my chin, so close I could smell it, but I couldn't do that to you."

Silence consumed the evening air. His words revealed another twist to his story, to our story. The history of my life had been pulled from the vault I had buried it in long ago. I could remember it all, the sadness and the pain of those years.

He swallowed hard. "I don't say that with any pride. If the best I could do for you as your father was to not leave you orphaned, that tells what an awful person I was. I am."

"I would've forgiven you, Dad."

"I never wanted you to forgive me. It was unforgivable, and I need to live with that each day."

I took a few steps toward him, my gaze piercing now.

"That's stupid. You left me on my own, crying myself to sleep each night, scared to death, all because you wanted to punish yourself? Didn't you realize that every day that went by, it just hurt me more and more."

"I do now. I'm haunted by that fact every day. At some point, the fog cleared, and I looked around at the destruction I'd left, and I figured it was too late. The best thing I could do was keep a roof over your head and stay out of your way. I didn't want to hurt you anymore."

"So, you were never going to tell me this? All these years. And then you just let me walk out that door last year, without so much as a goodbye, and never told me any of this? You were going to let me spend my whole life thinking my father hated me?"

"Is that what you think?"

"What else can I think, Dad?"

"I've never hated you, Brooklyn. I loved you from the moment that I held you in my arms. It breaks my heart to know that I've hurt you. I'm sorry."

My heart leapt. Two simple words I had waited ten years to hear. My eyes clouded with tears, not from his apology, but from the reality that it *was* too late. I was too far down the bumpy road of life my parents had set me on. My heart, unfeeling, had galvanized against hope and forgiveness.

"So, you're a changed man now? A church going man, I hear."

"I don't know. I'm trying, I guess. When you left Chatwin,

I couldn't stay there anymore. Everything reminded me of the past. I knew I couldn't do it anymore. I had this hope, small as it was, that I could start a new life where I would begin to put the past behind me. And then when I was sure, when I knew I had changed, I'd find you, and I'd ask for your forgiveness. So, I quit Chatwin Fabrication and sold the house. I moved to Fall Creek, and I'm trying to start a new life."

"What if I hadn't been able to find you?"

"I wouldn't have let that happen. I was never going to be more than a phone call away from you."

I turned my head and stared along the trail again. The shadows of dusk slowly stretched across the landscape.

"The problem is, Dad, we've done this before. You tell me you've changed, and you're going to be there for me now, and then things always go back to the way they were."

"I'm trying. I did drive across the state of Colorado to pick you up in the middle of the night."

I quietly chuckled. "Well, I guess that makes up for everything, doesn't it? One kind act and we're square, huh? I'm just supposed to forgive you now?" I shook my head and began walking toward the house. My heart pounded and my eyes burned.

"Brooklyn?"

I climbed the stairs and pulled the door closed behind me.

I turned to go back outside, I couldn't leave it like this, but hate had me firmly in its grasp. I threw the remains of my sandwich away, walked to my bedroom, and closed the door.

CHAPTER 34

I sat at the kitchen table, staring blankly at my laptop. I listened to the rhythmic hammering coming from my father in the backyard. He was building a shed, and the beat of the hammer reminded me of my childhood. The sounds of his work, steady and tranquil, matching the slow, happy life we enjoyed before the bad days came.

He was always building something in those days. Then he would come in, sweat clinging to his forehead, and wrap his worn arms around my mom. She would playfully push him away, but I think she enjoyed the game.

The dishwasher let out a chime, signaling the end of its cycle and bringing me back to the present. I looked again at my laptop screen. The browser was open to my Grand Mesa email. A collection of unread messages waited for my attention. My eyes drifted to the edges of the open tab. There was a picture of me and Brad taunting me in the background. I had set that the wallpaper months ago.

I could only make out the narrow ends of the photo, but I knew it by heart. The two of us on Abbot Peak, with the city of Carlson unfolding thousands of feet below. I'd give anything to go back to that moment, before everything became so complicated.

I slouched in the chair and clicked on the first email. I knew what it was before I read it.

To: Brooklyn Blair

From: GMCC Admin

Date: Thursday, September 15, 2025, 09:17:33 MST

Subject: Student Deferral

Brooklyn, we received your request to cancel your courses for the FALL 2025 semester and defer your schooling. Your deferment has been accepted, and you have been removed from all coursework this semester. Because this request was received before the add/drop deadline, you will not be charged for the selected credit hours. However, your $50 registration fee is nonrefundable.

Please understand that if you are receiving financial aid, it is your responsibility to contact their office regarding your deferment. Any interruption in your schooling may result in loss of your aid.

Thank you,

Becca Howell
GMCC Administration – Student Enrollment Office

My life was officially on hold; although, I knew the unspoken truth, it was over. My dreams had died the moment I stepped out of the Foster's front door.

I had replayed that scene over and over in my mind. My choice had been so definitive. Before that moment, I had been filled with uncertainty, but with my heart racing and the adrenaline pumping through me, I stood face-to-face with Nicole and chose the baby, our baby, over Brad. Yet, with each new day in the nearly two weeks since I left, my convictions were becoming more and more muddied in a sea of doubt.

I leaned forward and rested my head on the table. I felt the coolness of the wood against my cheek and traced my finger along the delicate patterns of the grain.

"What am I doing?" I whispered to myself. Had I really given up on school and walked away from my dream life to come home and be a single mother? To raise a child with Down syndrome? To live with my father? A man I couldn't seem to be around for any extended period without us stepping into a minefield of arguments.

My laptop pinged, and I raised my head. A notification appeared at the bottom of the screen.

NEW MESSAGE FROM: Dr. Cassidy Brown

I clicked on it.

To: Brooklyn Blair

From: Dr. Cassidy Brown

Date: Thursday, September 15, 2025, 11:17:33 MST

Subject: Checking In

Hi Brooke,

I haven't seen you in class the past two weeks, and I noticed this morning that your name has been removed from my student roster. I'm worried about you. Is everything all right with you and the baby? Please reach out and let me know how you are. If there is anything I can do, please don't hesitate to ask.

If you're still checking this email, and I hope you are, the Collegiate Association of Photography is running a contest focused on inspiring images. They are calling it Be the Change, and they are accepting submissions from anyone between the ages of 18-25. With your talent for capturing emotion in your photos, I believe this is right up your alley. You should submit one of your stills. They are offering a cash prize of $500, but the true reward is the publicity the winner receives. Each participating college and university will post the winning photograph on their social media platforms. Twitter, Facebook, Instagram, etc. It's an amazing opportunity! The only downside is submissions are due in two days. I'm sorry I couldn't get this information to you sooner; I just heard about it myself. If you're interested, please reach out to me, and I'll help you through the process.

Actually, reach out to me either way. I want to know you're okay.

All the best,
Cassie

I gently chewed the end of a fingernail and wondered if I could find an image and edit it within two days. I hardly wanted to get out of bed in the mornings, so having a deadline filled me with the anxiety of a seemingly impossible task. Besides, I wouldn't win anyway.

I scanned my memory, thinking of photos I had already captured. Some of them were good but seemed too amateurish. They might win a prize at a community college, but I had seen the work of talented photographers, and I wasn't at their level.

I left the kitchen and went to my bedroom. I slid open the closet door, its rollers rattling along the track. The closet was empty except for my sparse collection of clothes and the box I had brought with me from Carlson. I reached for it but hesitated. I wasn't sure I wanted to open it. Boxes tucked away in dark corners are put there for a reason. They hide the memories we want to forget. Unfulfilled dreams, lost loves, and the reminders of those who are gone, never to be seen again.

I pulled it from the shelf and lifted the lid to find the scattered remains of my life in Carlson. My headphones, a pack of gum, and a Grand Mesa T-shirt. I caught a slight, familiar scent emanating from the box. The fragrance of flowers mixed with a hint of cherry. It was Ellie, her perfume or lotion woven into the fabric of the shirt. I held it to my nose, and the aroma surrounded me. For a moment, I was back in our town house. So many laughs and so many cries, and so many laughs that had turned into cries.

Staring back at me, where the T-shirt had been, was a small silver frame. It held a picture of me, Brad, and Ellie, the three of us at Brad's birthday party. It had sat on the edge of my nightstand for months, where I had looked at it so many times. I removed it from the box and held it for a long moment. The smiles on our faces perfectly captured our genuine happiness. I missed those days. The longing like the ending of a good book, where one wishes they could start over and experience it all again. I wondered what they were doing now.

I put the frame down and pushed a few more items aside. There in the bottom, I found the camera Brad had given me. I sighed heavily and moved from my knees to a sitting position. I leaned my back against the wall and stared up at a set of transom windows in the bedroom. The sunlight streamed through them, reflecting off a frosted, silver water bottle sitting on my nightstand.

I wanted to take the camera and throw it against the wall. I wanted to see it shatter so I would never feel like I did right now. Yet, I also never wanted to forget how I felt when Brad gave it to me. To be loved. To be accepted.

I lifted the camera from the box and held it for a moment. It felt natural in my hands. I brought the viewfinder to my eye and smiled. I could remember looking through it and seeing Brad's excitement. I could also remember his words, "We're going to get years of use out of it."

"We," I said to no one.

If only I had a chance to talk to him again, one-on-one, without Nicole and all the other distractions, maybe he would remember us. Maybe he would see me again. He would feel that old spark and would realize how dumb all of this had been. Maybe he already felt all of this and was searching for me.

My mind caught hold of this thought and raced with the sliver of hope. I had updated my information on the GMCC database, but it didn't let me add a phone number. With the way we left things, it seemed unlikely he would show up at my door without trying to call me first.

I quickly put the other items back in the box and slid it into the corner. I paused, debating my thoughts, then walked to the backyard.

My father stood on a ladder, his ball cap turned backward, a hole in one of the knees of his jeans. He held a hammer in his hand and made steady, quick swings. Each nail he placed, slid effortlessly into the wood.

"Dad?"

He didn't answer, so I stepped closer.

"Dad?" I asked again. Still no response.

I stepped to his side. He hammered another nail in, causing me to flinch, and then he finally saw me. He pulled an earbud from his ear.

"Sorry."

"It's okay, what's going on?" he asked.

"Would you mind if I borrowed your truck for a couple of hours?"

"You're welcome to take it anytime you want."

"Are you sure? If you need it, I can…"

"Brooklyn, it's okay, you can use it anytime you need to."

"Okay."

"Where are you going?"

"I just have a few errands to run."

"Do you need help?"

"No, I should be okay, but thanks."

"I just topped it off with gas yesterday, so don't worry about that. Be safe, the cars come fast around that intersection at Elizabeth Street."

"I will."

I stepped away and walked back toward the house. The white lie I had told him was already gnawing at my conscience, made worse by his generosity, but it was better if he didn't know where I was going. He wouldn't understand.

I stopped at a convenience store and bought a water and a banana to fuel me on my journey. I wound through Fall Creek and was on Interstate 25 quicker than I expected. I turned the radio up and sang along as loud as I could. The excitement of hope seized my body.

My plan raced through my mind. I knew I couldn't go to the Foster's house.

Would I ever be welcome there again?

Instead, I would go straight to Ellie's. I would probably need to mend some hurt feelings, since I left without telling her. Although, my options had been limited, so I doubt she was too upset with me.

Once we were good, I would have her take me to Brad. I imagined the moment he would see me. A smile would roll across his face, lifting a bit higher on one side like it always did. I pictured myself in his arms, feeling the warmth of his chest against my face. Letting the sorrow melt away.

Of course, it wouldn't be that easy. I knew that. We had issues to work out, and it would take time, but if I could just talk to him, I could fix this. We could pick back up where we used to be, before all the drama. Just the two of us.

I could hear the conversation I would have with my father, telling him everything was okay. I would tell him that I was starting a new life, just like him, so I wouldn't need to live with him anymore. He'd likely be excited at the chance to move on without me. We would go our separate ways, but more peacefully this time. I'm sure we would talk on Father's Day and Christmas.

Then Brad and I would go to the Foster's. There would be an awkward silence, before Nicole would pull me off to the side. She would apologize, and I would be embraced in a friendly hug, just like she used to give me.

I would go with Brad back to our townhouse, snuggle on the couch, and begin to plan our future. The baby's room, our wedding, and the life I was promised.

The truck drifted slightly onto a rumble strip along the side of the road, the tires growling to the intermittent pattern of indents. I awoke from my thoughts and straightened the wheel. I checked my mirrors, traffic was light. I looked ahead to an approaching sign.

Denver   203
Fort Collins   268

The realization hit me; I was a long way from Carlson.

I started singing again, but my words trailed off, interrupted by a thought that played over and over in my mind. Something I had said to Ellie on the night I left. Words I wanted desperately to ignore.

"I saw it clearly in his eyes," I had told her. "He doesn't love me."

He did love me, though. I know he did. He couldn't have faked it, not for that long. He just needed to see me again and feel that connection. Yet, my lip quivered and my lungs tightened. The excitement fading as quickly as it had arrived. The exhilaration turning into cruel reality. Regardless of what my heart wanted to believe, when I said those words to Ellie, I knew they were true.

I quickly turned on my blinker and pulled the truck hard to the right. The tires rumbled across the hard gravel between the interstate and an exit ramp. The cab vibrated with a heavy bounce as the rear tires caught the edge of the asphalt. I slowed down, gained control, and straightened the wheels. I let the truck drift gently to the other side of the ramp and put it in park.

What was I doing? Was I so dumb and naive to think I could ever go back to them? They didn't let me walk out that door, they pushed me out.

"Why doesn't anyone want to be with me?" I said to the emptiness around me. "Why does everyone leave me? My mom, my dad, my friends in Chatwin, Brad and Ellie and the Fosters? Everyone!"

I pounded my fists against the steering wheel.

"And what am I going to do with a baby? I can't do this alone. It's too much this time. I can't do this anymore."

I rested my head against the side window, the sun-warmed glass pressing into my temple as the last thread of hope unraveled inside me. Everything in me felt heavy—hollow. I opened the door, climbed out, and slammed it behind me, the mirror rattling against a loose bolt. I balled my fists and screamed, raw and loud, then turned and kicked the truck with the sole of my foot. Pain shot up my leg, but I kicked it again, harder this time.

I clutched my head in both hands; another scream ripped from my throat as I staggered around the side of the truck. The air smelled of dust and hot sage. I wanted to run into the brush, into the thick forest beyond. To vanish. To erase myself from this place and everything it meant.

I leaned against the truck's hot metal side and slid to the ground, gravel digging into the backs of my legs. I pressed my cheek against the warm steel and closed my eyes. I sat there for a while, letting the stillness settle around me. In the distance, the hum of the highway droned on.

The storm of emotion that had built for days finally broke and began to ebb. It wasn't grief or rage, but something quieter. Something final. This was the end. I could feel it settle over me, as certain as the heat radiating from the truck. I wasn't going back to Carlson. I couldn't. It was over. It was time to move on.

I pulled myself up, brushed gravel from my palms, and rested a foot on the passenger-side running board. My shorts clung to the backs of my legs, and I tugged them straight before leaning against the window. I stared into the cab. The worn gray leather of the seat was cracked along the edge, peeling slightly where years of sun and use had taken their toll. My camera still there, exactly where I'd left it. I'd brought it hoping something along the way might spark my imagination.

I opened the door and slid onto the seat. In the heat, the interior smelled of dust and vinyl. I picked up the camera and powered it on. It came to life with a soft hum. I pressed the green playback button. The screen lit up, and the last photo appeared. It was the one I had taken of Paige, leaning over Luke's tiny NICU bed.

The feelings of that moment stirred in me again. *This* was the photo I needed to submit for the contest. This is what it's all about.

Life.

I had seen it disappear with my mom. The flame of another soul extinguished. Their worth never known. Their impact never realized. I knew how the loss of one life disrupted the harmony of the world. Every life sown into the collective fabric. There was no choice to be made. My daughter deserved the life that God had granted her.

I set the camera down, wiped my eyes, and moved into the driver's seat. I turned the truck around and headed south on Interstate 25.

It was time to go home, for good.

CHAPTER 35

The sun cast long shadows across the landscape. Its brightness, deceptive to the cool breeze that played through the rustling aspen leaves. Late summer was giving way to fall's grand entrance.

I pulled the collar of my jacket up and lowered a fleece headband over my ears, the warm fabric providing immediate relief from the chill in the air. I walked at a steady pace, my breathing calculated, as I rounded the bend leading to Brite Park. With each step, the horizon unveiled itself frame by frame until downtown Fall Creek appeared in front of me.

I stopped to catch my breath next to a monument that sat atop the downward slope of Main Street. I stared into the distance. The upper peaks above Shadow Lake popped with a chorus of yellow, orange, and red. The tapestry of fall drifting majestically down the mountainsides. I drew in a deep breath, the fresh air invigorating.

I strolled along the sidewalk past the storefronts. Their summer themes, once geared toward the visitors of the lake, had been transformed into a sea of golden colors, matching the changing seasons.

I pushed open the door of Essence Bakery. Its heavy frame hesitating and the hinges moaning as I made my way in. The bell above the door announced my entrance.

The store was empty, including the checkout counter. I walked quietly across the worn linoleum to the display case to survey today's treats.

"I'll be right with you," Cathy yelled from the back.

"It's just me."

The case boasted the usual assortment of desserts. Cookies lined the top shelf, with the seasonal addition of Sybil's pumpkin spice macarons taking center stage. The middle rack contained a variety of breads, and the bottom row held the sparse remains of a tray of cinnamon rolls and a line of fruit tarts.

Cathy came from the back. "Hi, Brooke."

"Everything looks amazing today, as always."

"Thank you."

She wiped her hands briskly and a puff of flour danced in the air. She dabbed at a narrow smear of chocolate below her eye.

"No Sybil today?"

"Not today, she's with her grandkids."

"That's fun."

Cathy walked over to a pitcher of water next to the display case. It stood atop a decorative pedestal. A layer of lemon slices floated effortlessly on top. She poured some into a plastic cup and handed it to me.

"Thank you."

"How are you feeling today?"

"Good. It's getting colder, and I feel like I'm moving slower, but I love my daily walks. They recharge my soul."

"How many weeks are we at now?"

"Almost thirty."

"The last trimester can definitely be an uncomfortable one, but you'll make it."

"I hope so."

She pulled a chair out from under one of the white, metal tables and motioned for me to sit. I welcomed the opportunity to rest my legs.

"Hey, people have been raving about the new pictures on the website, and the ones we've been sharing on Instagram."

A sense of pride flashed through me, and I worked to conceal a smile. "Really?"

"In fact, a woman just called yesterday afternoon. She saw one of our posts and ordered a cake for her daughter's sweet sixteen."

"That's awesome, I'm glad it's helping."

She slid open a door behind the display case and grabbed a small sheet of tissue paper from a box. The paper rustled in her hand as she bent down and reached into the case. She pulled out one of the macarons and brought it to me.

"Thank you."

She smiled and wiped her hands again, then reached for a narrow, pink tumbler next to the register and took a long sip.

"I've had some people ask about you as well."

"Really? That doesn't sound good."

She let out a hearty laugh and coughed as she tried to swallow the remainder of her drink. "No enemies," she said. "I promise. Just people wondering if I could recommend my photographer."

"No way."

"I'm serious."

"I've received a couple of random requests, too. I got asked to shoot a wedding next month, and a woman called just this morning, wondering if I would take their family photos."

"I told you, Brooke, we take care of each other in this town."

I smiled and took a bite of the pastry. I had never bought into the pumpkin spice craze that consumed the dessert world during the fall months, but Sybil was converting me into a true believer.

"So, are you going to take the jobs?"

"I think I know just enough to do the family shoot…at least I hope I do, but the wedding is a different story. I'm nowhere near that level."

"Brooke Blair, how many people need to tell you you're amazing before you start believing them?"

"I know, I know, I just don't want to mess up."

She walked to the table, sat down, and leaned forward to look right into my eyes.

"You just gotta believe in yourself. You've got this."

I took another bite of the macaron and followed it with a sip of water.

"Maybe, but I also don't know if I have the right equipment. Plus, will I even be able to do it when I'm super pregnant? I'll be like a month away at that point."

"Sweetie, it sounds like you've already talked yourself out of it. Just know, years ago I was overdue with Madelyn, my youngest, and was still working here at the bakery every day. I must have been two weeks past due."

"Seriously?"

"Okay, maybe not overdue, but it sure felt like it. I was wobbling everywhere, and my knees were aching."

She laughed again and opened her arms wide. She teetered back and forth, showing how she wobbled. I laughed and wiped at a crumb on my lip.

"And Maddie was my fourth, so I wasn't young like you. My point is, just because you're having a baby, doesn't mean that life has to stop. In fact, it's just beginning."

"I guess maybe I am only thinking of reasons not to do it. One thing to add to the pros column, I could definitely use the money."

"It's a big leap, but I know you can do it."

My phone rang, and I pulled it from my back pocket. "Sorry." I looked at the screen. Dr. Brown's name appeared. I paused and looked at Cathy.

"Do you mind if I get this?"

"Go right ahead."

I stood and swiped the phone to answer. I paced to the other side of the bakery.

"Hello."

"Hi, Brooke, it's Cassie."

She had asked me several times during my internship to call her by her first name, but I never got used to it. It seemed too informal. Every time she introduced herself, I stumbled for an awkward moment, not sure what to say.

"Hi."

"I'm glad I reached you, it's so good to hear your voice," she said. "Have you checked your email?"

"Not since yesterday."

"You might want to."

"How come?"

"Because you won."

I heard the words, but my mind couldn't register them. For a moment I wondered what she was talking about.

"Did you hear me?"

"I won?"

She laughed. "Yes, you won the photo contest. You did it, Brooke."

I turned and looked at Cathy. She was watching me intently.

"I really won?"

"Won what?" Cathy whispered.

"Yes."

Cathy walked toward me, her eyes fixed on mine.

"What did you win?" she asked again.

"I won the photo contest I told you about."

She screamed and made up the distance between us in one leap. She wrapped me in her arms, nearly knocking the phone from my hand. I laughed and felt the excitement pulse through me. I held on to her.

"Brooke, are you still there?" Dr. Brown asked.

I released our hug. "I'm here, I'm here, sorry."

"No, don't be sorry. Celebrate, you deserve this."

"Thank you."

"Can I read to you what the committee said?"

"Yes, yes, please. Let me put you on speaker so my friend can hear."

I held the phone out between me and Cathy. My hand was shaking.

"Okay, go ahead."

"Dear Ms. Blair, thank you for the submission of your photograph, *Nightly Miracles*. We are happy to announce that you are our 2025 winner. Congratulations! While we received many amazing entries, yours stood out in capturing the essence of the contest, *Be the Change*. There are many ways for one person to make a difference in the world, but we feel strongly that it begins with love. Your photograph tells the story of the pure love that a parent has. You captured so much in one still. From the darkened room, the glowing monitors, the nurse busy at work in the background, to the mother holding her infant's hand, with a single tear rolling down her cheek."

I could picture the image in my mind. Remembering the countless tiny adjustments that I had to make to allow the viewer to see what I felt in that moment. I had nearly edited out the tear, as my experience was a hopeful moment, not a sad one. Yet, in the end I didn't feel it was my right to manipulate the emotion. My job was to put the viewer in that moment and let it speak to them personally.

Dr. Brown continued, "If we could all let go of the things which divide us, and unite in the care, concern, and love for each other, we can change the world. Your photograph proves that one person can make a difference. Again, we offer our congratulations. Your cash prize will be mailed to you and please look for your winning photo to be spread throughout the social media platforms of the participating colleges and universities."

Cathy and I stood in silence. I looked at her as she shook her head, her smile wide.

"Wow, Brooke!"

"I'm really proud of you, Brooke," Dr. Brown said. "This is a big deal, I hope you know that."

"Yes, ma'am."

"I've already posted it on GMCC pages."

"Thank you."

"I don't know when we'll see you at Grand Mesa again, but I would love to have you present at one of my exhibits in Denver if you're interested."

"Really? I would love that. Anytime."

"Congratulations again, I'll be in touch."

"Thank you."

I reached to end the call, my finger still shaking, then I stopped.

"Dr. Brown?" I asked, hoping she hadn't hung up.

"Yes?"

"Thank you for everything you've taught me and for believing in me."

"You're welcome, Brooke. You deserve this."

The call ended, and my home screen reappeared. I held the phone out in front of me, unable to move. I looked at Cathy and grinned.

"This is amazing, Brooke. I can't wait to tell Sybil. She's going to flip."

"I can't believe I won. I mean, I know it's just a small contest and doesn't mean much, but…"

Cathy's hands shot to her hips. "Stop right there. Don't say that. Don't downplay this moment. Big or small, it doesn't matter. You took a piece of your soul, dared to share it with the world, and people loved it. That's huge."

I looked down at my phone and nodded. I couldn't contain my smile. "I can't believe I won."

"So, how can I see this winning photo of yours?" Cathy asked.

I smiled with excitement and unlocked my phone.

"Let me check GMCC's Instagram."

I opened the app and refreshed my feed. I slowly began to scroll through; my photo appeared near the top.

"Oh my gosh, here it is.

Nightly Miracles, winner of the Association of Collegiate Photography's 2025 Be the Change award!
By Brooke Blair, Fall Creek, Colorado."

I handed the phone to Cathy. She pulled a pair of glasses from the pocket on her apron and held the phone. She tilted her head back slightly, holding the phone farther away, and looked through the bottom of the glasses.

"Oh my, look at that."

"It's kind of hard to see on the phone."

"No, I can see it. It's beautiful. Who is the woman?"

"That's Paige. I met her at the hospital, right after we found out that our baby has Down syndrome."

She looked up from the phone and smiled at me. "There must be a story there. How did you end up taking this photo of her?"

"I was sitting outside the hospital, completely lost in my grief, and she appeared. Almost out of nowhere. She saw I was sad and wanted to make sure I was okay."

"Sounds like a nice woman."

"She was, and she started telling me about her son, Luke, who was born premature and all the challenges he was facing. We got to talking, and she invited me up to see him. I remember her telling me, 'Let him change your day,' and he did."

Cathy lowered the phone and handed it back to me.

"Wow," she said. "I swear, some things aren't a coincidence. That woman was meant to be there for you at that exact moment in time."

"It was right after I took this picture, after I left the hospital, that my boyfriend Brad told me he wanted me to have an abortion."

Cathy shook her head and took off her glasses. She reached for my hand and locked her fingers around mine.

"In a quiet moment, standing in this little boy's room, I saw this scene play out. I'll always remember it. How much he was fighting to stay alive and how much Paige, and everyone there, was fighting to keep him alive. Seeing that, I knew I could never give up on my daughter. I have to fight for her."

"And you took a picture of it and changed the world."

I laughed and dismissed her praise.

"I don't know about that."

"Maybe not the world," she said. "But someone is going to see this picture and it will change their life."

I looked at the photo again and smiled. The euphoria of the moment rose through me, its warmth filling me with emotion. My confidence silencing the voices of my critics, crushing the unspoken fear that lurked just beyond my consciousness. That nagging voice that told me I could never escape my past, my family legacy, my lot. I needed this win.

CHAPTER 36

clicked through a series of photos and couldn't help but laugh. Image after image was the same. A young couple, their smiles fresh, the woman's hair falling effortlessly in perfect curls, the man's shadow beard trimmed to a precise length, trying desperately for one perfect picture.

The woman held their one-year-old son in her arms, while their three-year-old daughter straddled the father's side, his arm straining to keep her from wiggling.

The child smiled wide, two baby teeth poking sweetly above his lower lip. It had been easy to make him laugh, but the daughter hated all of it and sat stone-faced, pressed against her father's shoulder. She didn't want to be there. She had complained that it was too cold outside, that she didn't have her treats, that she was thirsty, that her dress was itchy, and on and on.

We tried everything to coerce a smile, but nothing worked. Picture after picture, she held the same face. Brow furrowed, eyes heavy on the brink of tears, and a lower lip that hung with an angry frown.

I continued to click through the images. I only needed one smile, or anything that wasn't a scowl, then I could take it and transpose it over her pouting face and give this couple the perfect family photo to send with their Christmas cards.

Through the beat of the music in my ears, I heard the faint sound of the doorbell. I gave a questioning look toward my bedroom door and removed my earbuds. Except for the occasional solicitor, no one ever stopped by my father's house.

I heard his footsteps moving through the kitchen toward the front door, and the click of its handle. I listened closely, trying to catch the greeting. My father's voice rose to a higher pitch, and he laughed. It had to be someone he knew.

I put my earbuds down and quietly opened my door. I took a few steps into the hallway and paused.

"It's really nice to see you again after all these years," my father said.

"You, too," a woman replied.

I took a few more steps, my curiosity on full alert.

"Come in, come in," he said.

"Are you sure?" the woman asked. "I hate to show up unannounced."

"No, she's going to be so excited to see you."

They were talking about me, but who would come to see me? Who even knew I lived here?

"Brooklyn," my father yelled, but I was already walking into the room.

The woman stood there, rubbing the sleeves of her brown overcoat. Her blonde hair flowing out in strands underneath a gray beanie.

"Miss Amy?"

My hand flew to my mouth and my heart skipped a beat. She was here. After all this time, she was really here.

"Brooklyn."

She stepped toward me, but I had already made up the distance between us. I wrapped my arms around her and held her tight.

"I can't believe it's you."

"I can't believe it's you," she laughed.

She grabbed my shoulders and held me away from her. She looked into my eyes.

"Wow, look at you. You have grown into a beautiful woman."

I smiled so wide it hurt. She pulled me close again.

"How did you find me?"

"I saw the picture you took. The one that won the contest."

"You won a contest?" my father asked.

I glanced at him over Miss Amy's shoulder. The confusion on his face blended with a look of either embarrassment because I hadn't told him or sadness for the same reason, I couldn't tell which. I released the hug.

"Yeah, but it wasn't a big deal."

"It's a very big deal," Miss Amy said. "It's beautiful and it immediately caught my eye. Then I saw the name, Brooke Blair from Fall Creek, Colorado, and I knew it had to be you. I looked up your father's name and did a little detective work to find an address."

She looked at him and smiled.

"Then I drove here from Utah, hoping to find you."

"You're in Utah now?"

"Yes, we've bounced around the last few years, but I think we've finally found home."

"And you drove all the way here just to see me?"

"You've never been far from my thoughts, Brooklyn."

She took a step back, looked at me, and smiled at me again.

"What?"

"I can't believe I found you," she said. "That you're standing in front of me. I've missed you."

"I've missed you, too."

"And you're pregnant, how exciting."

I stole a sideways glance at my father, then looked back.

"Are you married?"

The question hung in the air. My mind raced for an answer. Something, anything, so as not to lose her respect.

"No," I looked down. "It's a long story."

Silence again. A moment later, I felt her arm gently caress my back. The same tender mercy I had felt from her years ago.

"Well, maybe I can take you to lunch, and you can catch me up. I mean, I am the proud owner of your first photograph."

My eyes widened. "You still have that?"

"Of course I do. It is the sweetest gift I've ever received."

I looked at her and saw the same caring eyes that once watched over me. This guardian angel who had protected me and shown me love when I needed it most.

"Do you have time for lunch?" she asked.

"Yeah, of course."

"David, would you like to join us?"

He looked at me, then to her, then back to me. I tried to hide my feelings, but I didn't want him there. I could be more open with her, without the fear of his judgment.

"No, you two go. I gotta finish up some work."

I noticed an understanding glance exchange between them.

"Let me just grab my coat."

As we wound through the tree lined streets of Fall Creek, I told Miss Amy about Brad and Carlson, and all that had taken place.

"It's been really hard."

"You never cease to amaze me," she said. "You've had wave after wave of life crashing over you, and yet you keep on standing."

"Honestly, I don't know how many more waves I can take."

She looked over at me, then reached for my hand and gave it a reassuring squeeze. She turned her car onto Main Street and pulled up to The Grove Café. The old blocks of the narrow building had been painted bright white. A rustic metal sign hung above a black awning, giving the space a modern feel.

"What do you say we go in and eat?"

"Sounds great."

The café was mostly empty; the lunch rush had moved on for the day. We stood in front of a white shiplap wall and stared at the menu written on a large, black chalkboard.

A woman behind a long counter approached us. "How are you ladies doing today?"

"Good, thank you," said Miss Amy.

"Have y'all been here before?"

Miss Amy looked at me, and I shook my head. "No."

"Well, welcome in. We love getting new customers."

"What do you recommend?" Miss Amy asked.

"I like to believe everything on the menu is good. The salads are great, and we can customize them anyway you like. People love our sandwiches. We also have our tomato basil soup today that's to die for. I guess it's whatever you're in the mood for."

"It all sounds so amazing," said Miss Amy. "I think I'll go with the cobb salad, and I'll take a cup of the soup as well."

"Great choice."

"What about you, Brooklyn? It's my treat."

"I'll get the Caesar salad, and I'll have the soup as well."

"Excellent. Have a seat anywhere, and I'll bring it out to you."

Miss Amy nodded. "Thank you."

We each got ourselves a cup of lemon water and sat down in one of the booths. I placed a straw in my cup and twirled its empty wrapper between my fingers.

"So, you're living with your dad again. How's that been?"

"Umm…he was probably my last choice, but I had no one else to turn to."

"That bad, huh?"

"I mean, no. He came and got me in the middle of the night, and he's given me a place to stay, no questions asked."

"That's nice."

"He even found me a doctor close by, for the baby. I didn't ask him, he just did it."

"It sounds like he's doing better."

I looked out of one of the large windows at the front of the restaurant. The sun reflected off a chrome hubcap, casting a beam of light through the glass and onto the ceiling.

"I don't think he'll ever change, really. He does this. He'll try and be super dad for a while, but he always goes back to his old habits."

"Is he still drinking?"

"No, I'd know if he was. He's been sober at least since I came back. He said he stopped soon after I left for college. Of course, he'd wait until I was gone."

"At least he's stopped." Her calm eyes rested on me.

"Yeah, it is. It's just…"

"It's just what?"

"There's just been so many years and so many bad things that have happened. I don't think I can ever forgive him. Is that bad?"

"No, it's completely understandable."

She reached across the table and held my hand again. She looked at me for a long moment.

"I've worried so much about you. I've thought so many times that I should have found a way to take you with me. To get you out of that situation."

"Really? I felt so dumb afterward, for even asking you. Like I actually expected you could just take me away."

"I almost stayed in Chatwin, just to be there for you."

The woman stepped to our table and placed the two cups of soup in front of us. Then she gently placed a spoon next to each one.

"Your salads will be out in just a moment."

Miss Amy turned to her. "Thank you." She reached for the pepper at the edge of the table and gave a couple of quick taps into her soup.

I followed her lead.

"I'm sorry I wasn't there for you. Things changed so quickly with my husband's grandpa, and then his new job took us out to California. I felt like I abandoned you."

"Are you kidding? You changed my life. I wouldn't be here without you. You taught me to dream."

"I'm glad. The one thing that gave me some comfort was that I knew deep down your dad loved you."

I stirred my soup wanting the comment to pass. I didn't want it to ruin the moment. She was wrong though. She didn't know how bad it had been.

"Chatwin was a strange town," she continued. "My husband and I have lived in a few different places now, moving our kids around as we've followed his career, and I've never been in a place like that. A miserable place. A place where people almost seemed to take pleasure in the failures of others."

"Good ol' Chatwin."

"Right? Don't get me wrong, there were many good people there, but there were a few who had so much to say about everyone else. So much to say about your dad. They made so many judgmental comments, but do you know what I saw?"

"What?"

"I saw a man who'd lost a baby and his wife all within the same year. I saw a man who was broken."

Her words exposed a truth my heart wanted to ignore. I had lost my mother, but my father had lost the hope of a new life and the love of his life. She was his confidant and his best friend.

She rested her elbows on the table, folded her hands, and looked directly at me. "I saw a man who came by my classroom every few weeks, to thank me for helping his daughter."

My eyebrows shot up and my eyes widened. "He did that? I didn't think he even knew about you."

"He did, and I could see it in his eyes, Brooklyn, he loved you. He just couldn't find a way out of the storm." She lifted her spoon and went back to her soup.

I pulled a napkin from a silver dispenser and placed it in my lap. I swirled my soup again and lifted the spoon to my mouth.

"Pain and grief aren't an excuse to stop living, or to stop loving," she said.

"But?"

"But they sure can be a monumental hurdle to overcome."

The woman appeared again, holding a salad in each hand. Both looked carefully crafted, with the ingredients stacked high. She placed them in front of us.

Miss Amy picked up her fork. "These look amazing. "

"Yes, they do."

"Thank you," the woman said. "Can I get you anything else?"

Miss Amy looked at me, and I shook my head.

"I think we're good for now."

"Enjoy," she said and walked away.

I stirred the salad around with a fork, spreading its contents, then carefully drizzled a small cup of dressing over the top. "So, you think I should forgive him?"

She paused, ready to spread her own dressing on her salad. She looked at me, her expression kind, but with more intensity.

"Yes, but not for the reasons you think."

"Then why?"

"You don't know this, but when I was a little girl, my father abandoned our family."

I looked up from my salad, her words instantly capturing my heart. A kindred understanding, deepening our connection.

"One day, he just decided he wanted a different life. He didn't want to be a husband or father anymore. He was gone long before my heart could comprehend it."

"I'm so sorry."

"He'd call or occasionally come around, and my siblings and I would desperately try and recreate the good times from the past, but it was never the same. He'd always leave again. When we got older, my mom married a great man who became a second father to me. A better father than the first. Life moved on, and my real father continued to bounce in and out of it. Then one day it seemed like he decided he didn't like his new life anymore. He suddenly wanted to settle down and reconnect, but me and my siblings weren't going to let him off the hook that easily. I mean, we invited him to all the birthdays, graduations, and weddings, but we treated him like an outcast. More often than not, he would end up sitting in the corner alone, watching us. I couldn't open my heart to him again."

"So, you know how I feel."

"I do. Maybe that's why the two of us connected so easily."

"Kindred spirits."

"Absolutely."

We both took a bite of our salads. I let the fork linger in my mouth for a second, surprised by how good everything tasted.

"This is so good."

"Mine, too."

I took a sip of my water and looked at her again. "So, have you forgiven him?"

"Kind of," she said. "I was always getting mad at him and he embarrassed me. I wanted him to be more involved, then he would try, and I would push away again. I wanted him to hurt, like he had hurt me."

"I know that feeling."

"Then he was gone."

"Wait, what? Are you serious, he left again?"

"Not exactly. He died suddenly of a heart attack a few years ago."

I studied her face, wondering if her father's death had brought relief or sadness. She poked at her salad and looked as if she were contemplating what to say next.

"I'm sorry."

"Thank you. What's funny…or sad I guess, is that as I sat there at his funeral, I realized I wasn't mad at him anymore."

"Like, you were relieved?"

"No, that wasn't it. I actually felt…empty."

"Empty?"

"Yeah. At that moment, I knew I would never get a chance to talk to him again. I realized how little I had accomplished by shutting him out. It didn't force him to be a better man. It didn't help me heal, and it certainly didn't help him. It was wrong of him to leave us, for sure, and he should've been a better father. All of that's true, but I always thought I'd have more time. It's like I wanted to punish him just long enough for him to give up hope, then I'd ease up. Except I ran out of time, and the regret I feel now eats at me more than any anger I felt toward him."

The café was quiet. My thoughts were captivated by her story. Her words turned in my mind, questioning what I thought to be true.

"I can't tell you how to feel, Brooklyn. I've never walked a day in your shoes, but I hope you'll come to realize that holding on to anger as a way to punish your father, really only punishes you."

I nodded. "You've always been able to speak right to my heart."

"That's the sign of true friendship."

I looked at her, then looked away.

"What are you thinking?"

"I think," I said, then paused. "Never mind, it won't make sense."

"Try me."

I looked down at my hands. I let out a slow, steady breath. "I think if I forgive my dad, then I'll have to face an awful truth."

"What's that?"

"That I'm really angry at my mom." I looked at her to see how she reacted to this revelation.

She stared at me with compassionate eyes and gently nodded her head.

"I'm mad at her for leaving me. I'm mad that she ruined our family. I'm mad at her for making me feel like I wasn't enough."

She put her fork down and slid around to my side of the booth. She gently put her arm around me.

"But the thing is, I can't be mad at her. I mean I am, but like I can't be, because who's going to protect her memory if I don't? That probably sounds stupid."

"No, it doesn't. You've been defending your mom's good name for a lot of years, so much so that maybe you haven't had the opportunity to process it and heal yourself."

"I can't turn against her like everyone else did. She has to be remembered for more than the last thing she did." I pushed a crouton around my plate with my fork, my mind hung up on feelings I had so often ignored. "But maybe she doesn't deserve to have her legacy saved, you know? She left me. What kind of mom does that? You don't do that to a child."

"I don't know, sweetie. Sometimes people do things that we just can't understand, and it's okay to be angry and wrestle with those feelings, but don't let how you think you should feel change how you actually feel. It's a gift to be able to find the good through the bad. Your mom should be here, and it's not fair that she's not, but with all the stories you've told, there's no doubt that she loved you and you love her. Don't go digging up skeletons of the past just for the sake of digging, do it to find understanding and forgiveness."

I rested my head against her shoulder. I hadn't realized how adrift my thoughts had become and how much I had missed Miss Amy's gentle guidance. I suddenly felt sad. "I don't think I can say goodbye to you again."

She gave me a tight squeeze and pressed her head against mine.

"This isn't goodbye, not this time. Face it, Brooklyn, you're stuck with me."

I laughed and reached for another napkin from the dispenser and wiped the tears from my cheeks.

"I do think, though, since we've got a lifetime of friendship ahead of us, that you can just call me Amy."

I laughed. "Okay."

"I can't wait to meet your daughter," she said. "You're going to be a great momma to this little girl."

"I don't know."

"I do. It'll be hard, but you were made for this."

"Thank you."

We sat like that for a while longer. A piece of my heart was put back into place. My soul healing.

I said quietly, "I've missed you."

"I've missed you, too."

CHAPTER 37

awoke to the sound of wind blowing the branches of leafless trees that rustled against the house. My eyes opened to the darkness of my bedroom, with a faint orange glow of a streetlamp streaming around the edges of my blinds.

I lifted a leg, my muscles tight from being in one position through hours of sleep. I reached across to my nightstand, searching for my phone. My hand swiped at the empty air, my fingers finally connecting with the wood top, tracing their way until I found it.

I held it up, and the screen came to life. My eyes fought to adjust to the light, focusing on the time.

Four twenty.

I moaned. Why was I awake? It would take me forever to fall back to sleep.

I laid on my back and stared into the darkness. I felt the inevitable pressure on my bladder. This uncomfortable urge seemed to be my constant companion now, and I still had two months left until my due date. I stepped out of bed and made my way to the bathroom.

I sat on the toilet longer than needed, the fog of sleep still hanging over me. Maybe I would be able to fall back to sleep.

I stood and rinsed my hands with cold water and started back to my room when a stabbing pain shot through my abdomen. I doubled over, catching myself against the door frame. I took a deep breath and the pain disappeared.

I stretched my back. It gave a gentle pop, and I rolled my shoulders, letting the fatigue melt away.

I took a few more steps, making it as far as the short hallway leading to the kitchen, when another shot of pain coursed through me. I placed a hand underneath my stomach and massaged the area. I took a series of quick breaths, clenching my jaw until the pain went away again.

My heart was beating fast, a slow panic overtaking me. My mind raced with worry.

I walked into the kitchen and began to warm some water in the microwave. The shadows of night stared at me through the windows. I grabbed a canister of hot chocolate from the panty and a spoon from one of the drawers. I stood next to the microwave, ready to stop it before it had a chance to beep and wake up my father.

I massaged my abdomen again. The pain seemed to have gone away. I pressed hard against my stomach, hoping the baby would return my pressure with a swift kick or a roll. She didn't respond.

Steam began to rise from the water, and I quietly opened the microwave door and removed the mug. I took the lid off the hot chocolate and began dumping heaping spoonfuls into the water. With the final scoop came another attack of excruciating pain.

The spoon crashed to the countertop. It rang through the kitchen, and a cloud of dry chocolate dusted the air. I grabbed the counter with both hands and took in another deep breath.

"No, no, no, what's happening? What are you doing, baby girl, it's too early for you."

I gingerly walked toward the kitchen table and pulled out one of the chairs. I sat down hard and arched my back, taking the pressure off my chest. After a few more deep breaths, the pain began to subside.

I pressed against my stomach again, feeling for any type of movement. Nothing. I lowered my elbows to the table and rested my head in my hands.

"Come on, Brooke, think. What are you going to do? What should you do?"

I stood up from the table, hesitated, then began to tiptoe toward my father's bedroom. I carefully navigated the dark hallway and approached his door. It was mostly closed, but through the small opening, I could hear the rhythmic breathing of his sleep.

I placed my hand on the doorknob and waited. I didn't want to wake him. I didn't want to run to him with every little problem the baby had.

I changed my mind, stepped away from his door, and walked back to my bedroom. I sat down on the edge of the bed, praying the pain wouldn't come back. I felt my stomach again, still no movement.

"Brooklyn," my father whispered, startling me from my thoughts. "Is everything okay?"

I looked up at him. He was standing in the doorway, his face barely visible in the faint light. He rubbed his eyes and stared at me. I wanted to lie to him, to hide my fear, but I didn't know what to do.

"No. I don't know. I'm feeling this weird stabbing pain, and every time I try and get her to move, she won't. She's usually always moving during the night, but now she isn't, and I didn't want to wake you up. I didn't want to bother you. I should know what to do. I need to learn how to handle things myself. I didn't come here to burden you…"

He walked into the room and reached toward me. "Woah, slow down. Just relax. Don't worry about any of that, okay?"

I nodded.

"Here's what we're going to do. I'm going to throw on some different clothes. You get your shoes and coat, then I'll take you to the emergency room."

I shook my head and moved to stand. "No, I'm sure everything's okay. I don't want to drag you all the way there in the middle of the night."

"I think it would be better to get you checked."

"But I don't even know if anything is wrong. I don't want to get there, waste money, and have them laugh at me."

"They're not going to laugh at you. Anyway, who cares if they do? Your safety and the baby's safety are the most important things right now."

I nodded again. "Okay."

"Do you think you can make it to the truck?"

"Yes."

"I'll get my stuff and meet you there."

The emergency room was quiet. A few individuals sat in the waiting area, staggered among a sea of maroon chairs. They all looked tired, with heavy eyes and matted hair, the exhaustion of the night appearing to wear on them. I wondered what brought them here. What tragedy were they dealing with?

My father stepped to the reception area. I followed close behind. A young woman in scrubs sat behind a large, orange desk. She stared at the screen of her computer and lifted a strand of golden-brown hair behind her ear. She looked at my father and gave him a bright smile.

"Hi there," she said, her voice surprisingly chipper, given the early hour. "How can I help you?"

"Hi, I'm here with my daughter. She's pregnant, and she's been having some pains in her stomach."

She nodded toward me. "Okay, is this your daughter?"

"Yes." I stepped closer to the desk.

"How are you?"

"Good, just a little worried."

"I understand. Can you tell me what's going on?"

"Yeah. I woke up and had to use the bathroom, and when I was going back to bed, I felt a sharp pain in my stomach."

I pointed to show her exactly where the pain occurred.

"Did you notice anything unusual when you went to the bathroom? Any bleeding or unusual discharge?"

"I had the light off. I didn't even think to look, I'm sorry."

"It's okay. I would have done the same thing. If I'm asleep, I'm leaving the lights off so I can stay asleep."

I smiled, my anxiety easing.

"Have you experienced any additional pain?" she asked.

"Yes."

"How often? Is it consistent or does it come and go?"

"Just a few times, and it kind of comes and goes."

"Does it feel like you're having contractions?"

I looked at my father. I didn't know how to answer.

"I don't know, maybe. I'm not really sure what to expect."

"That's okay. Did you call your doctor?"

My embarrassment burned within me, building, nearly choking my words. With each question, I felt more and more inadequate. The judgements that must be churning in her and my father's minds.

How can this girl be trusted with a baby if she can't even do the little things to take care of herself?

"No."

"No problem. Most clinics have a doctor on call at night, just for situations like yours. Who's your doctor?"

"Dr. Sutherland."

"Oh, perfect, her clinic is tied in with the hospital."

She reached for a clipboard and attached a form to it. She scribbled a few notes on it and placed it on the edge of the desk.

"I'm going to have you fill out this paperwork, then I'll go ahead and contact the on-call doctor and see what they want to do. Do you have insurance?"

Another question bringing to light one more failure. I didn't know if it was Brad or Nicole, but shortly after my first appointment with my new doctor in Fall Creek, the billing department called and informed me that my coverage was no longer active. The insurance that Jack and Nicole had promised they would pay for.

"Don't worry about it," they had said. "We got it. We want our grandchild to have the best care."

I wasn't surprised they had canceled it, but I had hoped that, despite their feelings toward me, they would open their hearts to their granddaughter.

I guess not.

I could sense my father's piercing gaze, waiting for me to answer the question. "I'm working on finding some insurance options, but I don't have any right now. I have some cash and…"

"You have insurance," my father said. "You're on mine."

He was already reaching into his back pocket for his wallet. He thumbed through it and pulled an insurance card out, handing it to the receptionist. I looked at him, my words failing me, and a burden lifting from me all at once. I held my breath, trapping it deep within me, fearing that if I let it escape, all the relief and emotion I felt at the moment would come rushing out.

He leaned against the reception desk and looked at me. "I got set up with some small business, group insurance plan. I don't know exactly how it works, but it's supposed to help with the rates. Seems like a pretty fair deal. I added you when I could, back in January, just in case you got sick or something up at school. I thought you knew that from the doctor's office. They sent a letter saying your previous coverage had been denied. I called right away and told them you were on my insurance. I thought they would have told you."

I shook my head.

"I'm going to take care of you, Brooklyn. So far it's just been a small co-pay, but I'm going to cover the other costs as well. Whatever the insurance doesn't cover."

I turned away, my heart suddenly full. I drew in another deep breath.

"All right, we're all set," the receptionist said. "They'll likely have us transfer you down to maternity, but don't worry about that right now. You just relax."

"Thank you."

We each sat down on one of the padded chairs, and I tried to get comfortable. My father thumbed through a stack of magazines but quickly gave up the search. He leaned forward and pressed his fingers into his palms, cracking his knuckles. He yawned and looked over at me.

"How are you doing? You're not saying much."

"I'm okay."

"Does it still hurt?"

"Not lately."

"That's good."

I rolled the pen attached to the clipboard between my fingers, pressing the cap off with my thumb and then pushing it back on.

"I feel stupid for not being able to answer her questions."

"Why?"

"I should have thought to call the doctor first. I should know what contractions feel like. I should know what to do. I'm supposed to be a mom, but I have no idea what to do. There's no way I can do this."

"You sound like a mom to me, doing whatever you can to make sure your baby's safe."

He leaned back in his seat and looked over at me. "That's the secret of parenthood that nobody tells you, we're all just winging it, hoping to do our best. I should know, I've made plenty of mistakes."

I looked at him, his words comforting me. He leaned forward again and stared at his hands. He had always been a man of few words, but when he did speak, when it was just him and not the vice of alcohol, he had a way of calming any storm for me.

A janitor wheeled a mop bucket past us, one wheel of the cart squeaking. He stopped where the edge of the linoleum floor met the carpet of the waiting area. He lifted the mop from the bucket, let the excess water rain down, and plopped it on the floor. He began to methodically move back and forth, slowly mopping the path of an endless hallway. The scent of his cleaning solution matched the sterile feel of the hospital. The white lights reaching into every corner, the hushed tones, and the unspoken fear that hung heavy in the air.

"I hate hospitals."

"Me, too."

"It reminds me of Mom."

He looked at me again. "Me, too."

"Do you remember much about that day?"

He looked away and stared into the distance. I feared I was stirring the ghosts of the past, reawakening the nightmares of my childhood, but I wanted to know how he experienced it. My heart longed for another soul to commiserate in the indescribable sadness. I watched him intently.

He took a deep breath and it escaped slowly. "I remember Juli-anne Timmons called me at work. I knew something was wrong before I even answered the phone, because we weren't allowed to take personal calls unless it was an emergency. She was very matter of fact. 'David, this is Julianne. Angela's hurt herself, and you need to get to the hospital right now.' I don't even remember how I responded, or if I said anything at all, but I had nearly hung up the phone when I heard her say, 'David, you should know, Brooklyn was the one who found her. She's with me, but she's pretty shaken up. Do you want me to bring her to the hospital?'"

A chill ran up my back, the memory suddenly so fresh. A wound that I thought had healed, still ached just below the surface. "I remember chasing the ambulance, begging them to bring her back. And I remember Mrs. Timmons arms around me and looking up at her and seeing tears running down her face. In a weird way I thought that was nice, that she cared enough about Mom to be sad."

"They were good neighbors."

"And I remember the sliding doors of the hospital opening and seeing you at the end of a hallway just like this one, talking to a doctor, then falling to your knees. I knew it was bad. I broke free from Mrs. Timmons and ran to you."

He nodded and looked at me. We stared at each other for a moment, sharing the sadness of our broken hearts.

"Things were never really the same after that."

"No, they weren't."

"I felt like, once I was on my knees, I could never get back up."

A woman wearing pink scrubs entered the waiting area, rolling a wheelchair. She was older, maybe my father's age, slender, with her hair pulled into a tight ponytail. I took a deep breath, pulling myself from the memory. She grabbed a clipboard from a pocket on the chair.

"Brooklyn Blair?"

"Yes." I raised my hand.

"Hi, my name is Hannah, and I'm one of the labor and delivery nurses. It sounds like you've been having a rough night."

"Yes, ma'am."

"I'm sorry to hear that, but we're going to take good care of you, I promise."

"Thank you."

"What we'll do first is have you get nice and comfortable in this chair, and I'll wheel you down to the maternity ward."

My father stood and took my coat. I looked at the wheelchair and waved a hand, dismissing it.

"I'm really okay to walk."

"Our number one priority is to make sure that you and the baby are safe. You just relax, enjoy the ride, and we'll get you hooked up to the monitors and see if we can figure out what's going on with this little one."

I sat in the chair, and she turned it around toward the elevators. She began to push, and my father followed close behind. As we passed the reception desk, the other nurse waved at us.

"Good luck," she said.

"Thank you."

She took me to a small exam room, its layout like the many I had visited over the past months. A gray cabinet with a small countertop and sink on top, two chairs, and an exam table in the center. The morning light burst through a narrow window at the edge of the room.

Hannah went through the standard procedure of checking my weight, my blood pressure, and asking a series of questions. She then connected a variety of monitors to me. One to check my heart rate and one to measure whether I was having contractions.

"Okay, now let's find baby's heartbeat," she said. "Lean forward for me. I'm going to strap this monitor around your abdomen."

She wrapped a soft cloth around me which held a circular

device in place. She applied a large amount of gel to my stomach and began to move the device around. One of a set of screens flickered to life next to me and a pulse began to track across it.

"There she is," Hannah said. "A good, strong heartbeat."

I let out a deep breath. I looked at my father; he was staring at the screen and smiled to himself.

"Okay, Brooklyn," Hannah said. "We're going to monitor you for a while. I'll come back to check on you soon."

"Thank you."

We sat, lost in our own thoughts, my father in one of the chairs, me on the exam table. His head was tilted back, resting against the wall, his eyes closed. I yawned, as the rhythm of the monitors mixed with the gaining fatigue of the early morning. He opened one eye and smiled.

"Tired?" he asked.

"Yeah, you?"

"I'm doing okay."

He closed his eyes again. Of all the people I thought would be with me at this time, he was the last one I expected.

"Thanks for being here, Dad."

"There's nowhere else I would rather be."

I laughed, which came out as more of a snort. My response automatic and unintentional.

He opened his eyes and looked at me.

"You say that as if it's normal for us. As if you've always been there for me."

"You're right," he said. "I'm sorry. Given all the ways I've let you down, I can't blame you for having low expectations of me."

His eyes closed again, and I watched him in the brightness of the sunlit room. I saw the pain or guilt or whatever he was feeling change his expression. A sadness pulled at his face.

"No, I'm sorry. This whole time since you brought me into

your house, I've never really thanked you. All I seem to do is remind you of the mistakes you've made. I'm the one who should apologize."

"You don't need to, I deserve it."

"No, you don't. Because no one else in my life is sitting here with me now. You're the only one. Everyone else has left my side except for you."

I was beginning to remember the man he once was. The man who used to swoop me into his arms. The man who played the hero in my dreams.

He leaned forward in his chair and placed his hand on mine. "I'm lucky to be that one."

I smiled, then turned to watch the monitors. Their lines and numbers were lost in the mix of my thoughts.

"I can't lose you."

"What?"

I turned and looked at him. "I can't lose you this time, okay."

"I'm not going anywhere."

"But you can't promise that, can you? I hoped for so long that you would change, but you never did. You would try and you would always fail. So, how can I believe you now? How can I open my heart to that hope again? Sometimes I feel like it's better to stay angry at you, so you'll keep trying. I feel like once I forgive you, you'll let your guard down. You'll fall again. And I can't lose you like that. You're all I have left, and I don't think I can do this alone."

He stared at me intently, his lips pursed. He squeezed my hand.

"I live with that same fear every day, Brooklyn. The fear that this version of me is an imposter. That the real me is just waiting for a slip up, and I'll return to being the man that I hate. That I'll lose everything again."

"So, what do we do?"

"We don't live in fear. God is greater than fear. When I left Chatwin, I left that man behind. I turned my heart over to God, all the pains and all the mistakes, and he gave me peace."

"What does that even mean, Dad? People say stuff like that all the time, but I'm sorry, I don't believe you can have one grand epiphany and suddenly change who you are."

"I agree, but when I say peace, I mean clarity. It was like I was given a glimpse of who I truly am, as He sees me. But that's all it was, a moment. The question is, what do I do with it? Do I see who I can be and fight like crazy to be that man, or do I accept being a lesser version of myself? You might not believe me, Brooklyn, but I was a good father once. You were my everything. Knowing I would come home to see you and Mom, would carry me through my day. That is the real me. A father who loves you and would do anything for you. I wish I could tell you that my demons will never come back, but all I can do is take it day by day, trade old habits for new ones, look ahead, and don't live in the past."

The door opened with a silent swing. Hannah stepped in, pumped a squirt of sanitizer into her hand, and walked over to the monitors.

"How are you feeling, Brooklyn? Any more pain?"

"No, not for a while."

"That's what we like to hear."

She pulled my chart from a file holder hanging on the wall and studied the monitors. She flipped the top page over and wrote down some notes.

"Everything looks great. The baby's heartbeat is strong, your heartbeat is strong, and we're not measuring any contractions."

A wave of relief flooded over me like I had never felt before. The tension drained from my shoulders.

"It's likely your body is just getting ready for the big day," she said. "You may experience more of this as you get closer, but that's normal. However, if you're ever worried, even a little, don't hesitate to call us."

"Thank you."

"I'll have the doctor stop by just to confirm everything and answer any questions you have, but I think we'll be able to get you out of here pretty soon."

"Okay, thanks again."

"You bet. Is there anything else you need right now?"

"No, I'm good."

"Okay. Well, hopefully we won't see you back here for another few weeks. That means everything will have gone as planned, and you'll be ready to deliver this sweet little angel of yours."

I watched as she left the room, then I looked over at my father. He was smiling.

"Big relief."

"Huge relief."

"I think I'll walk down the hall and get a coffee. Do you want anything?"

"No, I'm good."

He stood, stretched his back, and yawned silently. He walked gingerly toward the door, as if his legs hadn't quite woken up.

"Dad?"

He turned and looked at me.

"Yeah."

"I believe in you."

He nodded and turned away. I saw his shoulders rise, then fall. He looked back at me. "Thank you. That means everything to me."

CHAPTER 38

walked through the darkness, my direction unknown, each step a leap of faith. I felt the cool air swirling around me, sending a chill through my body. The inky black shadows of night fought against my footsteps and my mind, pulling me in confusing directions. I reached out, hoping for anything to hold onto.

A faint light appeared in the distance. It was only a speck in a sea of black, but its guidance was familiar. I fixed my eyes on it, my heart drawn toward the sliver of hope. With each step, the brightness intensified, the emptiness dissipating. The heavy clouds falling behind me, whisked away into the past. The light consuming the darkness.

I heard a familiar sound under my feet. The gentle crunch of pebbles and dirt. Walls of tall grass sprang from the landscape around me. I was back on the dirt road of my dreams.

The sun stood strong in the horizon, its brightness filling the world. I shielded my eyes from its reflection and searched for her.

"Mom?" I asked.

She stepped into view, a small silhouette in the distance. She paused and looked at me.

"Mom."

She turned and started walking away.

"Mom, where are you going?"

I ran toward her. I felt the familiar burn in my chest, a longing so intense I feared it might consume me. I needed to feel her touch again. Just one more time to be surrounded by her love.

"Mom, please wait. Don't leave me behind."

She stopped at the edge of the cliff and waved for me to come. My strides were long, the dust from the road lifting in small plumes behind me. Our eyes met, the gap closing between us. I pictured myself falling into her arms. I reached for her, and then she was gone again.

Suddenly the earth disappeared beneath me, and I was falling. My arms and legs flailing, the scenery cascading past me. I closed my eyes and braced for the end.

Then all at once, the world was quiet again. I heard the buzzing of a bee circling around my head. My senses were awakened to a sweet scent around me. I opened my eyes. I was surrounded by the sea of lilies. The vibrant colors stretching as far as I could see.

"Mom?" I asked but couldn't see her.

I stepped forward and a path appeared, the lilies parting as I moved along. Slowly, the scene became familiar to me. A street sign appeared, white letters against a faded green background. I recognized the sign. The way it hung crooked against a metal post, fastened crudely with an old, rusted hanger. I had walked past it every day of my childhood. Whitmore Street. I was home, I was in Chatwin.

In the distance I could see the Timmons house. I walked past it, expecting to see Sophie swinging on her porch swing, making faces as I went along, but the house was empty.

I looked ahead and could make out the dull green pitch of our roof, peeking just above the lilies. I dragged my fingers along the fence bordering our driveway, the red boards popping against the blossoms, looking as if it had been freshly painted.

I walked along the narrow concrete leading to the front porch. I expected the first step to creak, like it always had, but it didn't make a sound. The steps were sturdy, and the railing around the porch looked new.

The scent of fresh-baked cookies danced through the screen door. I heard my mom humming from inside the house. A forgotten relief flowed through my body. A hope from my childhood heart. She was having one of her good days. She was happy.

I opened the screen and entered the cramped sitting room. Everything was as I remembered it. The wood floors, a decorative runner stretching toward the kitchen, and a little loveseat tucked next to the picture window. I walked into the kitchen, toward my mom's humming. I paused in the entryway and watched her. She was busily working within the confined space between the narrow cabinets and countertops, as if she had always been there. As if she had never left.

"Mom?"

"Hi, baby girl."

"What are you doing here?"

"I'm making your favorite cookies."

She moved back and forth, dropping small rounds of dough from a mixing bowl onto a cookie sheet. I walked up behind her and wrapped my arms around her.

"Oh, thank you, sweetie," she said. "I needed that. Now don't let me get flour all over you."

"Can I stay here with you?"

"Did you see outside?" she asked. "Did you see the lilies?"

"Yes."

"You created that baby girl. All your hope, faith, love, and dreams. You created something beautiful."

"Can I stay here with you, forever?"

I felt her chest rise, then a deep sigh. My heart sank. She spooned one more ball onto the cookie sheet, a perfect dozen, and wiped her hands against her apron.

She turned to face me, her deep blue eyes looking into mine. She held my face in her hands.

"It's time for me to go."

"No," I said, backing away from her. "You can't go. You can't leave me again. I won't make it without you."

"I wish I could stay."

"Then stay."

"I can't, sweetie."

"Yes, you can. Why does everyone say that? Why does everyone wish they could stay, and then they always leave? Just stay, you don't have to go."

"I'm sorry, Brooklyn. I'm sorry I left you."

I stared into her eyes, my thoughts cutoff at the acknowledgement of what she had done. The unspoken breach. The ultimate abandonment.

"Why did you leave me?"

The question hung in the air between us. An insecurity that had sat in the dark corners of my mind, threatening the pedestal I had placed her on.

"Why wasn't I enough?"

She stepped toward me. I felt the warmth of her soft hands against my face again. I could smell lotion on her fingers. Her scent that always brought her back to life in my mind. I leaned into them, savoring the moment.

"You were my everything, Brooklyn. The light of my life. I didn't want to leave you. I just didn't know how to escape the pain."

I fell into her arms, and we held each other. I knew this was goodbye.

"I love you, Mom."

"I love you, too, baby girl."

After a moment, she pulled away and pointed toward the sitting room. I turned and looked. My father was standing there, hands in *his pockets. A little girl crossed in and around his legs, laughing as she went. I stepped closer, wanting to see her face. Then Miss Amy appeared, standing next to Sybil and Cathy. They smiled at me.*

"The baby is coming soon," she said. "I know you're scared. You need to know that you are not alone. I know you feel that way, but you have never been left alone. Someone has always entered your life just when you needed them."

The history of my life surrounded me. The past, the present, and the future. The memories of sadness and loss encircled with a lifetime of love.

"You have created this beautiful world for yourself. These people love you. Go with them."

I stepped toward them, then stopped and turned back to her. Our eyes met and our souls embraced.

One, two, three, four, five. Breathe.

"Goodbye, Mom."

Her eyes held mine and she smiled.

"I love you."

My eyes filled with tears. "I love you, too."

"And Brooklyn, don't forget about her."

"Who?"

She pointed again and I turned to look.

"Ellie."

CHAPTER 39

I stretched my legs along the narrow cushion of the window bench and rested my back against the wall. I watched as heavy snowflakes painted our neighborhood in gentle brushstrokes of white. I could feel the chill of the outside air pressing hard against the glass, opposing the warmth inside.

An older man walked past, just as he did every morning, taking careful steps along the sidewalk. He wore a red, plaid jacket, and a black flat cap. His golden lab followed dutifully beside him, their steps leaving tracks in the sugary powder.

I wrapped a blanket around my legs and looked at my phone screen. It lit up, and the lock symbol shifted. I scrolled up from the bottom, and I was back where I had left it, on Ellie's contact.

I had painfully let go of many things, but not her number, not Ellie. She had changed my life. I held onto a hope that somehow, she would find my new number. That my phone would ping one day, and I would unsuspectingly check who had texted me and see her name. My old friend would return. Yet, week after week, her text never came.

Still, I had never reached out. Not once. I missed her like crazy, but thinking about Ellie meant thinking about Brad, and I wasn't ready for that. Wherever she was, he was always nearby, part of her world in a way I couldn't handle.

My love for him was gone. I knew that. It wasn't coming back. But the little girl growing inside me was still part of him. Because of that, he'd never fully disappear.

Would reaching out to Ellie, if she even wanted me back, mean letting him in, too? I didn't think I could do that. But how many real friendships does a person get in life? The kind where you're not just yourself, but better. The kind where you know someone always has you. The kind that changes everything.

I pressed on the message icon and stared at the empty screen. Our history was blank. Maybe that's the way she wanted it, to forget the girl who had entered her life, stole her brother, and tore her family apart.

I held the phone in my hands and began typing.

Hi El! It's Brooke. Just thinking of you. I wanted to wish you a Merry Christmas!

I reread the words, wanting them to sound natural, not desperate or awkward. I wanted to pretend like nothing had changed, that we could forget the end and start again from the middle.

I rapidly pressed the backspace symbol, the words disappearing one letter at a time.

Hi El! I typed again. **It's Brooke!**

I deleted the words again and let out a frustrated sigh. Why was this so hard? I used to be able to tell her everything.

I exited the message screen and stared at her contact page again. An "EF" sat where her picture should be. Before I had time to think, I pressed on the call icon. My heart raced as the phone began to ring.

"Hello?"

I was frozen in the moment, her voice bringing a flood of memories with it.

"Hello," she said again.

"El."

There was a long pause. My hope faded with each passing millisecond.

"Brooke?"

"Hey."

"Oh, my gosh, Brooke. How are you? Where are you?"

Relieved, I smiled. "I'm good, how are you?"

"Hold on. It's too loud in here, I can't hear you. Hold on, okay? Don't hang up."

"Okay."

I could hear the sound of endless voices in the background, a crowd of people talking over each other.

"I have to go," I heard her say through the muffled microphone, then the phone went silent.

"Ellie?"

Did she hang up?

I held the phone away from me. The call time was still counting. I put it back to my ear.

"El?" I asked again, but it was still quiet.

"Ellie?"

"Brooke, are you still there?"

Whew?

"Yes."

"Good, I thought I lost you. Where are you?"

"I'm still in Colorado. I'm staying at my dad's house."

"Wait, you're living with your dad?"

"It's a long story, but yeah."

"Are you back in Chatwin?"

"No, he moved. It's a place called Fall Creek."

"Fall Creek? Where's that?"

"It's like a little past Denver and then over toward Utah."

She didn't respond. I pulled my phone away again, to make sure I hadn't lost her. I shifted my position on the bench, worried that my reception was bad. My mind fought to remember the things I wanted to say. Anything to keep the conversation going. I couldn't let it end so quickly.

"Listen, El, I just wanted to call and say I'm sorry for leaving like I did."

"Brooke, stop. I don't want to hear it."

My heart sank.

Was she upset?

I had always believed she would understand why I left like I did.

"What are you doing right now?" she asked.

"Sitting in my house, working up the courage to call you."

"Are you busy?"

"No."

"Then I'm on my way."

I stared out the window, my confused look reflecting back at me in the clear glass.

"Wait, what?"

"I'm getting in my car right now and coming to see you."

"Ellie, you're not going to drive across Colorado just to see me."

"Why not? I've already plugged Fall Creek into my maps. I'm on my way…unless you don't want me to come."

"Are you kidding? Of course I want you to come, but it's a long drive and it's snowing."

"Brooke, I've been searching for you for four months. I drove all the way to Chatwin, Colorado, just to find you."

"You went to Chatwin?"

"Yeah, and that place is kinda trash by the way."

I laughed. "I told you."

"Honestly, I can't believe I'm finally talking to you. Why didn't you call me sooner?"

I hesitated, searching for the right answer. Searching for the truth. "I'm sorry. I thought it would be better for everyone if I just left."

"Not for me. I'm supposed to be your best friend and you just vanished."

"I know."

"But I get it. After the way things went down, I would have done the same thing. I would have run from Carlson and never looked back. Sometimes I wish I could do that myself."

"If it makes you feel any better, I've missed you like crazy."

"I've missed you, too. And, Brooke, you don't need to apologize. I should be the one apologizing, but honestly, I'm done with drama in my life. I've had too many serious conversations lately. My family is trying to justify the choices they've made. I'm done with all that. They can deal with the consequences and figure out what to do. I just want my friend back."

"Good. That's all I want, is for you to be Ellie. The girl who asked a stranger she met in a bookstore to be her roommate."

We both laughed at the memory.

"Text me your address. The map says I'll be to Fall Creek in like three hours."

My entire face smiled. Of all the outcomes I had hoped for this morning, I never thought I would be seeing her in just a few short hours.

"Oh shoot. I just remembered that I have a doctor's appointment at one o'clock. It's like the final one before…"

I stopped myself, not wanting to open old wounds.

"Before the due date? December fifteenth, right?"

"You remembered."

"I haven't forgotten, Brooke. That's all I've thought about. This baby is my niece, you know."

My heart leapt. I hadn't thought of that. "I can meet you after the appointment. There's a cute little bakery in town that I like."

"Send me the address and I'll be there."

"Okay, perfect. It's called Essence Bakery. I'm sending the address now."

"I'm on my way."

"I can't wait to see you."

"Do you have to go? Or can you keep me company while I drive?"

I looked out the window and smiled as snowflakes playfully danced in the sky. "I'd love to talk."

I leaned back, crossed my legs, and just like that, we were us again.

CHAPTER 40

Delicate snowflakes danced effortlessly in the late afternoon sky as heavy clouds gave way to the approaching, blue horizon. I carefully rolled my father's truck down the steep slope of Main Street. A layer of snow covered the road, the asphalt barely visible in the deep ruts of narrow tire tracks. I slowed as I approached Essence Bakery, fearing I might slide right past it.

I gently maneuvered into what I hoped was a parking spot, the stripes long since buried in the powder. I saw Ellie's coupe farther down the road, parked as haphazardly as I was. The white of her car was covered in a layer of brown slush, the windows clouded over in a haze of dirty snow.

I turned off the engine, the excitement nearly consuming me. I climbed out and carefully stepped through mounds of snow to get to the bakery.

The bell rang as I entered, but the sound was lost among a boisterous conversation. Sybil and Cathy leaned over the display case, laughing with Ellie. I laughed. She was still Ellie, the girl that could talk to anyone, anywhere, and leave them feeling like they were her best friend.

"Ellie?"

She turned and looked at me, letting out an excited scream.

"Brooke!"

She nearly jumped over a chair, then twisted her way through the maze of tables. I clutched my keys and phone in one hand and ran toward her, wrapping my arms around her in a hug that was long overdue. We held each other, our feet tiptoeing as we tried to keep our balance.

Ellie stepped back. "Look at you! Nine months pregnant and you're still freaking gorgeous." She pulled me into a hug again. "Why am I crying?"

"You? What about me? I promise these are happy tears."

"Well, I understand why both of you are crying," said Cathy. "But I have no idea why I am."

We looked over at her and Sybil and laughed. They both brushed away tears.

"Guys, this is Ellie Foster, my best friend in the world."

Cathy stepped forward and wrapped an arm around Ellie's waste. "She got here a bit before you. We've had the pleasure of meeting, and it's obvious why you two are such good friends."

"Right? Ellie brings happiness wherever she goes."

I looked at Ellie and we both laughed.

"Why don't you two take a seat," Sybil said. "I'll whip up a couple of chicken salad sandwiches."

"No, you don't need to do all that. We can just have a cookie or something."

She placed an arm around my shoulder and gave me a gentle squeeze. "You're the only customers we're gonna get in here on a day like today, let me spoil you a little."

"Okay, thanks."

We sat down at one of the tables. I wiped away a dusting of snow that clung to the cuff of my leggings.

"So first, I have to tell you the craziest thing," Ellie said. "Something I've been dying to tell you but couldn't over the phone."

"What?"

"I'm engaged."

"Shut up."

She nodded and grinned, presenting her left hand. A small diamond sparkled against the lights of the bakery. "I'm serious."

"To who?"

"This guy I met in my Econ class."

"When?"

"Right about the time you left. I was so behind that I joined a study group."

"*You* joined a study group?"

"I know, right? And every time our group met, I just kept hanging out with this guy more and more. I don't even know how it happened. We just connected, and it feels completely right."

I held her hand in mine and admired the diamond ring.

"I'm so happy for you. What's his name?"

"Justin."

She looked down, tracing her finger along the rivets of the table.

"You totally love him, don't you? I can see it on your face."

"I don't think I've ever been happier, Brooke. Like honestly, I was just thinking a couple of weeks ago, the only thing that'd make my life better, was if you were still in it."

"I feel the same way. I've thought about you every day. I almost drove to Carlson one time to see you, although, I'm glad I didn't. I was going for the wrong reasons."

"Brad?"

"Yeah."

We stared at each other for a silent moment. Our shared history playing through my mind. The snapshot of his face as he watched me leave, seared into my memory.

"How is he?"

She straightened and turned her gaze toward the picture windows at the front of the bakery. "You know Brad, he's always had the ability to move on and never look back."

Her words hit with an unexpected hurt. My heart had moved on, but the reality that he could so easily forget me, forget us, made me wonder whether I had ever really known him.

"I can't believe he let things go down the way they did. Letting you get pushed out like that. I love my brother, but I don't think I'll ever be able to look at him the same."

I leaned forward and placed my hand on hers.

"Let me hate him and you love him. He needs you, El. You're the only person who truly knows him, the only one he trusts."

Her forehead wrinkled, and she shook her head, releasing my grip.

"I can't believe you're saying that. He left you and pushed you out the door. Doesn't that make you mad?"

"Of course it does. I was devastated when I left Carlson. I still am, honestly. I didn't think the sun would ever shine again, and I carry a constant fear with me that I have to do this alone. In my perfect world, he would be right here by my side, but you're right, he let me go and never came after me. You don't do that to someone you truly love. So, if he was here, out of obligation, I think that would be worse. He would be here but not here, you know? He wouldn't leave me, but he would always be finding reasons to escape, and I would still end up raising this baby alone, just in a different way."

"You're right. I think that's what he's doing now, running away. He left my dad's firm and started some extreme adventure business with Harrison. I think he's over in Africa right now."

"I bet your mom's not happy about that."

"Probably not, but who knows. She's really good at pretending everything's okay. It's going to take me longer to forgive her than Brad."

"Would she be mad that you're talking to me?"

"No, I don't think so. She'll never admit it, but I think she surprised herself with her own cruelty. It's like she's always believed she's this super kind and thoughtful person, but now she's kinda done this horrible thing and she knows it. If she knew I was here right now, I think it would actually make her feel better in some weird way."

Sybil stepped out from the back kitchen carrying two plates. She balanced both in one hand and grabbed a couple of napkins.

"Here you go, girls," she said. "Homemade chicken salad on fresh-baked croissants."

The croissants were big enough to fill the entire plates, each one piled high with chicken salad. The presentation capped off with a pickle spear on the side.

"These look amazing," Ellie said.

"Thank you," Sybil said. "It was my mother's recipe."

"Ah, that's sweet. Thank you."

"You're welcome, sweetie. Let me know if I can get you girls anything else. Cathy's just finishing up some cookies in the back, I'll bring out a couple when she's done."

"You spoil me too much."

"You're our favorite customer, so we get to."

Ellie smiled and looked at her croissant. She struggled to find the best way to lift it.

"These are huge."

"I know. I'm not even sure where to start."

I took a bite, the flavors melting in my mouth. I reached for one of the napkins and wiped my mouth.

"Enough about all of that. Let's focus on happy things, like you being engaged."

"I can't wait for you to meet him."

"I can't either."

She leaned back from the table and looked at me. "You look so cute pregnant."

I pushed my hair behind my ears. "Thank you, although, I feel gigantic."

"No way, you look amazing. How'd your appointment go any-way? How's the baby?"

"The doctor says she's doing really well. We had a scare a few weeks ago, but everything's been fine since then."

"So, when do they think you'll have her?"

"Honestly, it could be any day now."

"Wow, are you ready?"

"No." I looked at her and tried to dismiss my response, but my eyes couldn't hide the truth. "I'm just joking."

"No, you're not. I know you too well. You can tell me the truth."

"I can't, because I can't say the words out loud. If I do, then it makes me a horrible mom. I can't tell you that I'm scared out of my mind. I can't tell you that I secretly doubt my choices some-times. I can't tell you that I stay up at night, reading the discus-sion boards of other women with Down syndrome children, and their struggles. And then I realize that this is going to be my story, except I'm going to do it without a husband. Brad was right about one thing; this is a life sentence. And just by thinking that, by saying that out loud, it only reaffirms that I'm a horrible person."

She shook her head and placed a hand on my knee.

"You, Brooke Blair, are not a horrible person. It's okay to be scared. It would be weird if you weren't. Don't you think every new parent freaks out a little?"

"Yeah, for sure, but I think after a while they settle into a normal routine. I don't think there is any normal with special needs. Some-times I just don't think I'm the right one to raise this little girl."

"What if you're the only one? Like, what if this was all meant to be? Who else would fight for her like you have? Brooke, you gave up your dream life, to save her. You got in the face of Nicole Foster and told her she was wrong. Nobody tells my mom she's wrong. And look at everything that has happened. Do you think you would have reconnected with your dad without this?"

"No. No way."

"Do you think you would be entering and winning photo contests if this hadn't happened? Or starting your own photography business?"

"Probably not."

"Brooke, it's okay to be scared, but don't ever think that someone else can do this better than you. You lost your mom when you were a little girl. You know how precious life is. I've seen your strength, and I promise you that she's meant to be yours, not someone else's."

We looked at each other and our minds connected. We stood up at the same time and embraced in another hug.

"I've missed you so much, Ellie. You truly are my best friend."

"I love you, babe."

"And with that, I have to pee. For like the hundredth time today. I'll be right back."

As I left the bathroom, I knew what had happened, but I couldn't believe it was real. I stepped into the dining area of the bakery. Cathy stood next to Ellie, a fresh plate of cookies in her hand. They both laughed at something Cathy had said.

I slowly made my way over to them.

"Um, guys, I think my water just broke."

CHAPTER 41

The lights were turned low, casting shallow circles of faint light against the shadows of the room. The sounds from the day had given way to a peaceful silence, broken only by the occasional footsteps of the nurses making their rounds.

My eyes drifted toward the window. The city lights reflected brilliantly off the freshly fallen snow. The waning moon peeked through the clearing skies, casting a sliver of light across Ellie's sleeping face. She had offered to stay with me, relieving my father who had begun to fade as the minutes ticked past midnight. I smiled at my long-lost friend.

From the tiny bed beside me, my baby girl stirred. I turned toward her and watched her through the clear plastic of the bassinet. Her shallow breaths gently pulled against a swaddle blanket.

I sat up and reached for her. I carefully slid my hands beneath her, afraid that she might break, and I brought her to me. Her eyes opened, fluttering against the lights.

"Hi, baby girl. I'm your momma. I can't believe you're finally here. I've waited so long to meet you."

She wiggled then rested her face against my bare shoulder.

"I bet you're nervous about being in a new place. I know the feeling, but you already have so many people who love you."

I carefully turned her head toward the window.

"That amazing girl over there on the couch is your aunt Ellie. You're gonna love her. And your grandpa was here earlier to meet you. He cried when he held you."

I held her close to my lips.

"He never cries. And of course, you have me. I love you most of all, and I'll always be here for you."

I wondered if my mom had held me like this. In the stillness of night, what hopes had she whispered into my ear?

I gently unwrapped the blanket, laying her softly between my legs. Her arms wiggled with newfound freedom. Her pink skin rolled over her bent knees and elbows. She stretched, as if she were reaching for me. My heart skipped. She was real. She was alive.

"Everyone keeps asking me what I'm going to name you. You're a special girl, so it has to be something great, right?"

Her eyes closed and her body stilled. I felt the warmth of her tiny breath against my leg. I gently caressed the side of her face with the back of my hand.

"I'm going to name you, Zoey. Do you like that? It's a special name for a special girl."

I didn't know what the future would bring, but everything in my life had led to this moment. The loss, the sadness, the pain, leading to love, forgiveness, hope, and dreams.

I leaned close to her and whispered into her ear, "Zoey means life."

THE END

Dear Reader,

THANK YOU for spending time with my story. If it meant something to you, I ask one small favor—please share it. My hope is that more hearts will be reminded that every life has purpose. Together, we can spread light and hope farther than I ever could alone.

Visit the author's website:
authormjrichards.com

ACKNOWLEDGMENTS

MY HESITATION in writing an acknowledgments page is the fear of forgetting someone who deserves to be here. If I have, know that it was not intentional. I am grateful for all who have helped me along this journey.

First and foremost, this book would not be possible without my faith in Jesus Christ. He is my strength, and I hope I'm sharing His light in some small way.

I am grateful to the family and friends who have lifted me along the way. To my wife, Julie, and our four amazing children, thank you for believing in me and for letting me hide away for hours at a time to put the words of this book together. You are the best part of my life. Also, to my dad, who has always been there when I've needed him—and even when I didn't know I did. Thank you for encouraging me to take every risk and every opportunity to get better. Finally, to my brother, Steve, who in countless conversations said, "When you finish your book…"—never "If." Your faith in me mattered more than you know.

A huge thank you to Angie Fenimore, who taught me how "the magic happens in revision." You became not only an amazing mentor but one of my closest friends. Likewise, to Paige, Krisjon, Chris, and Rory, our little team that took a giant leap of faith to bring light into the world. All these years later, our work carries on.

To the voices in my head—I never knew my characters would speak to me. Thank you for helping me piece together your stories on countless long drives to and from my day job.

And finally, to the readers of this book, thank you. My greatest hope is that these words stayed with you, even after you closed the book.

ABOUT THE AUTHOR

M.J. Richards writes stories that reflect the power of forgiveness, the strength of family, and the gift of life. He makes his home in Utah with his wife and four children, where he finds inspiration in the everyday moments that matter most.